A Lonely Height

BRIAN CLEGG

Copyright © 2015 Brian Clegg

www.brianclegg.net

The author has asserted his moral rights.

No part of this book may be reproduced in any form, or by any means, without prior permission in writing from the author.

All rights reserved.

ISBN: **1517265576**
ISBN-13: **978-1517265571**

DEDICATION

For Gillian, Rebecca and Chelsea

CONTENTS

Chapter 1   - 1

Chapter 2   - 10

Chapter 3   - 23

Chapter 4   - 32

Chapter 5   - 41

Chapter 6   - 52

Chapter 7   - 61

Chapter 8   - 75

Chapter 9   - 86

Chapter 10   - 99

Chapter 11   - 111

Chapter 12   - 123

Chapter 13   - 132

Chapter 14   - 141

Chapter 15   - 151

Chapter 16   - 161

Chapter 17   - 172

Chapter 18   - 178

Chapter 19   - 188

Chapter 20   - 198

Chapter 21   - 212

Chapter 22   - 220

ACKNOWLEDGMENTS

Thanks to Margery Allingham, Colin Dexter, Susan Hill, P. D. James, Ruth Rendell and all the great British detective novel writers for giving me many hours of pleasure and inspiration.

CHAPTER 1

The cold points of starlight disappeared behind the tower, leaving him in total darkness. He paused, finding breathing difficult; the tightness in his chest came as much from his mind as from the steepness of the hill. His hands touched the stone, fingers scraping on the gritty, weather-worn surface. He couldn't use the torch, not yet. Not until he was inside the arch, hidden from the road below. He edged around the stone pillar, carefully sliding his feet, feeling for holes in the uneven flooring. He could not afford an accident. A fall could leave him trapped in the tower. It was worth the tediously slow, precise movements to avoid that.

Safe. The cold stone was behind his back: a shield, a welcome guardian. He slipped the thin torch, a metal cylinder no thicker than his finger, out of his pocket. It was a present, a bribe from the girl to keep his attention. She didn't realise that he was his own man. Feeling pleased with himself, he touched the end, splashing a narrow ellipse of light onto the wall behind him. He nodded in satisfaction and flipped the cylinder to point the beam straight ahead. But his hand betrayed him, coated in a thin film of sweat that told of the fear that he could not openly acknowledge even to himself. The torch slipped from his fingers and clattered onto the floor.

The sound of metal on stone was horribly loud. He held his

breath, waiting for someone to come screaming at him, waiting for the light to die, leaving him trapped in the darkness of nightmare. Nothing happened. The LEDs seemed to flicker as the torch hit the floor but the light remained stubbornly on, lighting the wall, throwing the pock-marked surface of the stone into the deep relief of shadow. He laughed aloud, determined to show himself that he was not afraid. Suddenly confident, he bent over slowly, holding his long hair out of his eyes, and took the torch again. It was own fault, he should never have taken it in his bare hands; he should be wearing gloves by now.

He slipped the end of the torch into his mouth and pulled a pair of driving gloves from his pocket. His nose was very sensitive; as he crumpled the gloves a faint scent of leather caught his attention. He would have laughed again, but the torch could have fallen. The bright spot flicked around the walls as he tugged at the leather. It was like an insubstantial night-time moth, a drifting spot of brightness in search of something solid. Finally he had the gloves on and could take the torch in his hand again. It sat firmly in the tight cup of leather at the base of his thumb, controlled now, in no danger of escape.

For the first time since he had entered the tower he turned the light towards It. His eyes, struggling in the contrast between the spot of light and the shadow black night darkness, tried to fool him into thinking that It moved, but he knew that It could not have. His gloves gave him confidence, the tight leather second skins seeming to caress his hands and lead him. He walked slowly, carefully across the floor towards It, towards the body. There: he had named It. The body that waited grotesquely in the corner. The body that was a sacrifice to her, for it was entirely down to her that these remains were lifeless. He took another step and the light went out.

His joints locked as his body rebelled against the calming attempts of his mind. He could feel his hair bristling. It's alive, a harsh voice said inside him, It's alive and It's going to get you for this. Only the gloves kept him going. It seemed as if they guided his fingers to drop the useless torch into his pocket, as if they tugged him forward another pace across the floor and stretched out his hands in front of him. He felt something soft give repellently to his touch. A bitter wave of bile surged from his stomach, filling his mouth with warm, sour liquid. He fought it back, swallowing; there mustn't be any evidence. He wasn't sure if they could track him down from his vomit, but he daren't leave anything behind.

In the reaction to the vile tasting mouthful, his fingers twitched tight and suddenly wetness was all down his arm and slopping to the ground by his feet. He jerked back, wary of leaving a footmark. There was only one thing left to do, one thing to be removed before he could leave the body and run from that place and never think about it again. The gloved fingers stretched out once more in the darkness.

~

I'm going to say something I'll regret, thought Stephen Capel. He shifted to one side, shading his eyes against the sunlight that streamed through the window of the chaplain's study. This was more like a job interview than a briefing. What gave Rhees the right to be so intrusive?

' ... I'm sure you'll agree, Father Stephen, that Thornton Down, especially the Church of England's little band of stalwarts in Thornton Down, is the last place to start such a scheme.' The older man's smile dripped with condescension.

'Just Stephen, please. I hope we don't need that sort of formality. Or Capel; most of my friends call me Capel.' That was good, Capel thought. Remarkable restraint. Anglo-Catholics like Rhees got up his nose, but he had no intention of showing it.

'Stephen, then.' Alan Rhees gave no sign of welcoming Capel's gesture of friendship. 'I don't claim to be an expert in the mysteries of modern parish priestdom, but I do know Thornton Down. I know what our little community wants.'

Oh, yes, thought Capel. What Thornton Down wants. If I'm

to believe him, what Thornton Down wants is to be left in some sort of time warp. 'I was hardly talking about radical change.'

'Radical is a relative term. Remember we're talking about the Mothers' Union of a rural village, not Wormwood Scrubs.'

'I don't believe they have an M.U. at the Scrubs,' said Capel. Damn it, that one had got out before he could stop himself. 'Look, you're probably right. You've been here a long time; I'm sure you know the people.'

'As well as it's possible with a full time job at the school,' said Rhees huffily.

Great, thought Capel, I try to be conciliatory and he takes it as an insult. Thornton Down wasn't quite the rest cure it had seemed after the open prison in County Durham where he had spent the first few years of his ministry. The village was in an apparently idyllic setting, far enough from Bath to have its own identity, but close enough to enjoy the benefits of the beautiful city. It was home to a minor public school, which, despite being the most conservative of establishments, added a faintly cosmopolitan flavour. And, in theory at least, it had the advantage of the school's chaplain, Alan Rhees, to stand in when the vicar was away. Rhees had been running the parish for the previous six months until Capel was appointed, something the older man seemed both to take pride in and to resent.

Capel nodded in what he hoped was an encouraging manner. 'Everyone says what a great job you've done in keeping things going. The parish couldn't have managed without you.'

'It hasn't been easy,' said Rhees. 'The pupils remain my first concern.'

'Of course,' said Capel, 'that's only proper.' He flicked through the remaining papers in the folder that Rhees had prepared for him. 'There isn't anything else urgent, is there? I have to get ready for my course.'

'I suppose you do.' Alan Rhees tilted his head forward to get a better view of Capel over the top of his half-spectacles. 'Unfortunate timing, going on a course in your first week. I'm surprised the bishop allowed it.'

'I don't know,' said Capel. He leant back as much as the hard upright chair would allow. The chair creaked uneasily. 'It was too good an opportunity to miss. I mean, a course on rural pastoral care when I'm moving to a parish like this; you could almost see it as divine intervention.' Capel saw Rhees's expression and hurried on. 'One more week without a vicar isn't going to devastate them after six months. You understand, don't you, Father Alan?'

'Alan is perfectly acceptable.' The chaplain looked as if he was eating burned toast. 'Of course I understand, it's simply a matter of timing.'

'It's only five days down at the Glastonbury Centre. Will you be able to manage evensong and the mid-week service?'

'Naturally,' said Rhees. 'I realise that you won't make a habit of swanning off.' He stood up.

That's telling me, thought Capel. 'Of course I won't. Thanks very much, Alan.' He stood and held out his hand.

'It's no trouble.' Rhees took the hand briefly, more a pat than a handshake. There was hardly any pressure from his warm, dry, almost crusty palm.

'I'll pop in to see you as soon as I'm back. Perhaps I can find you a stick of rock.'

'I'll look forward to that.' From Rhees's tone it was not clear what, if anything, he was looking forward to.

~

Capel sat on the side of his bed, turning a water glass as if he were trying to screw it into the top of the bedside table. He had been given a room in the George and Pilgrim, a solid, fifteenth century inn that had been modernised inside but still presented a dark mediaeval face to Glastonbury High Street. The Conference Centre, where he should have been staying, was being re-built. When he had signed in they had been very apologetic. The repairs had taken half the accommodation out of use; would he mind staying in the town? Capel had jumped at the opportunity. He loved buildings like the George, even though its touristy charm pushed up the price of the beer.

The glass rattled against the alarm clock. Capel moved it further away and continued to rotate it. It was worrying that he felt grateful for a chance to get away from Thornton. He'd been so sure that it was the right step. That was why he'd given up his career in the Home Office. He'd wanted an ordinary parish. The time he'd spent as chaplain in an open prison was only a stepping-stone. He was young enough, after all. Thirty-four was hardly too late to change.

He pushed the glass aside and picked up the tightly typed reading list. A lot had been written about rural pastoral care, but none of it looked thrilling. Not many best sellers there. He was going to have an early night with Margery Allingham - he couldn't go to sleep without reading something. In the morning things would look fresher. He was bound to feel a little odd about Thornton right now. It was simply first night nerves.

~

Midsummer's day was not far away. Capel had forgotten to draw the curtains, an invitation to the morning sun to burn its way into his sleep shortly after five. He tried to regain the shreds of his unconsciousness with little hope. Once he was awake, there was no return. The pillow obstinately refused to get back into a comfortable position; the unfashionable sheets and blanket tangled around his legs; the whole bed conspired to keep him awake. He looked blearily at the bedside clock. Five thirty. He knew from bitter experience that he could either waste the next three hours in a worthless daze, or get up and use the early morning light.

The slightly skewed hand of the clock flicked to 5.31. He forced himself to get out of the bed. It was his first time in Glastonbury; he shouldn't waste the chance to see the place at his leisure. If he worked hard enough at it, he could even consider waking early as a good thing. Almost.

The High Street was quiet, but not entirely empty. Capel walked up the hill, passing the old Tribunal and St John's with its strangely flattened thorn bush that was supposed to be descended from Joseph of Arimathea's staff. Any sense of mystery was dispelled by the flaking iron girders supporting the squat tree's branches. Across the road he caught a glimpse of the Abbey, surprisingly distant, a key-hole view pinched uncomfortably between the nearer brick buildings. He walked on. At the top of the hill the shops thinned out to the usual edge-of-town shabbiness; the more obscure names, the less well kept-up frontages. He was on the point of turning back to find the abbey gates when he saw the sign, an old sign built into the wall above a ruined drinking fountain. *To the Tor.*

A stylised hand pointed to the right, as if to challenge him to make the effort. It was the sort of challenge he found hard to resist. Besides which, it would make a good conversational opening with his fellow course members. 'I popped up the Tor before breakfast. The light was quite remarkable at six. So clear.' The sentiment was tongue in cheek, but the achievement would be real enough.

The narrow road led him past the Conference Centre, a disorienting find as he had imagined it to be in a totally different part of the town. Further along he reached an angled T-junction onto a bigger road. There was nothing to guide him, but he guessed that he should bear left. The surroundings grew more dingy with small, dark-windowed houses and a factory on the far side of the road. He began to doubt the sign. Things could have changed, streets could have been re-routed, since that sign was put up. This was too built up, too dismal for the Tor. Even the sun seemed to have gone into hiding.

A turn in the road exposed open ground on the left. Newly painted fencing surrounded some sort of garden, the Well Garden, and beyond it, the first rise of a steep hill could just be seen through the trees. His lack of faith had nearly defeated him. Not ideal for a priest. A tarmac path disgorged him onto the open hillside at the bottom of a well-worn track, wandering upwards in the direction of the tower at the Tor's summit. Capel set off at something approximating to a jog, but soon the steep slope had reduced him to plodding. He looked around sheepishly, hoping that it was too early for anyone to see how out of condition he was.

Not quite early enough. Someone was running down the path, out of control, careering down the steep slope towards him. Capel stepped onto the coarse grass at the side of the track. By the look of it, the man pounding down the hill would have little chance of stopping. A big man, with a full beard and long hair tied back with a rag. Reaction said 'hippy'; Glastonbury was famous for still having them. A peace person. But there was no peace in the relentless pace of the runner. In the momentary glimpse as he flashed past, Capel saw something disturbed in the maroon-flushed face. Fear or disgust, some profoundly felt concern.

Capel shook his head and breathed deeply of the clear, unpolluted air. People were at the centre of his business and his life - but he could afford time off from worrying about everyone else's problems. He shook away a large drop of dew that had brushed from the grass onto his toecap and stepped back onto the path.

Gradually the tower took form and detail. Capel resisted the temptation to stop for a rest at the bench part way up, continuing to put one foot in front of the other, concentrating on his breathing, trying to keep it at an even rate without great success. The tower was a surprise. He had imagined it a plain structure, a simple, ragged finger of stone marking the site of the long-disappeared St Michael's church, but the walls were finely decorated.

At the foot of the great archway he paused to look back down the slope, satisfied by his achievement. Glastonbury was a hazy mottling of yellow-white stone and muddy red brick on the undulating grassland of Somerset. Capel shivered. It could have been simply the hulking mass of the tower, but he felt that there was someone behind him, some early morning health freak, no doubt. He turned back with a smile, but there was no one. At least, no one obvious. He took a step forward, into the tower. By the stone bench at his right was a heap of... his mind clicked through the possibilities, suddenly efficient. It could be a bundle of clothes - but it seemed too solid. It could be a tramp, but why come all the way up here? It could be someone overcome by the climb, fatigued, perhaps even ill. All this passed through his mind in a fraction of a second. He knelt by the still form and pulled lightly where the shoulder should be. The body, and he was suddenly, awfully, certain that it was a body, rolled over to face him. It was a boy - a young man, rather - eyes bulging, face dark. Entirely dead.

CHAPTER 2

There was no wind. Nothing to stir the air in the open-topped tower where Stephen Capel was alone with a body. His ears strained to hear any movement, anything else alive up on the hill, but there was no company except the cold stone and the cooling flesh. He realised he was crouching in a pool of water, or rather a splash, too small to be there for long if the sun ever reached it in that shadowed space. It was pooled around the body's head: now he looked closer, that too was wet; dampness clung to the taut skin of the face; the hair was wild and thick with the sodden weight of water.

Capel jerked upright, took a step backwards towards the arch through which he had entered. He ought to fetch the police, to report the body before any more people trampled over the evidence. But he'd left his phone in the hotel room, and the scene held him in fascination. The red weal on the corpse's neck, lurid against the pallid flesh; the rough cut, jagged ends of the bright orange plastic cord that was fixed to some sort of peg in the wall. Capel's eyes, used to searching for details of personality, scanned the cracks and pits of the old stones, as if they could tell him something about what had happened, as if he expected the tower itself to spring up and confess an involvement in the crime.

It had to be a crime - even if it had been suicide, the young man could hardly have cut himself down and taken the rope away. Someone else had been there; someone else was involved. He thought of the man he had passed on the path, the man whose hair flew behind him as he ran from the devil. Perhaps he was the murderer? Capel scolded himself. For all he knew, the bearded man had found a suicide victim, cut him down to try to save him and even now was fetching the police.

There was only one way to find out. Capel took a last look around the tower and started back down the Tor at a controllable trot.

~

Glastonbury Police Station is not the busiest place at 7 am. Nor the most welcoming. Capel burst through the door, putting on a last minute spurt as he had been reduced to walking for the last few hundred yards. Like many such places, the interior was an uncomfortable compromise, a cross between the institutionalised decay of an aging hospital waiting room and a pawnbroker's - or at least how Capel imagined a pawnbroker's would be.

There was no one on the desk. Capel cautiously pressed the bell push, running through a few choice phrases in his mind. His experience as a prison chaplain would usually make dealing with the authorities a little easier, but this was not an ordinary circumstance.

'Yes?' A sergeant had appeared from somewhere and was looking at Capel with comfortable neutrality. He was short for a policeman - he looked as if he was too short, but that was the effect of a considerable girth, which made him seem squatter than he really was. It also made him look totally unflappable. He had seen it all and didn't expect to be surprised. There was none of the artificial respect that Capel's working clothes tended to generate; but then he was dressed for walking, not for benediction.

'I've found a body,' said Capel, favouring the straight forward, hit 'em between the eyes approach.

If he had been expecting the sergeant to be visibly shocked, he would have been disappointed. The thick-set man opened a book on the desk and flicked through to the current page.

'Perhaps I could have some details, sir, then we'll get a car to your body.'

'That'll be interesting,' muttered Capel, regretting it the moment he spoke. If there was one thing he ought to have learned in his job it was to think before he opened his mouth.

'I beg your pardon, sir?'

'Nothing, nothing at all.'

'I'm sure. Your name?'

'Capel - C A P E L.' He always spelled it out. It was an automatic reaction, formed in his teens to ward off the query. He never understood why it was necessary, it was a simple enough name, but people always asked. 'Stephen Capel.'

'Your address?'

'It's, er, oh, what the hell is it?' Now he was going to be considered devious, evasive. 'I've just moved in,' he explained, hoping to cover his embarrassment. 'It's the Vicarage, erm, oh, yes, Thornton Down. Thornton Down, near Bath.'

'Here at the Conference Centre, are you, sir?'

Capel awarded the sergeant a mental brownie point for not changing his attitude when he discovered Capel's occupation. It made a pleasant change to be treated as an ordinary person rather than a social innocent or an oddball.

'That's right.'

'And you've found a body - a human body?'

'Yes.'

'You're sure it was dead?'

'He was very dead, sergeant.'

'Nearly there, sir. We'll have a car and an ambulance off in a moment. Where exactly did you find this body?'

'On the Tor. In the ruined church - St Michael, isn't it?'

'It is indeed, sir. That's a bit of a bugger.' Capel added a gold star to the sergeant's brownie point for not apologising for his language as if Capel was some sort of feeble maiden aunt. 'The ambulance boys aren't going to like that. It's a long haul with a stretcher. We had a broken leg there a few months ago...' As he spoke he picked up a phone and dialled a short number. '... never heard the last of it. Ah, Bill, can we have a car at the front to go up to the Tor. Body found up there. And get the ambulance boys, you know how much they enjoy a good climb.' He smiled broadly at whatever Bill had to say to this. 'Won't they just.'

'Do you want me to go along with them?' said Capel.

'That would be helpful, sir. They won't be a moment.'

'Is there any chance of phoning the Conference Centre and letting them know I'm going to be late? It's supposed to be an 8.30 start.'

'I'll do that, sir. Morning, Perce - get you out of bed did we?' That was to a grey-haired sergeant, a very traditional looking policeman, were it not for the thick-rimmed glasses he wore.

The newcomer ignored the desk sergeant's remark with the ease of long experience. He stood upright by the door, a good six inches taller than Capel's five foot ten, waiting for some sense.

'Sergeant Moore will take you up to the Tor, Mr Capel,' said the desk sergeant, giving in gracefully. 'Mr Capel found a body on the top, Sergeant Moore.' The formality was obviously sarcastic.

'Very good,' said Sergeant Moore. He had a rumbling voice, the full Somerset drawl. 'Will you come with me, Mr Capel?' It wasn't really a question.

'Of course.'

There was a little more life on the street, but Glastonbury was in no hurry to come awake. There was nothing special about the day after all - except for Stephen Capel and a lifeless corpse on the lonely height of the Tor.

~

WPC Vicky Denning glanced out of the side window as the passenger neared the car, but she could see little detail. She waited, frustrated, as Sergeant Moore opened the back door for Capel, then lowered himself ponderously into the front seat, folding his apparently stiff, long legs slowly into the passenger space. Vicky looked the other way to conceal her irritation. It wasn't often there was anything worth rushing for in Glastonbury - now she had an opportunity, old Moore was infuriatingly slow. She wasn't looking for danger, but a bit of excitement now and again wouldn't go amiss, and Sergeant Moore was not so much methodical as geological.

'Reasonable haste, Denning,' said the sergeant, seeming to read her mind. 'No need for breaking speed limits. And no siren.'

'Oh, sergeant!' Vicky started the engine, but couldn't pull out as Moore had left his door wide open. She took the opportunity to glance in the mirror at the man in the back seat. Her first impression was bland. Mousy brown hair, nothing special about the face – nothing wrong with it, no beard or glasses, but nothing special. Slightly scruffy, casual clothes. But as she looked away, something about his eyes caught her attention.

She looked back. They were hazel, but as he turned they seemed to shift to green. And they definitely twinkled. She had never noticed it outside of a book before, but this man's eyes actually twinkled. It took a moment to realize that he was looking straight at her in the mirror, that he could see her pale blue eyes – no makeup, of course, or at least hardly noticeable – just as she could see his. Vicky turned quickly to face the sergeant.

'You can put the blues on,' said the sergeant, 'that's reasonable enough, but you are well aware of the standing instructions on the use of sirens. Especially this time of day. Just because you're up and about, there's no need to wake half the residents of Glastonbury. You use the siren if it is necessary to safely pass an obstacle, otherwise not at all. Is that clear, constable?'

'Yes, sarge.'

Moore harrumphed, perhaps suggesting that a more formal mode of address was appropriate with a member of the public in the back, but he left it at that and closed the car door. Vicky immediately let in the clutch, starting to pull out from the police station.

'Denning!' The sergeant was not pleased. He ponderously unreeled his seatbelt strap and clicked it in place. When he was certain of his security, and had glanced in the back to make sure that Capel was also strapped in, he nodded. Consciously not looking at their passenger, Vicky raised her eyes in silent frustration. With exaggerated care, she swung the car out into the thin early morning traffic and proceeded at a stately thirty miles an hour towards the Tor.

~

The ambulance had beaten them. Vicky raised her eyes again, a gesture so habitual that she was not aware of doing it. Capel, catching sight of her expression in the rear view mirror, smiled to himself. At the last moment, as they manoeuvred into place in the narrow lane that ran beside the Tor, a small three-wheeled car came rattling down from Butleigh Wootton. Vicky flicked on the siren for a few seconds, a gesture of pure defiance to the stolid sergeant.

'He might not have seen us, Sarge. Wouldn't have wanted an accident.'

Moore limited himself to a cough.

The ambulance crew were obviously old acquaintances of the sergeant. He went over for a chat with the driver, leaving Capel uncertain what to do. He was not in charge, it was down to the police to dictate the action, but it seemed to him that they ought to be haring up the hill towards the body. Moore turned from his friendly chat, seeing Vicky and Capel sitting uncomfortably in the car.

'Go on then, Denning,' said the sergeant. 'You accompany Mr Capel to the top, you've got younger legs. I'll follow on with these gentlemen.'

'Are you sure, Sarge? I've never...'

'You'll have to some time,' said the sergeant, more warmth in his voice than the words suggested. 'We won't be far behind.

You know what to do.'

Vicky glanced at herself in the mirror and flicked a finger along her fair fringe. She caught sight of Capel, once more looking straight into her reflected eyes from the back seat and hurriedly got out. Capel tried to open his door, but the child locks were on. Vicky opened it for him. Seeing her outside the car for the first time he revised his estimate of her age downwards. He smiled broadly at himself. Here he was in his early thirties - all right, if you insisted on it, mid thirties - and already the police were looking young. And, in this case, very attractive too. He had never understood the alleged appeal of uniforms, but Constable Denning was an exception. The black cloth set off her light coloured hair and softly blue eyes like dark velvet on a jeweller's counter. It was a shame about the shoes.

He realised that this was not the time to be eyeing up the police. 'Sorry,' said Capel, smiling again so the constable couldn't help but smile back at him. It suited her. 'I was miles away.' Not entirely truthful, but diplomatic. 'It's this way.'

'I know,' said Vicky.

'I'm sorry again,' said Capel. 'I'm telling you how to find your way around your own town.' They were silent until they had passed through the stile and were on the first, steep ascent of the Tor. Head down, concentrating on his footing, Capel noticed that the dew had already gone, leaving the grass by the path dry and flat. This wasn't good enough; he ought to say something.

'Are you on holiday?' asked Vicky, interrupting Capel's attempts to think of a suitable ice-breaker for talking to young, female police officers. 'You don't look like the sort to be here for the "mystical experience".' She surrounded the last two words with mimed quotation marks.

'You could say it's a bit of both. I've never been to Glastonbury - always meant to, you know what it's like - but I'm also here on a sort of mystical business. I should be at a conference at the Diocesan Centre.'

'You're not a vicar?' It was difficult to say just what Vicky felt; there seemed to be regret as well as the usual faint discomfort.

'It's not compulsory,' said Capel. 'You can attend a conference there without being one. But, yes, I am.'

'I used to go to church when I was younger. I just sort of ran out of the time for it.'

'We've got very similar jobs, you and I. Particularly the way we affect lay people. We make them feel uncomfortable - guilty, almost. And yet we're both there to help. We might as well recognise our similarities and get over the labels.'

'You don't look like a vicar. Sorry, that's the sort of thing you mean, isn't it?'

'I'll take it as a compliment. I don't suppose you look much like a policewoman out of uniform. It's another thing we've got in common; half the time people only see the uniform, they don't see the person.'

'That's certainly true, Mr Capel.'

'Stephen, please. Or Capel - that's what my friends call me.'

'Perhaps we could keep it to Mr Capel for the moment.'

'Sorry. You hit on a pet subject; my enthusiasm overcame my sense of occasion. I don't want you to think I'm always like this when I find bodies.'

'You don't make a habit of it?'

'It's only my second, and the other was very different.' He paused, his mind running off at a tangent as he caught sight of the lone tower of St Michael re-appearing from behind a fold in the ground. It was still high above them. 'Do you think they thought building up on the hilltop brought them closer to God?'

'That sort of thing's more in your line, isn't it?'

'What?' said Capel, momentarily at a loss. He stopped, watching the young policewoman stride steadily up the hill ahead of him, already showing her greater fitness. He struggled to catch her up, running clumsily on the uneven grass to circle round her. 'Not really. You must be interested in people's motivation. Why they went to the trouble of building the thing up here. It was a phenomenal effort, given the technology of the time.'

Vicky nodded, not sure what to make of the man. When she had last attended church her parish priest had been a humourless old sort, a remnant of a dinosaur breed who believed that his position in life depended on maintaining a clear distance between himself and his parishioners. He had longed for a time that he had never seen outside historical films, where the rector was a prominent member of society, a regular member of the squire's dining circle along with the doctor and the retired army officer.

'Whatever the reason,' said Capel, 'we should be grateful.' Vicky looked bemused for a moment. Oh, yes, he was talking about the church on the Tor, not fusty old priests. Capel carried on regardless: 'Without it, the Tor would be just another hill. The tower - it's strange how it's stayed when the rest fell - sets it off. Almost like it was put there as the finishing touch.'

'You don't have to distract me with chatter, you know,' said Vicky, wondering if Capel had picked up something of her uncertainty back in the car. 'I don't have to like bodies, but it's all part of the job.'

'Mine too,' said Capel. 'I said we had a lot in common.'

Vicky smiled, a genuine smile that came as much from her eyes as her mouth. 'If I didn't know better, I'd think you were chatting me up, reverend.'

'That's not a bad suggestion, constable.'

'It wasn't...' she stopped in confusion, a faint blush on her cheeks.

'Last stretch,' said Capel. 'Is there anything I can tell you about finding him?'

'Of course.' Vicky visibly pulled herself into official mode. 'Why were you up so early?'

'I couldn't sleep. I don't know about you, but once I'm wide awake in the morning, that's it. I might as well get up and do something.' He waited for a response, but realised that it could only lead to more embarrassment. 'So I came for a walk. As I said, I've never visited Glastonbury before. Coming to the Tor was a whim. I didn't realise how far it was; if I had, I probably wouldn't have bothered. I nearly gave up at least twice.'

'Did you see anyone else on your walk?'

'One or two people in the centre of town. You know, those sort of grey people who always seem to be about first thing in the morning, going about some mysterious business of their own. Then nobody until I was starting up the Tor. Well that's not true - I'm not being a very good witness - of course I saw lots of people, but they were in cars so I didn't see them, if you follow me. No one stopped, though. Then, when I was on the Tor, a man came down past me - running. I thought he might be going to the police, but it sounds like he wasn't.'

'Could you describe him?'

'Roughly - I know I'd recognise him if I saw him again, but I'm hopeless at verbal pictures. He was a big man, taller than me. Well tanned. A beard; reddish-brown hair - the beard was lighter, almost ginger - long hair, tied back with a strip of cloth. He looked like a traveller.'

'A hippy, you mean?'

'If you like. I'm not being evasive to be politically correct, it's just inaccurate. It's like calling someone who rides a motorbike and wears leathers a rocker, as if they still had battles with mods on Brighton beach.'

'Whatever. A peace person, if you prefer it. We have one or two in Glastonbury.'

'I don't particularly like "peace person", either. But I can't think of a suitable label. He had colourful clothes - they looked handmade, except for the jeans. Nothing else of note.'

'Earrings? Tattoos?'

'Possibly. He came past me very quickly. I'd say he was concerned or scared. That's why I thought he was going for the police.'

'And you saw no one else?'

'No one except the body.'

'How did you find it?'

Capel fought down the urge to say that he found it very unpleasant. 'I was going to walk round the outside of the tower, but then I saw someone, or something, inside. It sounds very petty, but I was irritated. I wanted the place to myself and I particularly resented that I'd been beaten to it. When I got a little closer, I was concerned. I thought he might have collapsed. You can just see him, in the corner there.'

The edge of the arch was darkened by a crumpled shape, unchanged as far as Capel could tell.

'Did you touch anything?'

'No more than I had to. I made sure he was dead, but apart from that I kept well away. The whole thing took less than five minutes.'

'Could anyone else have been here? When you arrived could someone have been hidden?'

'I suppose so; I didn't search the place. There was no one else inside the tower, that much was obvious, but someone could have been at the far side. I don't even know what's there, I never went through.'

'That's a pity.'

'I can see that.'

They walked the last few feet, Capel dropping back a little so he could observe the policewoman. As soon as she was in plain sight of the body she tensed up. Her fists clenched, paling at the knuckles. She looked back, her face whitened to a stark mask.

'There's no blood,' said Capel tentatively, trying to be reassuring.

'I've seen blood before,' said Vicky, resenting the implication of weakness. Capel had succeeded in reassuring her, but not in the way he intended. He watched as Vicky knelt by the body, looking closely at its neck, holding the shirt out of the way with the end of a pencil. 'That mark on his neck is very thin,' she commented, half to herself. The rubber tip of the pencil continued to probe the body's extremities, lifting the obscuring clothing like a curious insect. 'There are similar wounds on the wrists. Did you see them?'

'No,' said Capel. He crouched beside her. 'His ring's a bit of mess. It looks like someone's tried to force it off - the knuckle's scraped just above...'

'Could you stand back a little, sir. We wouldn't want to disturb anything before there's a chance to check it.'

Capel accepted her sudden formality, noticing the sergeant, his face a plummy red, steaming up the path towards them. 'I'll, er...' Capel gestured through the arch, 'I'll wait out the other side.'

Beyond the tower was a flat open space, worn to the bare earth by more feet than Capel would have expected to make the trek up there. He sat on the trig station, mind blank as he absorbed the clear views out to the distant hills. When solid footfalls approached from behind he hardly moved.

'Excuse me... Capel, the sergeant says would you mind waiting for the Chief Inspector to come up from Taunton. It'll be half an hour or so. You could go on down to the Conference Centre if you like, but the Chief likes to interview people on the spot.'

Capel smiled to himself, to the open air, at Vicky's hesitant acceptance of his name. 'I'm in no hurry. To be honest, now I'm up here I can't help thinking this is a better place to be than the conference. There's certainly a better view.' He turned to face the girl, smiling widely. Her eyes were screwed up in a frown.

'It's not such a nice place right now.'

'I'm sorry, I have an infuriating ability to appreciate the joys of creation even when I'm depressed by our ability to screw it up. Do you come up here often?'

'Not really. You don't, when it's local.'

'That's it - it's different through a stranger's eyes. Look, Constable Denning, this is going to seem a bit odd, I suppose, but you couldn't spare me some off-duty time, could you? I'd appreciate a local guide - perhaps we could get something to eat this evening.'

'Really, Mr Capel! It's hardly... respectful.' She nodded

towards the tower.

'Respect isn't about sackcloth and ashes. I might even be able to tell you something more about what I saw in a relaxed atmosphere. What do you say? Do your good deed for the day, help a bewildered clergyman.'

'Where are you staying, the Centre?'

'No, the George and Pilgrim.'

'Seven o' clock in the bar?'

'Good.'

'Denning!' The sergeant seemed to think she had taken long enough asking Capel to wait. 'Get the witness moved, please. No more trampling across the crime scene.'

'Coming, sarge.'

CHAPTER 3

Capel, banished to the edge of the summit, did not find it difficult to keep himself amused. There was something about him that appreciated solitude; he needed only a sufficiently varied vista to be able to marvel at the detailed complexity of it all. A friend of his, a chemist of some note who delighted in stressing his agnosticism, had put forward the complexity of life as the only possible proof of the existence of God. Capel personally doubted the logic of his friend's argument, and the need for it, but observation of the tiny details of the world around him could keep his attention indefinitely - the ladybird, scuttering across the surface of a single dandelion that grew defiantly from the base of the trig station; the subtle variations in granularity of the sandy soil; a bright blue tractor weaving along a track, its engine noise muted by distance to a dull burr. It wasn't that he was a solitary man, he was never happier than with people, but he had no problem with being alone.

'Mr Capel?' Vicky's voice dragged him back from contemplation of an errant patch of clover. There was a new formality in her tone. The Inspector must have arrived. Capel turned, his smile freezing despite every effort to keep it there.

'Funny place for a reunion, Stephen,' said the detective.

'Malcolm Davies? You're the Inspector?'

'Chief Inspector, Mr Capel,' Vicky corrected him.

'Better and better. I thought you'd be lucky to have three stripes by now. You must have got the special handshake down to a fine art.' He wondered if he had gone too far. Davies used to be touchy when he had known him, so long ago.

'Mr Capel!' Vicky, it seemed, was certain he had exceed the limit. It was rare enough to have the C.I. up from Taunton; now, when she was on the verge of applying for WDC, she could feel her control of the situation slipping away along with the plain clothes.

'Don't worry, er...'

'Denning,' Capel filled in, earning himself a black look from the policewoman.

'Denning. Mr Capel and I go back a long way, Denning.'

'I haven't seen *Chief* Inspector Davies since we graduated. I'd heard he'd entered the force, but I imagined him keeping an eye on the traffic on the M1 or something.'

'No thanks to Masonic mumbo-jumbo, I assure you. Perhaps we can have a drink when this is sorted.'

'It sounds a good idea, but not tonight.' Capel noted the silent pleading from Vicky and restrained the urge to torment her further. 'I've got some reading to catch up on.' It was easy to be economical with the truth. There had been no common ground between Capel and Davies at university. Capel, while majoring in psychology, had spent most of his time with a group of music students; Davies had stuck to the rugby club circle, his only ventures into music limited to droning a rugby song.

'Whenever,' said Davies, suddenly businesslike. He hadn't changed much from undergraduate days. Except for a short moustache, hiding a patch of his porcine, heavy-pored skin, he could have been on his way to a maths supervision. Even his clothes seemed a relic of a bygone era. And his hair was still too long. 'Would you mind walking me through it? How you found the body; what you saw.'

'I hadn't come far up the Tor...'

'You can leave that 'til later. If you'd come round to the far side of the tower, I'd like to step through the discovery with you.'

'Of course.' Capel followed the Chief Inspector meekly, stepping onto the newly positioned protective plastic walkway.

He paused at the corner of the tower, trying to remember where he had been when he had felt that intruding presence. Already his memory was hazy.

'I got about this far before I noticed anything. When I saw it - the body - I wasn't sure what it was to start with. Then I thought it could be someone who'd collapsed - I was feeling a bit rough myself after the haul up the hillside.'

'Exertion was never one of your strong points, was it? I'm surprised you came up here at all.' Davies allowed himself a thin smile.

'Just a whim. Anyway, I came closer, touched his shoulder, and I knew it was too late for any help.'

'You could pray for him,' said Davies.

Capel thought it typical of the man - Davies had done his homework very thoroughly and yet he managed to be unsubtle to the point of rudeness. 'I will, ' said Capel, 'I will pray for him. And whoever did it.'

'Ah yes, the caring church. So he was facing the wall when you found him?'

'Not exactly. His head and shoulders were twisted away from me, that's all.'

'What else did you notice?'

'There was the abrasion on his neck, of course. I assumed he'd hanged himself at first, going on his neck and that piece of orange rope on the wall. It looks like a climbing piton holding it up. But he must have got down somehow; he certainly couldn't have done that himself.'

'I'm sure your theories are very interesting. Was there anything else you actually saw?'

'There was water round his head.' Capel looked carefully past the photographer who was lining up yet another shot of the victim. 'It's almost gone now, but there was quite a lot of water round his head. His hair was very wet.'

'But there hasn't been rain in nearly a week,' said Davies, not contradicting, merely observing.

'It didn't seem like rain. Only his head was wet. His hair, his face and the floor round about.'

'What did that make you think?'

'What should I think? He had a wet head.'

'Anything else you noticed?'

'Nothing really. There's the initials, of course - they look quite recent, but they might have nothing to do with it.'

'Initials?'

Capel pointed silently at the wall a few feet below the shiny metal pin of the piton. The initials HM were scratched lightly on the grey surface, easily missed at a glance in the dim light that filtered down into the tower.

'Of course.' Davies absent-mindedly pushed the photographer out of the way to get a closer look at the mark. 'I believe you passed one of our unwashed, peace-loving friends on the way up the Tor?'

'Yes,' said Capel, frowning at this unexpected leap.

'I might have to ask you to identify the gentleman at a later date, but for the moment, that'll be all.' Davies turned stiffly, running a finger over his moustache. 'Haven't you finished yet?' he snapped at the photographer, Capel dismissed from his mind.

'I'll go down to the Centre, then,' Capel said, ignoring the abrupt termination of the interview. 'I ought to put in an appearance.'

'We'll be in touch, sir,' said Vicky. Her eagerness to avoid a reference to the evening was transparent.

'I'll look forward to that,' said Capel. To Vicky's relief he started off down the hill before he could be offered a lift.

~

Putting in an appearance proved to be all that Capel was capable of when he arrived at the Conference Centre. He picked up his course materials and sat quietly in the corner, unable to concentrate on the merits of greater lay participation in parish activities. It was a relief when the interminable discussion session finished and the day's programme closed. He felt an uncomfortable sense of release at the chance to go back to the George and put the course behind him. There was something very unreal, intrusive, about everyday life after an event like that morning's.

For a moment when he opened the door and saw the maid straightening the bedclothes a spasm of irritation passed across his face, then the professional smile of habit settled into place.

'Working late today?'

The girl - she must still have been in her teens - looked up in embarrassment, but couldn't help smiling. Capel's remark to Vicky about seeing past a uniform was more than a chat-up line; he had a simple gift of talking to the real person, whatever the role that hid them. He put it down to his time working in prisons, where expectations of the stereotype concealed everyone, prisoner and warder alike.

'I'm not supposed to be in today,' said the maid, 'but Linda - she should have been on this morning - she's got a bit of trouble so they rang me.' Her face was suddenly serious as she realised that she was being overly familiar with a guest. She flushed, her eyes crossing slightly under her dark fringe.

'That's very good of you, er...' Capel squinted to read the embossed plastic name badge, 'Andrea. Coming in at short notice.'

'I could do with the money. I had the weekend off because my boyfriend was over to stay. He's at uni in Bath. It was nice of him - he had to sneak out to see me - but it means I lost the pay.' It hadn't taken much reassurance to get back her openness, though Capel was particularly talented at winning confidences. 'Is it true?' she was apprehensive, but she was determined to carry it through. 'That you found him; Paul Schofield, up on the Tor?'

'I don't know his name, but I found a body.' It struck Capel that she was much of an age with the dead man. They could have been friends. 'Did you know him, this Paul Schofield?'

'Sort of. He was a couple of years ahead of me at school.

Used to go around with my brother Ben until he - Paul, I mean - until he got in with Kevin Blake and Dave Gunn. Our mum wouldn't let Ben go out with them. She always said they were gyppos, though they never are.'

'Do you know Paul's family?'

'There was only him - apart from his mum and dad, I mean. They live down in Leden Street, Mr and Mrs Schofield. A bit...' she looked puzzled for a moment, searching for a word. 'A bit reticent, they are. Old fashioned, but no harm in them.'

'Losing Paul will be a shock to them.'

'That's right enough. It wasn't a secret that they wanted him to settle down and get married so they'd have somewhere to go when they were getting on. They were already pretty old when they had Paul.'

About my age, no doubt, thought Capel. Pretty old. 'I don't suppose they thought too much of his friends, then.'

'Couldn't stand the bastards, if you'll pardon the language. I heard them yelling at him once - said he'd end up in front of the magistrate rather than the vicar if he hung around with those two. It was as good as encouraging him to make trouble.'

'Probably. Do you happen to know what number they live at?'

'Twelve, I think it is. Next to the old grain store.'

'I might go and see them tomorrow. I don't suppose it will help a lot right now, but it might later.'

'You must be brave... sir.' Suddenly, Capel couldn't see why, she was all bustling efficiency. She checked his supply of coffee sachets, gave the pillows a last pat and left, head down, without a further word.

Capel slumped on the bed, creasing the newly straightened cover. He marvelled at the effectiveness of the gossip circuit of a small town that could label him the finder of the body and bring him the name of the victim all in a day. He wouldn't be surprised if the chambermaid had known the cause of death as well. The telephone cut through his thoughts with a low, self-satisfied buzz.

'Hello, Stephen Capel here.'

'So it is,' said a deep, slightly sarcastic voice, losing none of its intonation through the tinny loudspeaker. 'How're you doing, honey-bunch?'

'Get stuffed, Ed,' said Capel with no malice.

'Love you too.' Edward Ridge and Capel spoke in a habitual code. 'I wondered if the C of E's answer to Father Brown needed a Doctor Watson.'

'That's a mixed metaphor, or something. And you'd make an appalling Doctor Watson, even if Fliss allowed you out to play. You're too self-opinionated, Ridge. The great detective needs a mirror for his genius, not a court jester. For that matter, I don't see how I qualify as Father Brown.'

'Finding the body, death in mysterious circumstances, all that sort of thing. I expect you're hot on the trail already.'

'Don't be ridiculous, Ed. An amateur detective is pretty unbelievable in fiction; it's ludicrous in real life. And how do you know about the body? Everyone I speak to already knows I'm the man who found the body. It's not fair, I'm missing out on the chance to tell anyone my big news. It's bad enough the locals knowing, but I didn't expect word to have spread to the hallowed glades of Sunningdale already. Was it on TV or something?'

'Not that I know of. We only listen to the wireless here. You're disappointing me, Holmes, I expected better from a man of your calibre.'

'Thanks Edward and good night. This isn't a joke you know, someone is dead.'

'Point taken. I rang the Conference Centre. I was hoping to scrounge dinner off you later in the week - got some business in those parts - they told me about it when I rang.'

'It'd be great if you could come. I might even know some more about what's happened by then - I'm seeing one of the police on the case this evening.'

'Late night interrogation, is it? Rubber truncheons, hoses, and "Whoops, did you fall down the stairs, sir?"'

'Not exactly. I'm taking her out to dinner.'

'Bloody hell, that's quick work, Capel.'

'We have no comment to make at this time.'

'I expect a full status report before I come down. Is Thursday night okay for you, or are you going to the cinema with the Chief Constable?'

'It's ideal. It's my last night of freedom before I get back to old mother Rhees at Thornton; consider it a sort of miniature stag night. A Bambi night. I'll book a table at the hotel here, the restaurant's pretty good if you can afford it - and you can.'

'I thought I was the one doing the scrounging - how come I'm paying?'

'Information is power. If you want to hear more, the dinner's on you. Humble parish priests don't get paid as much as Home Office mandarins.'

'Don't rush me, I'm little more than a satsuma so far. Does your bishop know about your expertise at touching people for cash? He ought to have you on the local fund raising committee.'

'Go and send yourself a memo,' said Capel.

'There's no point, I never read them. I've got an even better idea.'

'Saints preserve us.'

'Very Father Brown. Look, I should get most of my business concluded over dinner on Wednesday evening. That means I'll be free mid-morning on the Thursday. Why don't you bunk off your lectures and we can re-visit our youth and all that stuff. What do you think?'

'Get thee behind me, Satan. Though it's not such a bad idea; I've practically abandoned this course. I think I'm going to have to take it again.' Capel bit on the lower, fleshy part of his right forefinger, a habit when thinking that had stayed with him since childhood. 'You're on - you'd better come up to my room when you get here, I've tried meeting you at a set time before; it doesn't work.'

'Such faith.'

'Such experience. Now push off, I need to get ready.'

'You certainly need all the time you can get if you want to look presentable,' agreed Ridge. 'Good luck. I hope she's gentle with you.'

'Up yours,' said Capel and put the phone down.

CHAPTER 4

Capel scooped the last of his crême caramel from the pudding plate, his face showing nothing more than bland contentment. Across the small table, Vicky Denning pushed aside the remains of a chocolate mousse. The shape of her face seemed different, cheekbones softened by the outline of her hair. She had let it down to drape on the neckline of a well-washed dress that was too old to be fashionable, but too good to throw away. She kept touching the dark blonde strands, slipping her hand up to push them back from her face.

If Capel had felt any guilt at moving on to a significantly cheaper restaurant after a drink at the George, it soon faded. After all, the food was still excellent. They had managed to get through the meal without any mention of the morning's events, as if it were the sort of subject that should not be discussed over the dinner table. Now Capel pushed his chair back a little as he asked for some coffee and wondered if Vicky would feel constrained from talking about the murder.

'Do you know how Paul Schofield died yet?'

'It's weird...' Vicky put her spoon down and looked Capel hard in the eyes. 'How do you know his name?'

'Sources,' said Capel, 'I'm not without my sources.'

'Old boy network with the C.I., I suppose. Flashing the old university tie, were we?'

'Much too obvious, Constable. I can't say Malcolm and I were ever chums, though I could probably dig up a couple of unsavoury memories about college days which would liven up your rest room. No, I got the information from the chambermaid at the George. Probably significantly more reliable.'

'You'll have some gossip to pass back to her, then; I can't see it's going to stay a secret. He wasn't hung. That rope was nothing to do with it. He was drowned. On top of the highest hill in these parts, on a clear, dry night, a man drowned.'

~

There was something addictive about large quantities of food, Capel thought, and he was being given plenty of chance to indulge himself. Certainly there was no danger of him leaving Glastonbury slimmer. He scanned the panoply of the full English breakfast on the huge oval plate in front of him, wondering which magnificent, unhealthy item to attack first.

'Mr Capel?'

Capel looked up from the fat, brown, herb-rich Cumberland sausage that his gaze had settled on. He raised an eyebrow at Chief Inspector Davies, not trusting his brain to override his stomach, which was egging him on to make a brusque reply. A man should not be diverted from a breakfast of this magnitude. This was a serious breakfast.

'Sorry to disturb you, er, Steve.' The C.I. fingered his moustache defensively.

Capel was gracious, overlooking the strongly disliked 'Steve' - it was what he was called at college, so he could hardly blame Davies. He couldn't bring himself to use 'Mal' in return, though. 'It's no problem, Malcolm. How can I help?'

'I wouldn't normally bother you...' Davies paused. It struck Capel that the policeman would have been more comfortable in an earlier age when he would have had a hat to toy with. His hands were restlessly roaming in and out of his pockets. 'I was passing here anyway; there's been an incident at the Well Gardens. It may be connected with yesterday and I'd like you to come with me. Tell me if you recognise anyone, that's all.'

Capel looked sadly at the symphony of high cholesterol

excellence in front of him. 'And no doubt we have to go immediately?'

Davies nodded. Capel accepted the inevitable, grabbing a slice of toast as he passed an overloaded basket on someone else's table. He would have to make do with the continental breakfast this morning and leave the real thing to the next day.

There was an unmarked car waiting on the double yellow lines outside the hotel. The driver, like Davies, wore an everyday suit, though managed it with significantly more style. The younger man no doubt spent a lot of effort on choosing the right clothes; Davies looked as if he had picked up the first thing that had almost fitted him in Marks and Spencer's. Several years previously.

'Do you know anything about the well?' Davies asked conversationally over his shoulder as the car pulled out into Glastonbury's mild rush hour.

'Something to do with Joseph of Arimathea and the Holy Grail, isn't it?' said Capel.

'That's the story, that he brought the Grail over here and hid it in the well. Though from what I hear, it's a pretty modern idea. But I don't doubt that the well had some significance as a holy place before that. Whenever it started, it's become a bloody beacon to the usual oddballs and misfits. Like Glastonbury as a whole, I'm afraid. All crystal power and zodiacs and mumbo jumbo.'

'A lot of people are searching for something,' said Capel.

'But not looking in the right direction, eh?' said Davies, a sneer tainting his voice.

'Perhaps not - but at least they know that there's something to look for.'

The policeman limited himself to a snort. Capel watched the frozen faces of the pedestrians as the car slid slickly past. If expressions were any mirror of the soul, quite a few of them needed something to look for.

They pulled up by a wooden fence, newly painted a fashionably sober dark green. Capel got out of the car, following

Davies and the younger man, who'd identified himself as Sergeant Tobin, away from the Tor. At the corner, a tiny pay booth was crammed full with a large uniformed policeman and another man, a man who Capel immediately recognised as the person who had blundered past him on the Tor. Capel felt Davies's eyes fixed on him, looking for a reaction. He controlled his expression, reluctant to give anything away until he knew more of the situation.

'Well, Jackson?' Sergeant Tobin took the lead.

'This is him, sir,' said the bulky constable, hanging halfway out of the booth. He glanced at his catch as if expecting an outburst, but the other man sat quietly on the single seat in the booth, staring at the floor. 'I was called out by the caretaker, Mrs, er...' he took a quick glance at his notebook, 'Mrs Greenham. She came to open up and saw that the gate had been forced. When I arrived Mr Mal ... Mr Malkovski was still busy at the well.' He pronounced the name as he had written it, with a hard v. His prisoner looked up for a moment, then continued his study of the floor.

'Busy doing what?' asked Davies.

'He'd levered up the cover of the well with a crowbar - it's kept locked when there's no one here - and he was trying to get some water in a jam jar. On a piece of string.'

Capel suppressed a laugh that was bubbling in his throat. 'Why did you do that?' he asked the man.

'Why shouldn't I?' Malkovski looked him in the eye, his defiance tempered by Capel's mild tone. 'The water comes from the earth, everybody's earth. I'm as entitled to it as anyone else.'

'Where were you at six o'clock yesterday morning?' Davies asked suddenly.

'Me?' said Malkovski.

'You, Mr Malkovski. Henry isn't it?' Davies's voice became unpleasantly wheedling. 'I'm just looking for a bit of cooperation. Trying to get a few facts straight.'

'Yesterday...' said Malkovski. He scratched vigorously at the back of his head. 'Monday I go over to Wells. We've got a stall on the market there. Sell things we make.'

'You went first thing?' said Davies. 'You didn't go anywhere else, before you went into Wells?'

'No.' The answer was very quick. Malkovski glanced at Capel, uncertain of his part in the affair. He seemed not to recognise him.

'You didn't perhaps go for an early morning walk? Get some clear air into your lungs, stretch your legs before the drive?'

'Is anyone saying I did?'

'I just want to make certain, Mr Malkovski. I wouldn't want to think that I was confusing you with someone else. There's nothing the police like less than a case of mistaken identity. It looks bad on the news. Makes us look like idiots. You wouldn't want us to look like idiots, would you, Mr Malkovski?'

Malkovski seemed about to make matters worse. 'I was on the Tor yesterday morning,' Capel said quietly. He was rewarded with a glare from Davies.

'You asked me if I went anywhere,' said Malkovski. 'That's all I was saying. I didn't go anywhere. I started out for a walk, up to the Tor, you know, but about half way up I remembered something, so I came back down. Not what you'd call going anywhere.'

'So you never reached the top of the Tor?'

'Nowhere near.'

'You seemed in a hurry when you passed me.' Capel earned another black look from Davies.

'I said I'd forgotten something. I had to get back to the house.'

'What would that be, exactly? What did you forget?' asked Davies.

'Nothing to interest you.'

'Let me be the judge of that.'

'I don't think so. I don't think it's your responsibility to judge, Inspector er...?'

'Davies.' The policeman's face reddened. 'Don't play with words. You know what I meant.'

'I'm not playing. And it really is none of your business.'

Davies sighed noisily. 'It will be, Mr Malkovski, it will be. For the moment, perhaps you'd like to accompany Sergeant Tobin to the station. He'll take a statement from you about your movements since Sunday night. Do you think you might bring yourself to cooperate with that?'

Malkovski held out his hands dramatically, as if expecting to be handcuffed. The uniformed constable gently pulled him upright from his seat and out of the pay booth, handing him over to the sergeant. With nothing further to do, Constable Jackson loomed in the doorway of the booth like a sentry on watch.

'That wasn't very helpful, Steve.' Davies looked at Capel with a pained expression. 'I like to let them dig their own pits.'

'Perhaps that's the difference between our jobs. I'm supposed to help them out, not push them in.'

'I presume you do identify Malkovski as the man you saw on Monday morning? You aren't going to come over all coy with me, are you, Capel?' Chief Inspector Davies' attempt at firmness only made Capel feel more comfortable.

'I've no interest in obscuring the truth, Malcolm. I saw him on the Tor. I'm happy to identify him.'

'Thank you. I'm afraid Tobin has taken the car back, but I could get the constable to call you another.'

'Don't worry, I'll enjoy the walk. After I've looked round. I trust you have no objection to my doing a bit of sight-seeing, while I'm here?'

'Help yourself. The Greenham woman's skulking somewhere if you want to hear about the place. I've got a call to make. Constable!'

The uniformed man sprang to attention as Davies addressed him. Capel left them to it. He saw a maroon-jacketed figure leaning over the lid of the well, peering short-sightedly at something below ground level. Capel walked on the edge of the path, giving way to a silly impulse to approach quietly.

'Mrs Greenham, is it?'

The woman jerked round to face him. She was red-faced, a little overweight. Grey eyes squinted at him from behind pebble-thick lenses. 'Not again? Do you policemen never talk to each other?' Capel tried to interrupt, but was borne down in a flow of complaint, expressed in a melodious voice that sat uneasily with the woman's appearance. 'Don't you think there's a more efficient way of passing on information without every copper in the land pumping me for the story? It doesn't matter how often I tell it, you know, it will always be the same. I'm not some bloody woolly-brained widow, you know. You've no right to pigeonhole me.'

'I agree,' said Capel, managing to get it in when she took breath. 'And I'm not pigeonholing you. I'm also not with the police. I was hoping you could tell me something about the well.'

'I'm sorry. That's assumptions, you see. But you were with them.'

'Only as a witness. Have you been looking after the well long?'

'Since it was titivated a few years ago. To be quite frank, I don't hold with all this mysticism twaddle - a well's a well, as far as I'm concerned. It's a hole in the ground with a spot of water underneath. The garden's the interest for me. I get bored with my little plot back home; this is more of a challenge, that's why I took it on. That and the money. Widows' pensions don't seem to keep up with inflation, whatever they tell you.'

'But a lot of your visitors must be interested in the well itself.'

'Of course. Mind you, we get every sort of crank you could wish for. Serious historians too, I'm sure, but our main appeal is to the wide-eyed innocents who lap up this New Age guff.'

'Do you get many local people visiting, or are they all out-of-town types, like myself?'

'Mostly it's grockles we get, but there are a few old faithfuls. This town has more than its fair share of the... what can I say? Gullible, I suppose. Not real locals of course; outsiders attracted in by the Glastonbury reputation. There's even a girl writing a book on the well; she's one of the worst sort. More beads than baths, if you know what I mean. All floating hair and wistfulness, the sort of thing the intellectual Victorians went in for in a big way.'

'Do you know her name? I'm quite interested in New Age writing.'

'Really?' There was a new coldness about Mrs Greenham, as if Capel had suddenly plunged in her estimation. 'She calls herself by some silly name. Something Cooper - Lin... no, Lillith. Lillith Cooper. I can't imagine her parents christened her with a name like that. If they did, they've got a lot to answer for.'

'Do you know where she lives?'

'Certainly not. She comes here quite frequently, but I don't have any other contact with the girl.' Mrs Greenham's tone made it clear that Capel's credibility had sunk even further.

'Ah,' said Capel neutrally. A change of subject seemed politic. 'Is it the first time you've had a break-in?'

'It's the first there's been in my time. I've been here about five years; you should have seen the garden when I arrived. The problem is that the police don't really care about vandalism - not high enough in their priorities. Somebody smashed the original cover of the well years ago, I know that. But the only trouble I'd had until the weekend were a couple of holes in the fence, the sort of thing young men these days feel is necessary to prove their manhood when they've had too much to drink. You didn't get that sort of thing when we had national service.'

'I suppose not.' Capel paused, pulling together the facts from the tangled story. 'Something else happened at the weekend, then?'

'It's all of a piece with today. When I came to open up on Monday, I found someone had been tampering with the well. I let the police know, but of course they weren't interested. Too busy with something on the Tor to spare a car, they said, as if it isn't only a few yards walk. So I kept a watch out this morning. I thought he'd be back. When I saw him climbing over the gate I called the police again. They couldn't say "no" then, could they? Not with him here, red handed.'

'I can see what you mean.' Capel took a step forward so that he could look into the open mouth of the well. It didn't look anything special: a dark hole, speaking with the muted voice of the spring beneath. 'Thank you, Mrs Greenham, thank you very much.'

CHAPTER 5

Leden Street was a narrow road between houses that teetered between character and decrepitude. Capel had driven, and now he was regretting it. There wasn't the width for two cars to park opposite each other and a solid string of vehicles lined the left hand pavement. He crawled up the hill, looking for a space. Just as it seemed that he would have to go back round the block he found one, a tight gap near the end of the street. Capel sighed noisily. He didn't drive a big car - his stipend made sure that a battered Fiat was the limit of his aspirations - but parking in narrow spaces provided an uncomfortable threat to his manhood.

He pulled up alongside the forward car and prepared to reverse. As he turned to look over his shoulder his eyes met those of a boy, a scruffy youth of around ten, standing squarely on the pavement. Capel smiled, but it didn't seem to break through the boy's hypnotic fascination with Capel's car. Capel sighed again and started rolling back. Seconds into the manoeuvre, he knew he'd got it wrong. His rear wheels headed for the kerb as if magnetically attracted. The car pulled up with a rubbery thud, front wing protruding halfway across the narrow street. As he craned his neck to see if anything was coming up the road, Capel caught sight of the boy's eyes, still tied immovably to the vehicle. Capel frowned and pulled back out into the road. He lifted the gear stick for a second go at reverse. The gears grated painfully, refusing to engage. Capel couldn't help another glance at his audience. When he looked away he found that he had started to roll backwards down the steep slope, heading straight for the car behind. The engine revved wildly as he hit the accelerator, realised he was still out of gear and brought the car to a stop with a frantic jab on the brake.

The next attempt was totally anti-climactic. He slipped into the space with the precision of an automatic parking system. The boy was still there, waiting as Capel got out of the car and locked the door.

'There's something wrong with the gearbox,' Capel commented to the boy, who seemed to demand communication. 'I don't normally have trouble parking.'

The boy stayed silent.

'This hill's a bit of a swine,' said Capel, feeling increasingly defensive.

The boy finally looked away from the car's wheels. 'You just ran over a big slug,' he said with satisfaction. 'I heard it pop.' He ran off round the corner.

Capel studied the house numbers silently. He was outside number 46, a good distance from his goal. He plodded down the steep street, no one else in sight. Number 12 was a small cottage, brick with old beams lacing the front. Suitably restored, it would send an estate agent into raptures - at the moment a lot of imagination was required. There was no bell. He rapped firmly with the peeling black knocker.

'Yes?' The man who answered the door, though not beyond his fifties, looked quaintly old-fashioned. His shirtsleeves were fixed in place by the expanding metal bracelets that Capel remembered his father wearing. His trousers were baggy, his tie knitted and he wore a black armband above his left elbow.

'I've come about Paul,' Capel said carefully.

'Of course,' said the man, 'you'd better come in.' He shouted into the darkness behind him. 'It's the vicar, mother; about Paul.'

'I'm not actually...' Capel's voice tailed off as the man, Mr Schofield, ushered him into a small parlour, overheated by an electric fire with flickering red lights filtering through its fibreglass coals. The room was darkened by drawn curtains, lit only by a single standard lamp and the dull glow of the fire. Capel fingered his dog collar; he had worn it to make his presence easier for the couple, but this felt like deception.

Mrs Schofield, a pinched, thin-faced woman, dressed as much in a 1950s timewarp as her husband, looked up through sharp-framed spectacles at Capel. There was a handkerchief in her hand, screwed into a tight ball. She peered doubtfully at him. 'You aren't the vicar.' Her voice shook like that of a much older woman as she turned to her husband. 'He's not the vicar, father.'

'I should have explained,' said Capel. 'I'm not from Glastonbury, but I felt I ought to come and see you. I found Paul's body yesterday.'

Mrs Schofield's hand tightened on her handkerchief. Her husband came across and rested his hand on her shoulder. He stood well back from the chair, as if wary of consoling her too openly.

'My mistake,' said Mr Schofield, 'sit down.'

'Yes, sit down, please,' said Mrs Schofield. 'Would you like some tea?'

Capel, who always drank coffee and couldn't stand tea smiled warmly. 'Thanks, that would be wonderful. Perhaps I could get it for us?'

'No need to worry,' said Mr Schofield, 'Ian's getting it.' He raised his voice again. 'Can you get one more cup, Ian, we've got a visitor.'

'You have another son?' asked Capel.

'We only ever had the one boy,' said Mrs Schofield. 'Had. We've no one now. It's not right - it's not fair that he should be taken first.' She started sobbing quietly. Mr Schofield squeezed her shoulder, but he didn't move any closer.

'Ian's one of Paul's friends,' said Mr Schofield. 'The only one worth the time of day, if you ask me. Real yobboes, he chose to hang around with did our Paul. We couldn't understand it – they weren't even nice to him, except Ian. Our Paul was a good boy, worth ten of that filthy Gunn or Kevin Blake.'

'Paul spent a lot of time with them, did he?' said Capel.

'Every spare minute. Even if they left him alone for a night he didn't do anything worthwhile. He'd just read one of his trashy horror comics. We told him he ought to be doing something to better himself. Night school classes in something practical to learn a trade; he didn't want to be a porter all his life. But no, it was down to the pub with his mates. Or to the cinema, or more likely just hanging about the streets doing their best to scare people. They're animals are them two.'

'Was Paul with them the night he died?'

'He was earlier in the evening.' Mrs Schofield pushed up her glasses and mopped at her reddened eyes. 'Why does it happen, Mr...'

'Capel.'

'Mr Capel? Why does a boy like mine end up dying while hooligans like that can still strut around as if they owned the place?'

'I haven't got an easy answer, Mrs Schofield. I honestly believe that it is God's way not to interfere, to give us all free choice of action, good and bad, and that's sometimes very hard. But that doesn't mean there's no hope. In a sense, He can give us that free will because just once he did interfere, through his Son, to give us the hope of eternal life, and that's what you have to think of for Paul.'

The door swung open abruptly, crashing into the old fashioned sideboard, interrupting Capel. Ian Telfer stood in the doorway, a very pale young man, his hair nearly white, his eyelashes invisible, his close-set eyes the palest of washed-out blues. He held a tray in front of him protectively.

'This is Mr Capel, Ian,' said Mr Schofield. 'He was the one who found Paul.'

'Mr Capel.' Telfer's voice was low, a murmur, almost a whisper. He kept his head down as he slid the tray onto the sideboard. He looked more than concerned, more than upset. He looked frightened.

Somehow the police station was disappointing. Capel realised that he was expecting the sort of bustle that goes on in a murder mystery on the television. Perhaps everyday murders weren't like that. Everyday murder - not a pleasant thought.

'Can I help you?' It was a different man on the desk. He didn't recognise Capel.

'My name is Stephen Capel. I'd like to see Chief Inspector Davies, if he's available.'

'Chief Inspector Davies?' The policeman hesitated. 'Oh, the C.I. on the Schofield business. He's round the back. They've got an incident room in the car park, a sort of portakabin. They don't mix with us, more than they can help it.'

'Thank you.'

The car park was much closer to a TV show. A car was pulling out in a hurry, blue light flashing. A steady stream of people pushed through the narrow door of the temporary building. It was an ugly structure, a stark white box with a black chequered band at the top. The staff carried papers, boxes, all the paraphernalia of office life, down to chipped mugs and wilting plants. Two burly men in plain clothes stood right outside the door, deep in conversation, oblivious to the way they obstructed the path of the incoming goods.

Capel pushed through, following a small uniformed woman carrying a huge pile of wire mesh baskets. Inside the portakabin unbridled confusion thrived. Too many people were trying to do too much too quickly in too little space.

'How the hell can I set the computers up if there's no power on this socket?' a disembodied voice complained from beneath a desk.

Capel watched the chaos ripple around him for a while. It was soothing, like watching waves breaking on a shore. No one seemed to question the presence of a vicar - he hadn't had a chance to remove the dog collar - they paid him no more attention than the waves do a buoy, tossed disregarded by the storm. Capel realised he would have to take the initiative. He tapped the back of a nearby policewoman, who was attempting to plug cables into a small computer that nestled uncooperatively against the wall.

'Excuse me,' said Capel, 'I'm looking for Chief... Vicky! Constable Denning, that is.'

A number of expressions passed rapidly across Vicky Denning's features; confusion that a vicar should know her, recognition, mild embarrassment, all settling to a professional face, the sort of face that airline cabin crew come up with at the end of a long, difficult flight when the drinks have run out.

'Mr Capel. I didn't expect to see you here.'

'Me neither. You, I mean - I didn't know you were part of this.' He waved his hand in the air to indicate the whole scene.

'I'm in here for the duration.' Vicky seemed excited at the prospect. 'It's a real opportunity; I don't intend to stay in uniform for the rest of my career. I was lucky - being there when the body was notified, and then I've done this computer course so I was pretty well qualified.'

A young sergeant backed through the door with a filter coffee maker, barged alongside Capel and dumped the machine on the desk by Vicky. 'When you've finished that, love, rustle up some coffee for everyone. I've been on these jobs before; unless there's coffee on the go all the time it's like a madhouse.' He grinned at Capel and walked off.

'How can we help you, Mr Capel?' Vicky's face had set hard; all the enthusiasm of a moment ago had evaporated.

'I'd like to see Chief Inspector Davies, if he's available.'

'I'll check for you, sir.' Vicky gave the coffee maker a shove, rattling the jug, and threaded her way through the bedlam to a walled-off office at the end of the building. It was like being in a train, Capel thought. The long, narrow carriage; the end partitioned off like a driver's compartment - Vicky even adopted the sort of weaving walk that a train's motion imposes to get between her colleagues as they battled with the infrastructure of detection.

She was back quickly. 'He'll see you now.'

Several responses flicked through Capel's mind. His natural temptation was to tease her about the coffee, but sense prevailed. 'Thanks. Are you doing anything tonight?'

'Mr Capel!' She looked pleased. 'I'll be here 'til God knows when. There's no chance.'

'Tomorrow, then?'

'I don't know, I've never been involved in anything like this before. Can I ring you?'

'Here's my mobile number.' Capel handed over one of his newly printed cards. 'I'll be waiting for your call.'

'I don't know exactly when I'll be able to ring.'

'So? I've nothing better to do. It'll be worth it.'

Vicky turned her back on him, fiddling with the coffee maker. 'How do you like your coffee, Mr Capel?'

'White, no sugar. Thanks.'

Capel left it at that and picked his way down the portakabin. His foot caught a cable that was stretched across the narrow gap between a pair of desks. An angry head rose from behind the furniture. 'Watch where you're putting your fucking great... sorry, reverend. I thought you were one the lads.'

'So do I, sometimes,' said Capel. He knocked on the door, saw a movement behind the frosted glazing panel and pushed it open. The small space beyond was crammed tight with filing cabinets, a large desk and the bulky form of Davies, but it had obviously been set up earlier and was impressively calm after the main office. It had to be calm; it was so tight that Capel had to turn sideways to push past the cabinet by the door.

Davies looked up from the telephone, which was clamped between his chin and his right shoulder, and waved Capel into a seat that was squeezed into the only remaining floor space. 'Well get somebody up there! Not tomorrow, I want someone there today, this afternoon.' He smiled ominously at Capel. 'They've no idea... You, you George, you've no idea. Just get somebody onto it, all right?' He waited for a reply. 'Hello? George?' Davies rattled the telephone cradle. 'That's the last bloody straw.' He squeezed from behind his desk and flung the door open. 'Some bastard has cut through my telephone wire again! If it's not fixed in ten minutes I'll have someone's balls. For Christ's sake, what sort of an excuse for a police force is this?'

Capel coughed, wondering if Davies had forgotten him.

'These yokels need their heads banging together every half hour just to keep them awake,' Davies grumbled as he regained his chair. 'This place should have been set up yesterday, but they couldn't organise the proverbial piss-up. You know what the excuse was? We can't get the mobile incident room until tomorrow, sir. It's tied up. They'd only lent it to some bloody TV company to make yet another tedious bloody murder mystery - for Christmas. Can you imagine that? They call this sort of thing entertainment for Christmas. Christ, what a shambles.'

'I'm surprised you came here if that's the way you feel.'

'I didn't have much choice.'

'I didn't mean on the Schofield case.'

'Neither did I. It's my previous Chief Constable's policy. Supposed to make a better leader of you, if you move around a lot. If he had his way, you wouldn't get past C.I. without serving on two or three forces.'

'I can see the point,' said Capel.

'There's a lot to be said for being on your own patch, for growing in place. You get a finger on the pulse. And I wouldn't be working in a deadhole like this.'

'I like it.'

'You would.'

'And don't knock being moved about, we've gone that way in my organisation too. You don't see half as many of those ancient vicars who've been in the same church for the last fifty years and have no interest in the way their parish is developing. It works.'

'I don't suppose you came to discuss parishes,' said Davies grumpily. 'What do you want?'

'Just to see how things are going. I've been to see...'

Vicky came in with a small, battered tray. The cramped layout of the room forced her to stand right by Capel's seat. He couldn't help enjoying the innocent proximity.

'Put them on the desk, er...'

'Denning, sir.'

'Denning. Aren't there any biscuits?'

'Not yet, sir. We haven't had time.'

'Make time, Denning. I expect biscuits.'

'Yes, sir.'

'See what I mean?' said Davies, as if the lack of biscuits was the final mark of having left civilisation. 'What where you... Christ! There's no sugar in this, the stupid cow.'

'It's probably mine. You didn't give her a chance to say which was which.' Capel switched mugs and forged on quickly, not trusting himself to get into an argument about Vicky Denning. 'I went to see the boy's parents, the Schofields.'

'Good for you. Gave them a bit of comfort, did you?'

'I tried to. One of his friends was there, Ian something - Ian Telfer. It seems Paul was with him and a couple of other lads, rough types, the night it happened.'

'Give us a bit of credit, Steve. That bunch of no-hopers out there might be incapable of putting a simple incident room together, but we can manage the basics of detection. In fact I've a good mind to haul in those friends of Schofield's and charge them straight off. It'd save me the hassle of getting this place sorted.'

'You think that Paul's friends murdered him?'

'It seems the best bet to me - in my humble, insensitive opinion. And I'll get a confession out of Telfer. The other two, Gunn and Blake, they're hard bastards; they're the ones that'll have done it, but Telfer'll crack. He'll tell me all about it.'

'You've got proof? That was quick.'

'Proof, nothing. They're savages, Gunn and Blake. They deserve to be pulled in, even if they didn't do this one. Don't get me wrong, I've no intention of faking up evidence - naughty boys in the force tend to get caught these days. But I reckon if we prod around a bit, we'll find what we need.'

'What about Henry Malkovski?'

'Our happy hippy? We just gave him a talking to. I've not eliminated him, but I can't see it, myself. All bluster and self-importance. He'd no connection with Schofield, no reason for wanting him dead. Mr Malkovski's harmless enough.'

'Has he told you why he was running down the Tor?'

'No. That's one of the reasons I doubt he was involved. If he had a murder hanging over him, he'd be only too willing to cough up a story. You see what I'm saying? He's treating the whole thing too casually.'

'What about the initials?'

'Initials? Oh, your great discovery. Life is rarely so generous, Steve, even with divine guidance to help you. They could have been scratched there any time in the last week or so, there's plenty of opportunity up on the Tor. HM could be our Henry, but I doubt it.'

'You're probably right. Would you mind if I called on Mr Malkovski? I feel like I owe him an apology.'

'I can't see why, you were only doing your public duty.' Davies opened an orange file from a pile on the corner of his desk. 'Here you are, this is the address. He lives near the well; there's a terrace opposite the leather factory.' Davies shut the folder firmly, his body language indicating that the interview was over.

'Thanks, Malcolm.'

'Just don't tell them I gave you the address. They're the sort who're only too willing to jump on the police harassment bandwagon.'

'They?'

'He lives with a couple of women. Dodgy setup, but nothing more than you'd expect. Be good, Steve.'

'You too.'

The outer office was settling into a measure of order. Vicky was by the door, frowning as she tapped at the keyboard of the computer. Unconsciously she brushed at her fringe with her left hand. Capel didn't disturb her. They both had plenty to do.

CHAPTER 6

It seemed a good idea for Capel to lose his dog collar before he visited the Malkovski household. He walked along the uneven pavement of Chilkwell Street in jeans and the more disreputable of the two sweaters he had brought for his course.

It was difficult to suppress a twinge of guilt about playing truant, especially as once again he had walked past the Centre. But it was his duty, he assured himself. He could always go on another course; it was highly unlikely that he would ever again find himself tangled up in a murder.

He hesitated outside the small house. The door opened straight onto the pavement, a raised walkway reached from the road by a short flight of stone steps. In the window a small, faded poster announced a series of lectures on crystal healing. The door itself had been painted with a crude but bright dragon that started at ankle level and curved its way sinuously to a head with a knocker as a mouth. While Capel was trying to see past the net curtain a scruffy sparrow landed on the windowsill. It looked up from pecking at an unidentifiable blob of brown material to gaze speculatively at Capel.

'You're right,' Capel said to the sparrow. 'But I'm still doing it.' He knocked firmly on the dragon.

After a long wait, the door opened a few inches. 'Yes?' It was a female voice, edgy, unhappy. Capel caught a glimpse of whiteness through the gap.

'Hello. My name's Stephen Capel. I was at the well this morning when Mr Malkovski was caught. And I was on the Tor the day before. I wondered if I could have a word with him.'

'Are you police?' Very flat, still edgy.

'No, nothing to do with them, honestly. I just happened to be in Glastonbury. But I seem to have got caught up in this business with the Tor and the well.'

The door opened slowly. The woman was short, no more than five feet. She stared at him with open curiosity, her very large brown eyes emphasised by the short, spiky, brilliantly white hair that showed through mousy brown at the roots. She wore a loose top, dark blue splashed with paint, and faded jeans. Her earrings were chunky, intricate designs, enamelled like something out of an Egyptian tomb. 'You'd better come in, Stephen Capel.'

'Just Capel.'

' If you like. I'm Harriet Watson - just Harriet.'

Capel smiled. 'If you like.'

The house was a mixture of the predictable and the surprising. Parts of it reminded Capel of university life. The faded carpets and the plank and brick shelves that supported row on row of books along one side of the hall and the faint herbal odours. But then there was a modern, comfortable looking lounge, with nothing to suggest the bohemian life except a line of esoteric paintings, executed in the same bold hand as the door.

'Sit down. He's not here right now. Can I get you a coffee or something?' Today everyone seemed intent on offering him hot drinks.

'That's very kind of you. Thank you.'

'Well done.' The big brown eyes widened expressively. 'I'd normally expect more obvious suspicion that you were going to be plied with illegal substances. It's very ordinary decaffeinated coffee. Fairtrade, of course.'

'I wouldn't expect anything else.'

'Sorry, I tend to evangelise if I'm not restrained. I won't be a moment.'

Capel stood as she left the room and looked closer at the painting opposite him, a study of the Tor with something like the beams of a searchlight radiating from the ruined St Michael's tower. It had an unnerving quality that drew his eye to the base of the tower, where a tiny figure seemed to be spread-eagled against the wall. He forced himself to look down at the bookcase below, crammed with yet more paperbacks. The taste was catholic. New Age Wisdom and Celtic Heritage rubbed up against Ruth Rendell and Henry Cecil. Dean Koontz shared a shelf with the Mabinogion and P.G. Wodehouse.

The door clicked behind him. Capel looked up quickly at the painting. 'It's very good. Did you paint it?'

'It's not my sort of thing - one of Harriet's.' The voice was new, a husky woman's voice with a touch of county set or Chelsea about it, quite different from Harriet's warm but brittle tone.

Capel swung on his heel. In appearance the woman in the doorway couldn't have been much more different from his hostess. Long, carefully crimped auburn hair streamed over her shoulders and down the back of a flowing dress, decorated in an Indian style. She was pure pre-Raphaelite, even down to the patrician, melancholy features. And her pose, leaning slightly against the door frame, would not have disgraced a model in Vogue. She appeared very self-aware.

'Hello, I'm Capel.'

'Well, hello to you, Capel. I suppose Harriet is bringing you something? She's good at domestic trivia.'

'She is. Getting me a coffee, I mean.'

'Excellent.' The woman moved into the room and sat in an armchair, leaning forward towards Capel. Her smile was very broad and slow, cat-like below mocking eyes. Capel eased himself down onto the sofa, wondering if this was how a rabbit felt when hypnotised by a stoat.

'I came to have a word with Henry Malkovski.'

'That's not me, I'm afraid. Henry's prettier.'

Capel couldn't think of an appropriate reply.

'I'm Cooper, Capel. Lillith Cooper. I like Cooper Capel - it sounds like one of those old sports cars, all running boards and huge, dazzling headlights.' Again that slow smile. A heavy perfume came to Capel's attention for the first time. 'What are you for, Capel?'

'For?' Capel sat back against the cushions. He felt uncomfortably as if he was on trial. 'Freedom? Happiness? The American Way? Is that the sort of thing you had in mind?'

'Not entirely. What's your function, your reason for existence? What do you produce, Capel?'

'Do I need to produce something to have a reason for existence? I suppose you could say that I produced service to others, but that sounds crass. What do you do, Lillith?'

'You weren't supposed to need to ask that.' Harriet had come back while Capel was locked in the other woman's hypnotic stare. 'Not of Lillith Cooper, the woman who single-handedly discovered the Glastonbury dragon.'

'Harriet's too kind. Much too kind.'

Capel took the coffee he was offered. 'Thanks. I'm afraid I haven't heard of the Glastonbury Dragon, but then I'm new to this sort of thing. Is it part of the Zodiac?'

'Oh, my dear, you have been reading the wrong things,' said Lillith, punctuating her speech with another slow smile. 'There's no doubt about the existence of the Glastonbury Zodiac, but that's a toy to keep children amused. The Dragon is much older, the real power of Glastonbury that all the latecomers like the Zodiac and the Abbey feed on.' She suddenly lost interest in the subject. 'I'd be careful, Harriet, inviting strange men into the house; Henry could be jealous.'

Harriet Watson's glare at Lillith was undiluted hatred. Her eyes seemed to widen until they wiped out anything else in her face. 'Lillith is here, in my house, to write another book, Capel.' She did not take her eyes off the other woman. 'Another masterpiece; this time it's to be on the well. She's a very effective parasite on Glastonbury, is Lillith. Comes as she pleases, takes what she wants. She is the great Lillith Cooper, after all.'

'Harriet is very generous.' Lillith's studied composure seemed shaken. 'She looks after Henry and myself very well.'

'It was Henry I came to see,' said Capel. 'Did he come to Glastonbury with you, then?'

'Oh, hardly.' Lillith had recovered. 'Henry was already here with Harriet when I arrived.'

'Like I said, Lillith takes what she wants.' The tension between the women was practically tangible.

'I was there this morning, at the well,' said Capel. 'When the police took Henry away. But they say he's been released. I expected to find him here.'

'He'll be back in his own time,' said Lillith.

'Do you know why he broke into the well? Was it something to do with your book?'

'I did ask Henry if he could get me a sample of the water. I can't complete my outline without a chance to do a magical analysis, to break down the power elements within the water, to understand its influence.' She bit her lip. 'White magic, of course. The real earth magic, not men's crude tampering.'

'I'll take your word for it,' said Capel. 'Was this morning Henry's first attempt on the well? I hear it was broken into at the weekend.'

'Henry's only tried the once,' said Lillith. 'I asked him yesterday. He's always willing to indulge my little whims.'

'Isn't he just,' said Harriet, venom colouring her tone.

'Was he on another errand for you yesterday morning?' said Capel. 'When he was up on the Tor? That's mainly why I called, he seemed in quite a state.'

Harriet's eyes flicked from Lillith to Capel for a moment. She didn't speak.

'Not on Monday, dear man. Monday's his day for playing Harriet's good little domesticated helper and taking their trinkets to the market. Harriet makes very good trinkets, she's not limited to her daubs and making coffee.' The consonants in 'trinkets' had sharp, needling edges that made Harriet wince.

Capel nodded. 'I just thought you might have asked him to do something before he went to the market, that's all. It doesn't matter.'

'You're welcome to wait,' said Lillith, 'but he could be some time.'

'Don't worry,' said Capel. 'I'll come back. Hang on a sec.' He produced one of his new cards, the first time he'd use one, and scribbled a number on the back. 'My mobile number's on the front, and that's my room at the George and Pilgrim. If he wants to talk to me about anything, I'll be around to the end of the week. He'd be quite safe, I'm not from the police and I wouldn't tell them anything he didn't want them to know.'

'The integrity of the confessional,' said Lillith. 'You should be a priest. You'd make a good priest.'

'I'll bear it in mind,' said Capel. He stood up and half turned his back on Lillith, making it clear that he was addressing Harriet. 'Thank you very much for your hospitality.'

'I'll see you out,' said Harriet. As they entered the hall, he heard her mutter 'Christ, that woman,' under her breath.

'Thanks again,' said Capel.

'Look, there's something...' Harriet's eyes flicked towards the sitting room door. Lillith was watching them, draped decorously in the doorway. Harriet shook her head tightly, an almost imperceptible motion that sent sympathetic ripples through her long, vibrant earrings.

'I'll call some other time, when it's more convenient,' said Capel. 'To see Henry.'

When Capel looked back, well down the street towards the centre of Glastonbury, Harriet was still there in the doorway, her eyes seeming to plead with him to return.

~

Wednesday morning. By now he should have been well into the course. So far he'd spent maybe two hours on it, and that without any concentration. Capel found it difficult to feel any regret. He was returning to his room after breakfast. The night before he had told himself that he had done enough, that it was time to leave the investigations to the professionals, but now, with a good, solid breakfast inside him, he wasn't sure. He certainly needed to see Harriet again. And Henry Malkovski. He might as well ring the course administrator and withdraw; there was no point pretending that he was carrying on.

The door to his room was standing open, creased bedding half-blocking the entrance. Capel cleared his throat noisily.

'Sorry, I've got a lot to get through this morning.' Andrea, the maid from the other night, popped her head round the bathroom door. 'I can come back later.'

'Don't worry about me,' said Capel. 'I'm just getting a few things together, then I'm off out.'

'Okay.' She disappeared into the meat-red, tiled womb of a bathroom. Capel dug into the bottom of his suitcase, which was poised on one of the contraptions that hotels provide as a stand for cases, a metal and webbing monstrosity that was no more functional, but a lot less attractive than a simple table. His fingertips touched the slippery case of his camera before it disappeared into a clump of socks.

'Did you go?' The maid's voice, coming from behind him, was just enough of a surprise to dislodge his fingers from their minimal grip on the camera strap.

'Sorry?' Capel looked round to see the dark head, once more craning round the bathroom door frame, as if she was still legitimately working as long as her feet remained on the tiles.

'You don't have to tell me,' she said, 'I mean it's none of my business really, just tell me to shut up if you think I'm speaking out of turn, but I was wondering if you did go and see Paul's family. I'm Andrea, you know, you spoke to me the other evening.'

'Of course I remember,' said Capel. 'You were very helpful. Yes, I did see Paul's parents. And his friend, Ian. Do you know Ian as well?'

'Oh, him.' Her feet strayed unconsciously out into the room and she perched on the edge of the writing desk. 'I know him, all right.'

'A friend?'

'Not likely. Not for want of trying on his part though.' She looked down at the cloth she was holding and twisted it between her hands. 'I think he used to fancy me.'

Capel suppressed the urge to say 'You can't fault his taste, then,' all too aware how easy it was to be misinterpreted. He limited himself to a smile in reply.

'How were they?'

'Paul's mum and dad were very upset, of course. It's not easy to come to terms with, something that pushes you out of the normal way of things. It's bad enough when your children die before you from natural causes, but to have your son murdered...'

'Have you children, then?'

'No. Not yet at least. If you know Mr and Mrs Schofield well enough to go round there, it wouldn't be a bad idea to see them. They might not seem very welcoming, but they may well need support with the everyday things.'

'I could do that.' Andrea pushed her hands under her thighs, sitting on her fingertips.

'Then there was Ian Telfer. He looked like he was pretty shaken too. He could do with a bit of comfort.'

'What do you think I am, a teddy bear?' She wasn't angry, more amused.

'I just thought he could do with someone to listen to him. Paul's parents can't help him - they've got too much on their plates to worry about Ian - and I'm a stranger. But he obviously needed someone to talk to. He wasn't just upset, he was frightened about something. I just wondered if you were up to it. It could help him a lot.'

'As long as he doesn't get the wrong idea. He's a creep, you know. And my mum wouldn't like it if she thought I was leading him on. Neither would Phil, for that matter?'

'Phil?'

'He's my boyfriend.' Andrea's cheeks glowed, a pair of perfectly round blushes. 'Phil Hayes. He's never liked Ian. They were in the same class at juniors, but then Phil went into the fast stream at the High School. He's very clever is my Phil.'

'It was just a suggestion. I'm sure it'd help for him to talk to someone like you.'

'I'll think about it. Maybe, if I happen to see him.' Andrea pushed herself off the desk, the cloth still clamped in one hand. 'I'd better get on, I've got another twelve rooms to do, yet.'

Capel smiled and turned back to his bag, capturing the evasive camera with a surprise attack through his shirts.

CHAPTER 7

He had intended to visit the Abbey. That was why he got the camera out. Phones were okay, but he liked the feeling of professionalism that using a real camera gave him. Capel headed up the High Street towards the gap in the stolid shops that faced St John's church, where he had first caught a glimpse of the towering ruins, but it became obvious when he got there that there was no entrance into the abbey grounds. He would have to retrace his steps, down to the bottom of the High Street and beyond.

Capel was reluctant to turn back. He had made a start towards Harriet Watson's - perhaps he should continue. Her plea to speak to him again was genuine, of that he was sure. While his brain was still weighing the odds, his feet took over and continued up the hill towards Chilkwell Street and the raised terrace. Familiarity made the distance seem far shorter than the day before.

'You again? That was quick.' Harriet smiled warmly. She seemed less edgy than on his last visit.

'I got the impression you wanted to talk to me about something. And I'd still like to see Henry.'

'Wouldn't we all.' Harriet's mouth twisted up at one corner. 'He came back yesterday afternoon, stayed all of half an hour and hasn't been seen since. Probably on another of Lillith's errands.'

'Is your lodger in?'

'Lillith? Not Lillith. Wednesday's the day I like to clean the place - and you don't see Lillith for dust, if you get me. She'll be off down the library or taking psychometric readings at the Abbey, or some other showy pantomime for the benefit of her book. Come in. Can I get you a coffee again, Mr... sorry, Capel?'

'Only if I can help you with the cleaning. I'm a mean hand with a duster.'

'No need, I've done it already. My idea of cleaning's more functional minimalism than attention to detail.'

'A woman after my own heart. Well, at least let me make you a coffee. The only work I've done so far today is shovelling down the breakfast at the George.'

'That seems fair.' She lead him to a small kitchen lined with a jumble of everyday cans and exotica.

'I'm a bit surprised by your remarks about Lillith,' said Capel, pushing a large scale map of Glastonbury out of the way to make room for two mugs. 'I thought you were into New Age yourself - "showy pantomime" is hardly flattering.'

'She's not someone I'm in a hurry to flatter.' Harriet flopped onto an ancient kitchen chair and pulled up one leg so that she could fiddle with the embroidered toe of her slipper. 'Do you believe in anything? Anything beyond the obvious physical world, I mean?'

'Yes, I'd have to say I do.'

'Okay, well, that doesn't make you sympathetic to everyone who believes in the same things, does it? And it doesn't mean that you implicitly trust their motives for parading that belief. Lillith's only interest in the mystical side of life is to earn some more royalties. The trouble is, she looks the part. They lap her up on chat shows and at literary lunches and festivals and God knows what. The publishers'll print anything she can scribble down. She really is very popular.'

'And that's part of what you have against her? As well as trying to take Henry away from you.'

'Thanks.' Harriet took the mug and gestured at the other chair, sipping the coffee tentatively. 'Don't feel you have to go easy on my feelings, will you? Oh, Henry's just weak like that - he's a man, let's face it - I'm not much competition for her, am

I? I can cope with her desperate urge to own everything and everyone in sight - and to belittle them if she can't control them - it's her cynical attitude to other people's beliefs that makes me sick.'

'And that's why you wanted to see me again, without Lillith around?'

'Not particularly... oh.' For a moment she had forgotten the day before, forgotten the strange urge to confide in this stranger. 'No, it was something about Henry. Am I being stupid? Why am so I certain you aren't going to go running to the police with the first little thing I tell you? Do you always have this effect?'

'Very infrequently. But it's true. I'm not working with the police, I have no official connections. But I would like to see the truth come out. If you tell me something I think that Inspector Davies ought to know - he's the man in charge of the case - I'll try to persuade you to tell him, but it's not my job to pass on confidences. And I'd like to help you if there's any way I can.'

'I'm worried about Henry. I know why he came back from the Tor on Monday morning - it wasn't anything to do with the murder. I already said Henry can be a bit weak. He's been selling my jewellery on the market for a couple of years now and he got in with some people I don't know. They persuaded him to help move some weed - you know, grass. Nothing sordid, not real pushers, just friends helping other people to get what they need. And Henry sees it like he's Don Quixote or something and he's making this big stand against *them*, the establishment, by keeping this stuff on the move.

'I won't have anything to do with it myself, Henry knows that, so he's been trying to do it under my nose without me finding out about it. I think his idea's to protect me. Anyway, these friends of his were dropping off a little parcel Monday morning for him to take over to Wells. And being Henry, he'd forgotten all about it and he'd gone for a little walk - probably casing the well so he could do his obedient puppy dog act for

Lillith - then he suddenly realised that even I couldn't fail to notice the stuff if it was shoved into my hands, so he rushed back and arrived here about the same time as his friends. That's all there was to it, but he isn't likely to tell the pigs.'

'I can understand that.'

'Will you tell them?'

'No. I agree with you about drugs, and I'm damned sure there's no such thing as innocent drug dealing, but it's not for me to go to the police. Do you think Henry would talk to me about it? I might be able to sort something with...' Capel stopped, interrupted by a heavy rap on the door.

'We're popular this morning. I'd better see who it is.'

Capel sipped the coffee, still hot enough to numb his lips, and waited comfortably. Harriet was not gone long. She backed into the room, talking hesitantly to another visitor.

' ... seen him since. Perhaps you know Mr Capel already?'

'Oh, I certainly know Mr Capel,' said Chief Inspector Davies, following her closely into the room. 'I don't seem to be able to spend five minutes anywhere on this case without bumping into Mr Capel. I'm beginning to suspect that all I need to do is follow Mr Capel around and I'll get to see everyone involved.'

'You're too kind, Malcolm,' said Capel. 'I knew Inspector Davies at college; you have to forgive him his sense of humour.'

Harriet smiled nervously and picked up her coffee. She sat in the other chair, leaving Davies hovering by the door. Capel suspected that there was no malice in her action, but wouldn't have put money on it. He wondered how the three of them, Harriet, Lillith and Malkovski, managed with only two chairs. Perhaps they never ate together.

'Now Mr Capel has put me in my place, perhaps I could ask you a couple more questions, Miss Watson. It is Miss, I take it?'

'Harriet. Ms if you insist on a label.'

'Of course, I should have known. When did you last see Henry Malkovski?'

'Nothing's changed. It was yesterday when I saw him. Some time in the afternoon, maybe four thirty or five.'

'He hasn't been back since?'

'I'd have seen him more recently if he had, wouldn't I?'

'I don't know, Miss... Mizz Watson. He could have come home when you were out of the house, or when you were in bed.'

'He could have, but I don't think he did. Check with Lillith Cooper if you want to know if he came in during the night. She'll be back here this evening. He certainly wasn't here when I got up.'

'I'll do that. That's *the* Lillith Cooper, is it?'

'I didn't have you down as a mystic, Malcolm,' said Capel, who had been sitting very quietly, watching Harriet.

'You should know, Mr Capel. Thorough research, that's all.'

'Yes,' said Harriet, 'the one and only Lillith Cooper. She's staying here while she researches a book. I thought I told you yesterday.'

'So you did. I like to keep things straight. I don't suppose you know what Mr Malkovski was doing at 3am on Monday morning?'

'You'd better ask...'

'Ask Lillith Cooper. Yes, good. One final question, Mizz Watson. Did you have any reason to believe that Mr Malkovski might have some sort of business arrangement with Paul Schofield?'

'I told you yesterday, I never met Schofield.'

'That's not what I asked.'

'I think Henry knew him, but I don't know why. We don't live in each other's pockets.'

'Thank you for your cooperation, Mizz Watson. Do let me know if Mr Malkovski should reappear. You've got our number.'

'I think so.'

'No, don't get up; I'll see myself out. All the best Mizz Watson, Mr Capel.' Davies shut the kitchen door firmly behind him. A moment later they heard the outer door slam.

'He doesn't intend to be intimidating,' said Capel, somehow

feeling that his shared background made him responsible for Davies.

'Yeah, right.'

'Maybe you've got a point.' Capel swallowed the last of his coffee. 'Look, I'd better get on. I'd still like to speak to Henry - and the offer remains open; if there's anything you need to talk about, just give me a ring.'

'I will do. If we'd had a vicar like you, I might have stayed with the church.'

'Who said...?'

'Let's say I'm psychic. Good luck, Capel.'

'I'll vote for that all round. I hope I see you again, Harriet.'

'Who knows?'

They said good-bye at the kitchen door, Harriet turning to clear up the mugs and Capel walking down the short passage. Outside a chill wind had sprung up. Capel pulled his jacket tighter round him and closed the front door.

'Could you spare a moment, Steve?'

Capel jerked round, caught by surprise, looking for Malcolm Davies. The voice was unmistakable. He realised that it came from the road below, down the little flight of steps from the raised pavement to the tarmac. The back door of Davies' car loomed open and the big man was leaning out, leering up at Capel.

'Anything for you, Malcolm.' Capel's heel caught noisily on a stone as he stepped down to the road.

'Get in. Going back to town?'

'Yes. I thought I'd look at the Abbey.'

'Much more appropriate occupation for a man of the cloth, if you ask me. What are you trying to do, Steve, pick up a bit of rough? I wouldn't get involved with the Watson girl. Flaky type, not your sort.'

'I'm not getting involved with anyone,' said Capel mildly. 'At least, no more than my duties require me to be. Why are you still trying to find Malkovski? I thought you'd eliminated him.'

'Not eliminated. He started out a long shot, but we've

received some new information since yesterday. You weren't the only one who fancied an early walk by the Tor. We've got an eyewitness who saw a man coming down the path around three o'clock on the morning of the murder. A big man with long hair.'

'And a beard?'

'It's dark round here at night. Really dark. The witness saw the hair, but couldn't swear to any features.'

'That's impressively conclusive, Malcolm.'

'There's more. We've gone over Schofield's room again, this time more thoroughly. We found some rather interesting reading tucked away behind a skirting board. It seems Master Schofield was an enterprising lad. Quite the young entrepreneur. He kept neat little books of his business activities. And he had regular incomes from some very surprising people. Like Henry Malkovski. The sort of regular income you can squeeze out of a juicy piece of information. The sort of regular outgoing that could drive a man with a very limited source of funds to murder, especially when he has a new lady friend to entertain. One with expensive tastes.'

'What was Schofield blackmailing Malkovski about?'

'I was hoping our Henry could tell me that. Schofield didn't go into sordid details in his accounts. It was just a neat little balance sheet, very business-like. It wouldn't surprise me if he had it regularly audited.'

'So you think the initials in the tower were significant after all?'

'They could well be. Here's the abbey entrance. Enjoy the sightseeing and try to keep out of the police's way, will you? You could give us a bad name.'

'Thanks for the lift, I think our police force is wonderful. I can't help but be involved, but I assure you that I have no intention of interfering with your work. Have a good day, Malcolm.'

Capel slipped out of the car and shut the door before the Chief Inspector could reply.

~

The entrance to the Abbey was quite new, an uninspiring but not unpleasant attempt at modern conformity to ancient lines. Capel passed by the gift shop and the museum, following the twisting path that skirted another ragged thorn tree on the way to the main abbey ruins. He had to stand back under the sagging branches of the thorn as a boy, a young boy with none of the self-consciousness of a teenager, came solemnly down the path carrying a clear plastic bag.

He held it in front of him like one of the three kings in a nativity scene, bearing his gift as if it were the most precious thing in the world. Capel suppressed a smile. In the bag, swimming jerkily in the water that filled the bottom half, was a goldfish, a fat, solemn goldfish. Which king was supposed to have brought the gold? Capel thought. He couldn't remember. The boy went past as if Capel wasn't there, his attention focused wholly on the bag, determined to avoid a disturbance in the still surface of the water. He disappeared around the corner, becoming a tableau in Capel's memory, the sort of event that sticks in the mind long after the rest of the day has faded into a blur of sameness.

With the boy gone it looked like he had the place to himself. Capel walked slowly down the centre of the nave to the towering ruins of the transepts. The wind was less obvious now. Standing at the crossing, Capel wheeled slowly round, imagining the great walls, the aisle arches, the lofting roof beams high above. He completed a circle and walked forwards into the choir, up to the doubtful but touchingly romantic grave where the twelfth century monks had claimed to have found King Arthur's remains.

'Rex Quondam, Rex Futurusque,' said Capel softly. The Once and Future King - a rather unsettling concept, when you got down to practicalities. He paused, staring at the outline of stone. There was something nagging him about the confused mess of people he had been involuntarily involved with in

Glastonbury. Some detail that he needed to think through, but which his mind was stubbornly refusing to dredge from his memory.

He turned suddenly on his heel. In the midst of the struggle with his reluctant memories, he had sensed someone, standing close behind him. There was nobody there. The long lawn of the nave was empty. He was jumping at ghosts. About to return to his contemplation of the grave, he paused, his eye caught by a distant movement. A flash of vivid colour in the Lady Chapel, the most complete part of the church. He stood very still, staring intently. There it was again, a deep orange-red patch that swirled in the doorway then disappeared.

Capel began to walk down through the remains of the church, eyes fixed on the point where he had seen the form. As he drew nearer it appeared again and the mystery dissolved. A woman was bent over, her back to him, doing something on the wooden bridge that spanned the missing floor over the crypt. She was dressed all in black. In the dimness of the building only her hair showed in incandescent flashes when she tilted her head back. Capel rounded the carved walls to the entrance of the chapel, a humble archway behind a bald patch in the grass where the relentless feet of visitors had worn through to the soil. Inside, apparently unaware of his approach in her intense concentration, Lillith Cooper stood like a magnificent painted Victorian tombstone, her red tresses streaming down the severe black cloak, her classical profile pale, almost ghostly, against the dark fabric.

Feeling obtrusive, Capel cleared his throat noisily. She had to have heard him, yet she remained frozen on the dull planking, staring into the rear wall of the chapel.

'Miss Cooper, isn't it?' Capel took a step forward onto the bridge. Although the structure was solid, he felt it quiver in sympathy with his footsteps. Lillith moved her head from side to side dreamily and turned slowly to face him, cupping something that glittered in her left hand. Her smile broke the spell. It was too wide, menacing almost, and sent the echoes of

Burne Jones and Rossetti splintering into nothing.

'Oh, yes, it's Harriet's little friend. Caper? No, Capel. The very just Mr Capel. What does this say to you?' She made a flamboyant gesture taking in the church, the Abbey, perhaps all of Glastonbury.

'Do you ask questions like that to be provocative, or because you want an answer?'

'Can't it be both?' She perched lightly on the handrail, hanging over the dark cavity of the crypt with apparent lack of concern. Capel noticed that there was a whitening of her knuckles where she gripped the rail, a sign that the nonchalance was an act. 'You don't get away that easily, Capel.' She beckoned to bring him closer, her right hand clasping tighter on the unvarnished wooden rail. Her perfume hit Capel's usually insensitive nostrils like a small, velvet-covered sledgehammer. 'What does it say, Capel?'

'Peace, I suppose. The order of things, the simple regularity of monastic worship; the short-sightedness of our ancestors, to destroy such a beautiful building; the fickleness of life that it can seem more beautiful ruined than whole. But mostly it says honest, solid, stone-carving craftsmanship. Did I get it wrong?'

'In almost every respect.' Lillith slid forward a little towards him on the rail, sending a stronger wave of musk to envelop him. 'What about the mystical aspects? Is there no mystery for you? No spirituality?'

'Yes and no. The reasons for this place being built were certainly mystical - you don't get much more mystical than God's son being made human and dying for the sins of humanity. And I am certain of the spirituality of many of the men who lived in the community here, not to mention quite a few of the visitors. But I don't see anything mystical about the setting or the stones. It's all good, solid geology.'

Lillith laughed for the first time, a deep husky laugh, all throat and no heart. There was amusement in her eyes, but a condescending amusement. 'Oh, the ruin of our worldly society. I suppose you say that Mona Lisa is just daubs of pigment, that music is simple, everyday air vibrations and nothing more? Have you heard of dowsing?'

'As in water divining? Finding wells with bits of twig?'

'At its most mechanistic, yes. By dowsing we can tune into the vibrations of the earth itself, the forces that lie beneath the commonplace world. That's what I was doing when you arrived, I was dowsing.'

'You must have collapsible divining rods.'

'Not at all. Being in touch with the ancient truths doesn't cut you off from modern techniques, it just makes you aware of their limitations. I write my books on a laptop, not with a quill pen. No, I use this.' She slipped her hand inside the cloak and produced a small device with a narrow wooden handle and two pieces of wire, linked by a couple of beads. 'It's more sensitive than traditional rods and much less obtrusive.'

'I wouldn't have thought being obtrusive was ever a problem for you.'

Lillith laughed again. 'There are times when it's inappropriate to be flamboyant.'

'And did you find any water?' asked Capel, moving back to safer ground.

'I wasn't looking for water. Or at least, no more so than to feel its influence on the force lines. What most people don't realise is that the ancients had a much clearer idea of the real powers of the earth than we have nowadays. They were closer to it. It was life or death; they had to be more sensitive to it. Many thousands of years ago, adepts forged a new pattern at Glastonbury. Something much more powerful than can be accounted for by the mere natural occurrence of water lines and blind springs. The pattern I've called the Glastonbury Dragon.

'And it's only recently that the knowledge has died out. The masons who built the Abbey were well aware of the power of the earth force. They built to conserve it and focus it. This building is like a lens, concentrating the spirals of power into a sink in the crypt below. The rod almost jumped out of my hand.'

'And that gives the stones power?'

'That and the way that they've been carved. A thousand years ago, decoration was much more than a matter of aesthetics. The slots and reliefs, every marking and channel on those stones, are practical devices to focus the earth forces.'

'I only see a beautiful ruin of a building designed by very ordinary if wonderful craftsmen with no special knowledge that we have somehow mysteriously lost.'

'Are you really so blind? Do you see everything around you as mechanistic and soulless?'

'Not at all. Quite the reverse, in fact.' Capel looked up for a moment to the sky. 'I see the forces that you endow these things of earth and stone with all around me, every day. I acknowledge the forces of physics that make solid matter out of insubstantial atoms. They're impressive. But even more impressive is the force of life in the children battering hell out of each other in the playground. I see spirituality in the woman behind the counter in Woolworths and real mystical power in human relationships. Which of us, do you think, has the mechanistic view, the one who sees power in an arrangement of stones, or the one who sees power in people?'

Lillith looked as if she wanted to applaud, but her precarious position made it impractical. She reached out with her free hand to stroke his cheek. 'A touching lecture. You ought to be on television, you'd wow the housewives.'

'Thanks. Maybe I should review my career options.'

'And meanwhile we agree to differ. All I can do is respond to my feelings and the genuine interest there is out there in the power of the stones.'

'And the genuine money behind it, ready and willing to cough up for books. No...' Capel held up his hand as Lillith seemed about to interrupt, 'I'm not judging. You're meeting a need. Everyone has to make a living. Like your friend Henry. It amazes me that he scrapes together enough to exist on.'

'Henry has his means - but you have to realise that we live differently from you, our needs are simpler.'

Capel looked at the elegantly styled hair, the expensively severe cloak. Henry's needs might be simple, but 'our' was stretching a point. 'Of course. I'm only trying to help him, you know. But Harriet seems very protective, as if she was trying to cover up for something.'

'Harriet has a touching, canine devotion to Henry.'

'What about you? Do you understand what's going on? Why Henry won't say what he was doing?'

'I understand nothing because I have no interest. I'm only the lodger, you know. A humble visitor like yourself. What Henry gets up to is his own affair.'

'But he did break into the well for you.'

'Water lines are very significant as conduits of the earth's power. The well is fed by a particularly powerful source, which is why it forms the Dragon's mouth. There was no secret about why Henry was there. No study of the Dragon would be complete without analysing the well water.'

It seemed that she was going to say something else, but suddenly her expression changed; her eyes and mouth widened; her body started to slump backwards over the rail, poised over the drop. Capel saw the fingers of her hand loosening the grip that held her in place. He jumped forward, catching the tall, slim form and easing her off the rail. She pressed against Capel for a moment as he stood, clasping her like a lover, then pushed away from him.

'I'm sorry, I don't know what happened - I think I must have over-tired myself, surveying the site.' She steadied herself on the rail. 'I'd better go home. Will you excuse me?'

'Of course.'

'Our paths will cross again. I like to keep up with men who save my life.'

'Will you be all right getting home?'

'Don't worry, I'm feeling much stronger already.' She slid past, gripping his arm for a moment. 'Thank you. You should try to uncover more sympathy with the earth - it could bring you happiness.' And she was gone. Capel had no proof, he couldn't even pin down why he was so sure, but he was convinced that the whole thing was an act for his benefit. There had been something about her pose on the rail, something about the tiny flash of a smile as he caught her, that spoke of an act.

Capel stayed another hour at the Abbey, tracing the site of the cloisters, enjoying the quirky, soaring abbot's kitchen, but he had lost his connection with the atmosphere of the place. He would have to come back another time.

CHAPTER 8

The hotel phone's unfamiliar ring disturbed his half-conscious reverie. Capel struggled to identify the tone. The insistent jangle continued. Since he had slumped on his bed to think things out darkness had fallen. He fumbled on the bedside table for the light, knocking over something that sounded like glass. The light clicked on, a painful glare to his unaccustomed eyes. Groggy, Capel picked up the phone, making use of the delay to pull himself upright.

'Hello?'

'Capel? Is that you?'

'Vicky. Sorry, I must have...' No: it would sound too middle aged if he admitted sleeping. 'I must have missed the phone for a moment, there. I was in the bathroom.'

'It's me who should be apologising; I should have rung sooner. I've been at home nearly an hour, but I was dead on my feet. I'm afraid I sat down for a moment and dropped off. And I have to apologise about this evening, too. I'm back on duty in a few minutes. Things are hotting up on the murder.'

'That's why I wanted to see you.'

'Really?' She sounded disappointed.

'Of course it's not the only reason. Couldn't you call round when you come off duty?'

'I wouldn't be surprised if we're in all night. I reckon we're close to collaring Malkovski.'

'And you think he did it?'

'The Chief does, I'm pretty sure.'

'What about you?'

'It doesn't matter much what I think. How does the Archbishop of Canterbury feel about your opinions?'

'Yes... though Malcolm's hardly in the Archbishop class. A Canon at the most. A minor Canon. I don't think he did it.'

'Who? The Archbishop? I'm losing track.'

Capel sighed noisily. 'Malkovski. I don't think he was the murderer. I've been talking to the women he lived with... and I can't believe that Henry was involved.'

'Perhaps we'll know a bit better when we find him. Going to ground is hardly a sign of innocence.'

'I'm sure Henry has the normal share of guilt, but it doesn't make him a killer. Do you ever go to the Abbey?'

'Talking to you is like trying to play pin the tail on the kangaroo with a real kangaroo. I suppose I've been sometime, though I can't remember when I last went. I think I had a look round when I first came to Glastonbury... it might not have been since then. Why?'

'Pin the tail on the kangaroo? That's seriously bizarre. We must go to the Abbey together sometime.'

'The only place I'm liable to be going in the day time at the moment is the station - and I'd better be off there now.'

'Okay, okay... look, before you go, could you make dinner tomorrow night? I've got an old friend coming, Ed Ridge - I'm sure you'd like him. We're having dinner here at the George. It'd be wonderful if you could make it.'

There was a long silence at the other end, so long that Capel was about to ask if she was still there. 'I'll do my best. You know what it's like right now.'

'Of course. Eight o'clock, here in the hotel, if you can make it, but we'll go ahead quite happily if you can't.'

'Are you sure you wouldn't be happier just the two of you, talking about old times, all that stuff?'

'Don't be silly. I'd much rather you were there and Ed's good fun. Much more entertaining than me. Please.'

'I'll do my best. Be good, Capel.'

'I'll do my best.'

~

It was late enough to go to bed, but Capel couldn't face it yet. He rattled down the stairs and through to the bar of the George, taking a pint of bitter over to sit in the recess of the deep, stained-glass window. The panes were dark now, except when a car headlight caught the colouring and sent a fancy, Christmas light, night-on-the-promenade twinkle to tantalise the corner of his eye. Capel realised that he was staring at the anonymous back of a woman sitting alone at the bar. He looked down into the clear depths of his beer. He didn't normally have trouble with women. The censorious part of his mind bridled. Who did he think he was, 'have trouble with women' – it verged on objectification.

Capel shifted uncomfortably on the plain wooden seat and stared again at the woman at the bar, defying that inner voice with deliberate provocation. He couldn't keep it up long. The absurdity of looking at another person as if he was checking out a horse to be purchased was too much for him. He smiled at himself. Trouble was the wrong word, then. The censor nodded silently. What he really meant was that he was being thrown into contact with a number of women who were fated to be more than just part of his everyday life; who, one way or another, could manipulate his emotions.

Vicky was obvious - that's to say, he understood what he felt and he was happy about it - but Harriet and Lillith were very different. He liked Harriet; something inside him demanded that he put himself out to help her, as if she was some defenceless child, which she clearly wasn't. And then there was Lillith... He was sure that his reaction to her was not the automatic, knee-jerk lust that she assumed as a right from a man, but equally it was not something he liked or had adequate control of. Perhaps she was right; perhaps there was something in those stones.

The woman at the bar swivelled and looked directly at him. Capel felt a flush rising in his cheeks. He was still staring at her and couldn't force his eyes away before he had taken in the glaring eyes and hard, straight mouth. She pushed off the stool, heading towards him. Capel mentally rehearsed an excuse. The woman walked straight up to him and past to the next table.

'Where the hell have you been?'

She'd not been looking at him, but at the small, sandy-haired man beyond, pinned into his chair by that steel gaze. Capel sighed. Whatever his conscience said, he was having trouble with women.

~

There was a knock, the bored, pre-emptory knock of someone who knocks on a few dozen doors a day and Capel heard a key rattling in the lock. He struggled out of the tangle that the bedclothes had spontaneously developed during the night. There was something to be said for duvets.

'Er, hello?' Capel shouted, unable to think of anything more constructive to say in his waking daze.

The door swung open, revealing Andrea, an uncertain figure in the doorway. 'I'm sorry.'

'That's all right,' said Capel, straining to see his watch in the dim curtain darkness. 'You couldn't open those curtains, could you?'

'I'm not supposed to...' Andrea hesitated. 'Oh, bugger it, why not.' She pulled her trolley into the room, closed the door behind her and made her way unerringly across to the window, pulling the curtains open with a flourish. 'Sorry about that - swearing - I've had a horrible morning.'

'It's me that should be apologising. I never oversleep in a hotel room. I never have before, I should say. Would you like a cup of coffee or tea? I'm dying for one.'

'Mrs Clinton, the housekeeper, she'd crucify me.'

'She'd have to find you first, and I've no intention of letting her into my room. I'm a respectable clergyman, you know, I can't have a woman come in here with me in a state of undress.'

'Why not, then? I've had enough of this job, I can tell you.' Andrea made a move towards the kettle.

'No, leave it. My treat. You sit down.' Capel sprang out of bed and pulled on a florid dressing gown, patterned with a garish, abstract set of patches.

'That's... er, that's unusual,' said Andrea. She sat on the very edge of the armchair.

'A leaving present from my last congregation. They had limited resources. So what makes this morning particularly bad?'

'It's nothing different - just the same as every morning. I went to see the Schofields, by the way.'

'Were they glad to see you?'

'I think so. They talked enough, anyway. I suppose that counts as glad.'

'It's good if they can talk about Paul. It will have helped them. Tea or coffee?'

'Tea please. Milk and two sugars. I suppose you're right, though half the time it was Ian Telfer they were on about. "Ian's done this; Ian did that." You'd think he was theirs too.'

'It's natural enough,' said Capel. 'Having lost Paul, they're bound to fix on to Ian. It shouldn't be a problem as long as they don't get obsessive about it.'

'It wouldn't surprise me if they do, said Andrea darkly. 'Oh thanks.' She took the tea and settled back into the chair, folding her legs up on the seat with the unconscious ease of the young. 'Mrs Schofield was going on about him as if he was a baby. Did I think he ate properly; was he getting enough fresh air... I think she was even out to match us up. She said I should try to get him to go out; take his mind off some older woman he's got a crush on. Mrs S's got another thing coming if she reckons I'd go out with him.'

Capel sipped his coffee. 'Did she say who the older woman was?'

'No, I don't think she knows. One of these hippy types who wish they'd been around in the sixties, I think. When I say older, I don't think she's really old, not forty or anything like that, just older than Ian.'

'Right. If you happen...' Capel was interrupted by a sharp rap on the door.

'Oh, shit!' said Andrea, 'it's Mrs Clinton. I told you - she's like a bloody bat, she's got radar. Can I hide in your bathroom?'

Capel had an instantaneous flash of memory of a teenage holiday where he had struck up a friendship with a girl in the hotel. Her parents were very defensive, rarely leaving her on her own. He had panicked and hidden in a wardrobe when they'd called round one evening while he was innocently playing cards with the girl in her room. He had got away with it, but afterwards had realised how much worse things would have been if they had discovered him.

'No,' said Capel, 'it's better to brazen it out.' Before Andrea had time to reply, he was opening the door.

'Hello, sailor.' Ed Ridge breezed into the room, a picture of business efficiency in a stylish double-breasted suit and immaculately polished shoes, the picture only slightly marred by the sort of tie that only eight-year-old daughters think appropriate for the office. He was a big man, bigger than Capel, but with the physique of a regular gym user. Ridge took off his wire-rimmed glasses and wiped them briefly on his tie, taking in the scene.

'Morning, Ed,' said Capel.

Ridge carefully looked around, pointedly noting Capel's dressing gown, the obviously uncomfortable girl in the armchair. 'Whoops,' said Ridge, 'am I disturbing something?'

'Don't be more of an idiot than comes naturally,' said Capel. 'Can I get you a cup of something? Ah - forget that, they only provide two cups.'

'That's all right,' said Andrea. She struggled out of the chair and got a pair of clean cups from her trolley. 'Thanks for the tea, I really ought...'

'You don't have to rush off,' said Capel.

'Yes, I do. Oh, just a minute.' She searched distractedly through the pockets of her uniform. 'Here we are. This is Phil's number - my Philip. He's at college in Bath; he's going to be a teacher.'

'That's nice,' said Capel.

'Yes.' Andrea obviously agreed. 'I was talking to him on the phone, telling him all about Paul Schofield, and he said he'd like to speak to you. That's his number there. It's usually voicemail, but he'll get back to you.'

'What did he...?'

'He didn't say. Thanks again.' And she was gone.

'Quite remarkable,' said Ridge, taking the vacant armchair. 'I'll have tea, by the way. Green if possible. Coffee makes me woozy in the morning. Absolutely incredible. Is there anyone else I should know about?'

'Sorry?' said Capel, distracted by the kettle.

'I knew you were going out with most of the local constabulary, but I hadn't realised you were intimate with the hotel staff as well. Just how big is your harem?'

'Jealousy, always jealousy. I'll sell you my secret some time. Actually, I think Andrea's a bit young, even for your debauched tastes. Are you free then? Day's work over by...' Capel peered at his watch, '10.15 is it? I'd forgotten what it was like to be nationalized.'

'I thought Henry the Eighth did that for you. Yes, I'm all yours sweetie.'

'Spare me. It's bad enough that you should be here at all at this time of the morning, let alone that you should be jovial. I think you need a spot of healthy exercise, or cold showers or something.'

'That would depend on who I was sharing them with.'

~

The top of Glastonbury Tor seemed part of a different world. Even the weather contributed to the impression. It was a brilliantly sunny day without a sign of the blocky clouds that had marred Wednesday. When Capel and Ridge had left the centre of Glastonbury the temperature was already rising into the mid-twenties and felt even hotter, the air thick and unpleasant, like a bag of silica gel that had settled over the town. Up on the Tor the sun was still there, but its effects were concealed by a brisk wind which could not be bothered to crawl into the crevices and contusions of the town, but contented itself with attempting to blast St Michael's tower from the hill top.

'Very nice,' said Ridge, 'what does it do?' He shivered as a particularly inquisitive burst of wind attempted to penetrate his shirt.

'You've no soul. Just look at the view. You can see everything, the whole world laid out below you. Look, man, look!'

'The view's wonderful,' said Ridge, 'now can we get out of this wind.'

'Philistine,' said Capel, leading the way into the tower. Shreds of tape still hung from the wide archways, where the police had sealed it off. Ridge stood in the very centre, looking straight up the funnel of the tower walls at the blue rectangle of sky above.

'It's full of "why"s, isn't it?' he said.

'Don't you mean full of wisdom?' Capel sat on the stone bench near where the body had sprawled on the rough floor.

'They don't get any better, your jokes.'

'It's all a matter of tailoring to the audience. You should hear me when I've got someone intelligent listening to me.'

'Ha, ha. Doesn't it strike you like that though? Why has only the tower survived? And why did they build a church up here in the first place? It must have been a hell of a job, building up here, it's hard enough walking up to see the place. And think what it was like for the congregation. No roll out of bed, slip on the clothes, and a five minute stroll across the village green for them. They probably had to pack provisions to keep them going.' Ridge looked back up the tower, adopting an expression of extreme imbecility. 'It makes you think, doesn't it? It really makes you... you know, sort of... think.'

'The same thing had struck me. But it'd be a breakthrough of significant proportions if anything made *you* think.'

'You smooth talking bastard, you. You really know how to make a girl feel wanted.' Ridge was suddenly serious, her voice dropping in volume, his tone softening. 'Where was it?'

'Just here,' said Capel, pointing with his foot. He stood up, his eyes searching the wall. 'And there, that's where the spike with the rope was. There's nothing left now, just those initials, and I'm beginning to think they had nothing to do with it.' He traced the letters with his finger.

'We're back to why,' said Ridge. 'Why come all this way to kill someone?'

'It's quiet,' said Capel, 'I can't imagine there are crowds up here at night time.'

'But he still had to be drowned first, then dragged all this way. That doesn't make any sense. They couldn't hope to fool the police that he'd hanged himself for long.'

'They who?'

'What? You're burbling, man.' Ridge's stern look was patently artificial.

'They who? You said they wouldn't think the police would be fooled.'

'They who did it, of course. You don't imagine one person, not even your muscular hippy, could haul a body up here from the well on his own do you?'

'No...' Capel was staring at the wall, distracted, his finger still sliding slowly over the slight roughness of the cut stone, weathered by years of exposure.

'What is it?'

'A sort of opposite of deja vu - when you see something you know you've seen before and yet it's totally unfamiliar.' Capel smiled suddenly. 'Come on, I'll race you down the Tor. Last one to the gate buys lunch.'

~

'I want to go in the shop.' Ridge announced definitively as they passed through the abbey entranceway.

'It's all right by me, I didn't get there yesterday - at least it means I've something new and interesting to see.'

'So glad I can bring a much needed spot of light into your life. But more importantly, the girls wouldn't forgive me if I didn't take them something back from my travels. At least, I think that's why they're always so glad to see me leave.'

The shop had the usual mixture of books and country crafts that fill the right sort of gift shop from the smallest National Trust establishment to the largest cathedral. There might not have been much that anyone would actually want, but very little of it would cause offence. The only oddity was a pile of leaves from the Glastonbury Thorn, the collected leaf-fall of autumn, gilded to make souvenirs. There was a hint of pilgrimage about them, Capel thought, a tiny echo of the ancient pilgrimage industry that had flourished at Glastonbury - and not just the secular business that sprang up to support and fleece the pilgrims, a touch of mystery remained about the leaves of the Thorn.

'There's a book on dark doings and murders at religious sites here,' said Ridge from the bookshelves. 'Do you think they'll include yours in the revision?'

Capel was about to deny any intention of being murdered on a religious site - or anywhere else for that matter - when the shop assistant, the only other person in the building, who could hardly fail to hear Ridge's loud question, coughed hopefully.

'I couldn't help noticing you mention the murder,' she said. She was a lady of the hazy age that comes between mature and elderly. Her attire fitted the shop perfectly, a cross-breed of Liberty and Barbour with just a hint of Paris. It was hard to imagine she was doing the job for the money.

'Oh yes, I'm sorry,' said Capel aware of something of the embarrassed pleasure of being a minor celebrity. 'I happened to have...'

'Are you interested in such things?' asked the woman. There was a certain hopefulness about her that Capel couldn't understand. And a delicate glow of pride.

'In a way,' said Ridge, putting the book back on the shelf.

'My friend here...'

'I just wondered if you were,' said the woman, 'because I found the body.'

CHAPTER 9

Neither Ridge nor Capel could think of anything to say. The straightforward statement left no room for misunderstanding; the woman seemed quite - almost excessively - normal; yet there was a gulf of reality between her words and what they knew to have happened.

'I hope I didn't offend you,' said the woman, disconcerted by their dumbstruck reaction.

'No, er...' Capel thought back to that morning. Perhaps she had also been on the Tor; it was just possible that she had found the body before him, or while he was looking for the police. 'Had you gone for an early morning walk?'

Now it was the woman's turn to look puzzled. 'Just coming to work as normal. It was a working day.'

'I know,' said Capel, 'I was there. You must be very fit to walk over the Tor every day.'

'Walk over the Tor? I drive to work from Polsham, quite the wrong direction. I think we're talking at cross purposes.'

'You could be right,' said Ridge, feeling he had been quiet for much too long. 'Because it was Mr Capel here who discovered the body.'

The woman shook her head. She took a step backwards, pressing against the shelving behind her. 'No,' she said, 'I would have remembered. It was a beautiful, clear day; I couldn't have missed you. I went out to check round the Abbey - I do most mornings, just to make sure no one's left anything behind. Not bombs or anything, you know, we don't get that sort of thing at the Abbey. But there's often a coat, or a kiddie's toy or something, and I bring them back to the shop. That's where they come to ask, so much more friendly than the museum or the ticket desk, I think. And there, in the crypt of the Lady Chapel, there was the body. It gave me quite a start, you can imagine. Took me weeks to get over it.'

'When was this exactly?' asked Capel, gesturing to Ridge to keep quiet.

'Oh, let me see, what with... and mm... It was September last year. I know it was September because Rosamund had come back from holiday with that unfortunate rash. It's her own fault for taking a package tour. I couldn't put an exact date on it.'

'Not this Monday?' said Capel.

'Oh, I see,' said the woman. 'You must think me really stupid. Now I understand what you mean about the Tor. You meant that boy, while I was talking about Isobel Hunt. Lady Isobel Hunt.'

'The photographer?' said Ridge. 'The one with the TV series?'

'Exactly,' said the woman. 'A mugging, they called it. Horrible word, mugging - so American. She was a fascinating woman. So alive, and now...'

'She's not?' said Ridge untactfully, unable to control his mouth.

'No, it's my fault,' said Capel, trying to cover for his friend. 'I found Paul Schofield's body on the Tor on Monday. So when you said that...'

'You must have thought I was barking mad,' said the woman.

'Not at all,' said Capel. He picked up a flimsy brochure and waved it around in a vain attempt at getting the air moving. 'I think, if you don't mind, we'll go out and a get a bit of fresh air. It's so hot in here.'

'I have repeatedly said that they should get air conditioning,' said the woman. 'Only last week we had a girl faint right where you're standing. It's like a greenhouse when the sun's strong, with all this glass. Would you like me to show you where it happened? I feel we have a bond as finders of corpses.' She said it with the sort of jolly, convivial tone with which she might invite them to see her lupins.

'That would be lovely,' said Ridge at the same time as Capel said 'I wouldn't want you to desert your post.'

'It's no trouble,' said the woman eagerly. 'I like an opportunity to get out and we're hardly rushed off our feet today. You're the first I've had in since nine thirty. I've got a sign somewhere, for when I need to pop out.' She began rummaging in a pile of papers underneath the till.

'What are you doing?' Capel mouthed at Ridge.

'Don't be a spoilsport, it'll make her day,' Ridge whispered back. 'Anyway, the good detective is always looking for evidence.'

'But this isn't our murder,' Capel hissed.

'Ah, here's the little blighter,' said the woman, waving a piece of cardboard in the air. 'Follow me.' They followed.

The sun was almost directly overhead, splashing unmercifully into the open crypt below the Lady Chapel. Capel stood on the wooden bridge next to their guide, less than a foot from where he had saved Lillith from her dramatic plunge. The light was stark; every detail of the stonework stood out in fine, crisp profile.

'It was here that I first saw her,' said the woman. 'Below, in the crypt. She had been photographing a carving down there.'

'She specialised in architectural peculiarities, didn't she?' said Ridge as they were led over the bridge and down a tight flight of stairs into the crypt.

'Yes,' said the woman. 'Be careful there, there's a bit of a gap. She was very fond of oddities. In a technical sense, I believe Saint Mary's Chapel is quite unusual. A kind of mixture of Norman and Gothic, you see. But Lady Isobel would have come anyway. She was commissioned to take the photographs for a series of postcards. It's something we like to do now and again. Different photographers, different visions, you see. She was lying here. Hit over the head with a lump of rock. Very messy. And such a lovely, long, flowing, rather classical sort of frock she had on. Not many people could carry it off.'

'How terrible,' said Capel, interested despite himself.

'Oh, I don't know,' said the woman, 'classical styles are making something of a come-back.'

'Was anyone charged?' said Capel.

'The police hadn't got a clue. Lady Isobel had a key, you see.'

'Oh, yes,' said Ridge. He raised expressive eyebrows at Capel behind the woman's back. Capel shrugged.

'She was on her second week. Came in early, regular as clockwork every morning. She wanted to catch the place before it got crowded. So there was nobody here, nobody to witness it. They did their best, I'm sure, combed every inch of the grounds, but they didn't get anywhere.'

'She'd been here a week already?' said Capel.

'That's right. From dawn to dusk - she liked to experience a location in different lights; said it brought out the features better. A really lovely woman, you know, not a hint of airs and graces about her, though she was the real thing as far as the aristocracy is concerned.' She cocked her head to one side. 'Did you hear something?'

Capel listened carefully. There was a faint rumble of traffic from the town, a jet's roar, muted by distance, and voices. Nearer, other voices; no words, but mocking, aggressive tones. 'There's somebody looking round,' he said. 'I don't suppose it's very unusual.'

The woman was already bustling up the stairs, her lips tightly pressed together in a grim expression that produced unpleasant little wrinkles around her mouth. Ridge bounded after her, leaving Capel alone for a moment in the crypt. Despite the disturbance, the place had an unshakeable feeling of peace about it. Lillith's fancies were easy to understand. He wondered if Lady Isobel had felt that atmosphere of peace as the rock was about to strike her skull. Above him, voices penetrated his thoughts. He recognised Ridge, voice raised. Time to rejoin the world.

'Are you deaf?' Ed shouted.

Capel emerged from the doorway to see Ridge facing a couple of young men. Though he was shouting, there was an unnatural calm to his voice that made it seem particularly menacing. The men, both in their early twenties, didn't look worried. It was hard to believe that they were capable of worry. Under skull-caps of tight-cropped hair, one fair, one earthy black, their eyes were screwed up against the sun, their mouths trying to out-sneer each other, their fists clenched ready and hopeful.

'Piss off, you poof,' the smaller man, said. His neck was bright red, a thick column of flesh that seemed to stretch the neck of his T-shirt, a uniform red except where swathes of uninterpretable tattoo disappeared under the material.

'Don't be stupid,' said Ridge. He was taller than either of his opponents and stood casually, seemingly unworried by the encounter. Capel stopped alongside him. 'Just go now, okay?' Capel thought it best to remain silent.

'We'll be watching for you,' said the blond man. His voice was just a bit too high pitched. 'Don't go down any dark alleys.' He tried to turn away, but the other man held him in place. There was a whispered exchange, the smaller man spat in Ridge's direction and they ran out towards the entrance, out of sight.

'Thank you so much,' said the woman from the shop. Capel realised that she had been alongside Ridge all along, but his focus on the conflict had excluded her from his awareness. 'I don't know why they come here. Last summer there were a few young louts always hanging around the Abbey; slipping in when no one was watching; upsetting the visitors. I thought we'd got rid of them - the police certainly scared them off when the Lady Isobel business happened, but now it looks like we've got some more. I can't see what attracts them, they can't possibly be interested in the buildings.'

'They were taking some of the thorn tree,' said Ridge. 'Probably intend to sell it on the market.'

'Are these the same ones who were here last summer?' said

Capel.

'I don't know,' said the woman. 'I don't think so. I can't remember a lot about last summer's louts, but they had long hair - disgusting, you could tell it was greasy without looking at it. I think they must have been different, but the intent's the...' She was interrupted by the sound of glass breaking. 'Oh, no! Excuse me please.' She hurried off, an infuriated bundle of tasteful blues and greens.

'I suppose we should go after her,' said Capel.

But there was nothing to deal with when they got there. There was only the remains of a lager bottle, smashed on the stone wall.

~

Glastonbury's shops are fine for the needs of a small market town, or the curious, wanting to explore the wonders of crystal power, but don't stretch to sophistication. After leaving the Abbey, Capel and Ridge had prowled round them, Capel trying to find the answer to a nagging question, Ridge simply looking for the entertainment he could find anywhere and everywhere that there were people going about their everyday life.

They had settled in a small book shop that mixed the arcane and the mysterious with piles of those peculiar paperbacks that breed in airport bookshops, the ones with covers half-obscured by brightly coloured metal foil. Capel was deep in the architecture section, while Ridge browsed casually, splitting his attention evenly between the book spines and the people.

'Guess who?' A pair of cool hands had blinded Capel's eyes. He felt a slight pressure on his back; whoever had caught him was holding him close to her. Not that the voice left any doubt.

'Hello again.' Capel gently detached the fingers from his face, feeling an unexpected roughness to the woman's skin. Lillith had very long fingers that looked out of proportion to the rest of her hands. He turned to see the already familiar predatory smile. There was nothing warm or friendly about that smile, but something that stirred unpleasant skeins of sexual darkness.

'Reading up on the Abbey, Capel? Finding out about the power of the stones?' Today Lillith had abandoned black for a long, pale, sheath-like top over jeans. Her hair hung loose, always moving, magnifying the slight motions of breath and speech.

'In a way.'

Ridge had witnessed the meeting. He came up to join them as much as the restricted aisles of the shop allowed. 'Policemen have changed a lot since my day,' he said in a bland undertone.

Lillith frowned. 'Is he with you?'

'Unfortunately, yes,' said Capel. 'Ed Ridge, Lillith Cooper. Lillith's a writer, she's here doing a book.'

'An excellent thing for a writer to do,' said Ridge. He blinked several times, as if he had something in his eye. 'Let's see... horror is it?'

'Non-fiction,' said Capel. 'She's into ancient powers and mysteries.'

'Ah,' said Ridge, 'fantasy.'

'I can see I'll have to work on you as well as Capel, Mr Ridge,' said Lillith. 'But I'm afraid I haven't got the time right now. I only slid in here to hide from Harriet's repulsive little admirer.'

'You've seen Henry Malkovski?' said Capel.

'Not our darling Henry. There's a spotty local youth who's been hanging around the worthy Harriet. Impressed by her so-called art, no doubt - it's hard to believe it could be anything else. Ian something. Like the bridge man.'

'Ian Telfer?' said Capel.

'Exactly. I was nearly right. I'm surprised you move in such circles, Capel. Now I must be off, once I've done the necessary.' She turned full face to Capel and put her arms on his shoulder, stroking the back of his neck. 'This is for yesterday.' She kissed him full on the mouth. Capel wasn't sure how to react. By the time he had decided she had pushed away. 'Til next time, then.' She blew them both a kiss and left the shop.

Ridge shook his head, his mouth slightly open. 'Admiration

is not enough,' he said slowly, still shaking his head. 'If I had a hat, I would take it off to you. Forget that; show me the nearest hat shop and I will buy a hat.'

'Very funny.' Capel turned back to the shelves. He slid a book from the tight jumble and began to thumb through it.

'I'm not trying to be funny,' Ridge said. He seemed quite happy to talk to Capel's back. 'I'm genuinely envious. Is it something they teach you at Theological College, being fascinating to women? It certainly isn't the Home Office's idea of development training. More's the pity.'

'Don't be crass, it's all tied up with this murder. I went round to see somebody who's involved. He shares his house with a girl...'

'And it happened to be the lovely Lillith? That doesn't explain why she was thanking you. Does it? Capel? Oh, bloody hell, Capel, there's another one, isn't there? Lillith isn't the girl with the house - that must be Harriet. You're a marvel.'

'Let's start out all over again, shall we? You're obviously much more cut out for detection than I am. I thought you said you wanted to be my Watson? Look, I just want to finish looking through this book, go back to the hotel and have a shower, and I'll explain it all over a drink. Does that suit you?'

'Eminently. What've you got there?' Ridge reached over Capel's shoulder and tilted the book so that he could see the cover. It featured a row of gargoyles, with a woman leaning over the stone balustrade between them, as if trying to become one of the set. She had strong features, and looked straight into the camera with a determined expression. The title, which ran neatly along the cap of the balustrade was 'Hunt's Treasure', sub-titled for the hard of understanding 'One Woman's View on the Vagaries of British Architecture'. 'Ah. The late Lady I.'

'The same. She really had an eye for these things. Just look at that.' He pointed to a photograph of a huge, gothic monstrosity of a summerhouse.

'What are you trying to find?'

'I don't know. I can't imagine I'm going to find anything.

This book was published in... just a minute... in 2007, ages before she died. I was interested in her style.'

'You have a good wallow,' said Ridge. 'I'm going to take in the rest of Glastonbury's undoubted delights. I'll be in the bar by the time you've got them in. Mine's a G and T. No ice.'

~

In fact, Capel had been sitting on the plain wooden chair in his adopted corner of the bar for at least fifteen minutes before Ridge made an appearance. Capel liked his corner. He liked the big, clumsy tables and the use-darkened wood of the seats. He was at ease. Cleaned up from the heat of the day, changed, and with half a glass of tonic water inside him, Capel was happier with life.

Ridge came in with a sly smile decorating his face. He walked straight to Capel's table as if he was aware of where his friend would choose to sit as soon as he entered the dim room. He seated himself solidly in the chair facing Capel, picked up his drink, stuck out his long legs as far as the table would allow him and sighed deeply. 'Rural bliss. Why don't I move out here?'

'Because you're a stick-in the mud career person, because you appreciate all the distractions and entertainments the capital can offer you, and because you're a wimp.'

'No, don't spare me. Tell me what you really think. Even better, tell me about your bevy of beauties.'

'You've taken up headline writing for the tabloids, haven't you?'

'If I had, I could do much better than that. Pretty Pair for Parson? Vain Vicar in Vicarious Vice? Cosy Cleric Caught Out? Bishop Blasts Priest for Bonking Bimbos?'

'Watch it, sunshine. This is the fabrication of a warped mind.'

'Since when have those sorts of papers let the truth get in the way of a good headline? Anyway you've no room to talk. It's common slander, suggesting that someone's got a case of the tabloids.'

'I won't give that the false sense of respect that a response would imply. I've already told you that Vicky's something special - I'm sure you'll get to meet her, even if she doesn't turn up tonight...'

'Got some dark secret, has she?'

'She's liable to be on duty. Lillith you've already... encountered. She's a law unto herself, but I can assure you that you have just as close a relationship with her as I have. Then there's Harriet who she shares a house with. She seems a more approachable sort of person, but she's just someone I've come across through this murder business, that's all.'

Ridge nodded in an infuriating, patronising, thoroughly disbelieving style. 'Of course, that's all.' He leant back, pushing his chair onto two legs. 'And yet, the prosecution puts to you a very different picture, Mister Capel. Let me take you back to Wednesday afternoon, this very afternoon. Were you or were you not in a small book shop in Glastonbury?'

'Of course I was, but...'

'Just answer the questions, Mister Capel. That way we will get to the truth. Did you have an encounter in that bookshop with a Miss Lillith Cooper?'

'She spoke to me, yes.'

'And I put to you that Miss Cooper kissed you, saying "This is for yesterday."'

'Allegedly.'

'Do you deny the matter?'

'No.'

'No. Exactly. And yet you stand before the court and have the brazen cheek to suggest that there is nothing between you.'

'Yesterday I saved Lillith's life - that's what happened yesterday. She nearly fell into the crypt at the Abbey; I caught her. And that's all there is to it.'

'I see. And I suppose you are going to suggest that there is nothing between you and the maid?'

'What maid?'

'Oh, come on, Mister Capel, how many maids do you know?

Did you phone her Phil, by the way?'

'Who?' Capel was genuinely confused.

'Your maid friend's paramour. The one who wanted to speak to you. Dark secrets revealed, etcetera, etcetera.'

'Oh yes. Well, no - I rang, but he didn't pick up. Just voicemail. I said I'd call back.'

'He probably wants to warn you off his girl. He's heard how you've been chatting her up in your best silk pyjamas.'

'Game over,' said Capel, quickly. 'Here comes Vicky. I want you on your best behaviour.'

'Me?' said Ridge, suddenly the picture of innocence. He stood ponderously and turned to face the door. Vicky had just come in, still in her uniform and flushed from running from the police station. She looked uncomfortable.

'Hi,' said Capel, smiling in what he hoped was a welcoming way. 'Vicky, this is Ed. And vice versa.'

'I'm really sorry,' said Vicky, 'I didn't mean to come like this. I've only just got away, there wasn't time to change, and I knew I'd be late anyway, so I came straight up.'

'Don't apologise on my behalf,' said Ridge.

'I'd better go home and change,' said Vicky. 'I just wanted you to know I hadn't abandoned you.'

'There's no need,' said Capel. 'You're no doubt ready to eat - I certainly am - and by the time you'd got back it'd be getting late. I know you can't socialise in uniform, but couldn't you just get rid of the bits which most obviously belong to the Somerset Constabulary?'

'I'll look like a waitress. Go on, then. Give me a couple of minutes.'

'Spoilsport,' said Ridge as soon as Vicky was out of earshot. 'You know what a woman in uniform does to me.'

'Not now, Ed, there's a good boy.'

'Okay. I have to admire your taste in police officers, though. I had something more robust in mind. Police women and thick ankles go together wonderfully in my mind.'

'I don't know why I bother trying to educate you.' Capel

stood up as Vicky came back into the bar, looking much younger without her uniform jacket. 'Now do your bit and feed us, I'm starving.'

~

Vicky didn't have much chance to sample Ed's hospitality. They had just started on the first course when her phone rang. She mimed sorry, pulled it out her bag and stepped away from the table into an empty alcove to take the call.

Ridge took a large forkful of his starter, waving his fork in Vicky's direction. 'Delicious,' he said to Capel, 'entirely delicious.'

'I give up all hope of reforming you,' said Capel.

Vicky came back over, her irritation remaining. 'Your Mr Davies is a pain in the arse.'

'Quite so,' said Capel. 'And he's your Mr Davies. I make no claim to him. I presume he wants you back.'

'No kidding. They've just lost half the database and they want me to sort out the computer for them. Honestly, they expect people to use these things without training, then they're surprised when things go wrong.'

'Should we wait?' said Ridge.

'I wouldn't. I don't think I'll get back. I'm sorry, Ed. Some other time, I hope.'

'So do I,' said Ridge. He watched her out of the room. 'You've got a problem there, old son. Conflict of job and private life. Want to watch that.'

'You're telling that to a vicar? I can live with it.'

'Just so long as you've got your eyes open. Now, you were telling me about these other girls.'

'Like hell I was. You've had all you're going to get on that subject. Fine sort of Watson you're turning out to be. More interested in the females involved than the case itself.'

'I seem to remember that old JW had that problem himself a fair amount of the time.'

'Oh, yes. John, wasn't it? John Watson. You tend to forget he had any other first name than Doctor. I think he would suggest we reviewed the case. Okay?'

'Fine,' said Ridge. 'Only pass the black pepper first, will you?'

CHAPTER 10

Reviewing the case seemed to last half the night. On second thoughts, Capel realised as he struggled through the final, reluctant strands of sleep that stuck to his mind like over-worked chewing gum, it *had* lasted half the night. Although it was easy enough to lapse into silly banter with Ed, he was someone that Capel felt totally happy bouncing ideas off. And for the first hour or two after dinner they had even made sense. Perhaps it hadn't been such a good idea to take the bottle of port back to his room.

Capel slipped out of bed and took a first, tentative step towards the bathroom, his arms in front of him to ward off the contents of the room in the thick darkness that the hotel curtains provided. Something blocked his foot a few inches off the ground, giving under the pressure of his weight.

'Ow! Get off!'

Capel wobbled as the ground shifted under him. He stepped back, crashing into the bedside table. A crystalline pain played happily round his hip. Capel winced. 'Ed? Is that you?'

'It's not a bloody talking carpet,' said Ed's voice from the depths of the darkness.

'Sorry, I forgot you were there. Why are you there?' Capel's outstretched hands found a pair of curtains and dragged them open, letting a stream of light in to splash sadistically into Ed Ridge's half open eyes.

'Thank you very much,' said Ridge. 'Just what I needed. It's not enough to cripple me, you want to blind me as well.'

'Don't change the subject. Why are you there. Here.'

'Because I was invited to stay over by a disgrace to the church, who was clearly so pissed out of his skull that he doesn't even remember doing so.'

'Of course I remember inviting you,' said Capel, 'I just don't remember you accepting.' He eased himself onto the end of bed. It was the old fashioned type, high enough to leave his feet dangling above the carpet. 'In fact I definitely recall you declining my offer. Kind offer, I think you called it. Something about being too old for sleeping on floors. It's all coming back to me now. I got ready for bed, because it was obviously the only way I was going to get rid of you, and you went to the bathroom, and said you'd turn off the light on your way out. Does that ring any bells?'

'You shouldn't talk forcefully to a man in my state,' said Ridge, levering himself up into a sitting position. 'I haven't the constitution for it. I suppose there's an element of truth in what you say. I did switch the light off. But then the whole business of finding my way out and back to my hotel - I was supposed to be staying in another hotel you know, not this one - it all seemed a bit much. And the floor was there, ready for use. And it seemed remarkably soft.' He groaned and rubbed his shoulder. 'Then. It appears to have firmed up overnight.' He twisted his neck tentatively. From the wince that distorted his face, it was an unwise experiment. 'When did we get middle-aged, Capel? I could have sworn I was still a young man yesterday.'

'With a hairline like yours? Sorry, beneath the belt. Look, be a hero, Ed, put the kettle on. You're nearer than I am.'

'There must be an answer to that, but I'm in no state to come up with it.' Ridge looked as if he was about to stand up, grimaced and crawled across the floor to the kettle, which perched coyly underneath the television set.

It wasn't the safest place to keep a kettle, thought Capel. He considered commenting on this to Ed, but suspected that he would be told of a safer place to stick it. 'Well done. I suppose it would be asking too much to expect you to do a quick web search for me as well?'

Ridge didn't reply. He didn't need to. The look was enough.

'Of course it is. Stupid of me to ask.' Capel slid across the cover and grabbed his phone from the bedside table. He brought it back to the end of the bed and proceeded to thumb through to Google.

'Why the search?' asked Ridge.

'I thought I'd look up... just a minute,' said Capel, running his finger down the side of his phone as he read.

'I'm in no hurry,' said Ridge. 'I could even work on standing up.' He helped himself upright with the corner of the television set. 'Nothing to it, when you're used to it. I bet I could do this every day if I tried.'

'What, sleep on the floor?' said Capel, continuing to search down a second page of results.

'No, stand up. Wow, isn't the world so much more interesting from this height?' A knock on the door interrupted him. 'It'll be your friend, the maid.'

'I told you, she just works here,' said Capel. 'Oh, thank you, I've lost my place now.'

'Blame me, why don't you?' Ridge took the few steps to the door with ample caution. He opened it with a flourish. 'Hello there, perhaps you'd like a cup of tea on my lap this morning.'

'Really!' said an unfamiliar female voice. Capel looked up. A heavily built lady filled the doorframe. She was not the sort of woman you invited to take tea on your lap. Not if you cherished your personal safety.

'I'm sorry,' said Ridge, genuinely unhappy at having upset her, but equally concerned for his health. 'I thought you were someone else.'

'Yes,' said the woman. The single syllable said it all. It might have been a short remark, but it had plenty of force. Flowers have wilted at less. Her gaze took in the two men, the empty bottle and dirty glasses on a side table, Ridge's dishevelled state. Her mouth pursed tightly, forcing little mounds of flesh to rise alongside her lips. Ridge, who was much nearer than Capel, found himself fascinated by her mouth, the fascination that a lethal weapon at close quarters can bring.

Capel cleared his throat. 'Can I help you?' he said. He had to say something; Ridge and the woman seemed happy to stay there all morning.

'I am the housekeeper,' said the woman. 'I came to apologise about the irregularity of the maid service this week.' Her tone made it clear that, while she might have come to apologise, she had no intention of doing so any more. 'We've had sickness.' But nowhere near as sick as the goings on in this room, those compressed lips seemed to say.

'Thank you very much,' said Capel. 'It's very kind of you. But there was no need to apologise, the service has been excellent.'

The housekeeper grunted and closed the door without another word.

'That was a salutary lesson to us all,' said Ridge.

'Shut up and get on with making the drinks,' said Capel.

'And what is sir doing in the meanwhile?' said Ridge. But he did turn the cups over onto the little doilies in the saucers.

'Detecting. It was what you wanted, wasn't it? I'm googling Ian Telfer.'

'It's no use trying to blame me for the detective work. You don't take sugar, do you? You're just as interested in this murder as I am. More, really. You aren't going to find out much beyond an uninspiring Facebook profile.'

'You're probably right, but I suspect he lives with his parents, and they may well be old enough to still be in the phone listing.'

'So you know his address?'

'No, but I can't imagine there are too many Telfers in Glastonbury. I could ring Paul Schofield's parents and ask them, but I'd rather not bother them. Good grief, there are ten of them.'

'All in Glastonbury?'

'No, but in the area. We don't know for certain he lives in the town, but it seems likely. That cuts it down to three. A.P., Simon and V. I've always wondered why some people have names rather than initials listed in the directory. It looks strange.'

'Try V. first. He sounds like someone with a V. for a parent.'

'It's as good a reason as any. No, hang on, V. is a Telford. It must be one of the other two.'

'If they've got a phone and they're not ex-directory.'

'Don't be too optimistic, will you. Thanks.' Capel took a sip of his coffee and put it down on the bedside table. He dialled A.P. 'Engaged. Is somebody trying to tell me that this isn't such a good idea? Let's try Simon.' Capel straightened suddenly, going through the mental equivalent of straightening his tie. The phone was ringing. 'Hello, is that Mr Telfer? My name's Capel... No, I'm not... Really, I'm not... Mr Telfer, I am not a salesman. I wanted to have a word with Ian... Ian Telfer; look, I think I may have the wrong number... There really is no need to take... Well, thank you, Mr Telfer.' He put the phone down.

'Not our Mr Telfer?' Ridge asked, peering over the top of his teacup with a passable imitation of a superior look.

'That seems a fair assumption.' Capel scrolled back through his call list and hit redial. 'No, A.P.'s still on the line.'

'Keep at it,' said Ridge. 'I'll get dressed, make myself beautiful, that sort of thing.'

'It could take a while,' said Capel, touching the phone screen once more. 'It might be easier to make a hippopotamus - ah, good morning, is that Mrs Telfer?... My name's Capel, I'm trying to get in touch with Ian... No, you wouldn't know me, Mrs Telfer. I met Ian at the Schofields' after Paul's tragic...' Capel performed an aggressive thumbs up for Ridge's benefit. 'No, nothing like that. I'm a vicar, Mrs Telfer. I was the one who found Paul's body. I wondered if I can have a word with Ian, because I think we can help each other... No, really, there isn't... All right, can I get in touch with him at work?... Where's that?... I understand. Thanks very much, Mrs Telfer. I appreciate this... Okay, thanks. Goodbye.'

'He's at work,' said Ridge, coming out of the bathroom towelling his face.

'Correct,' said Capel. 'Glastonbury Woodcraft, to be precise. It's some sort of DIY shop in one of the side streets. She seemed a bit nervous, but it's understandable.'

'Good stuff. Let's get off then.'

'I would like to get dressed first. I find it projects a better image if you're wearing clothes.'

Ridge sighed heavily. 'Get on with it then. That's the trouble with you clergymen, you're not used to working a full day, except on Sundays. You don't expect to do anything before midday during the week.'

Capel glared and got on with it.

~

Glastonbury Woodcraft was one of the old-fashioned sort of DIY shops that somehow manage to keep a shaky grip on solvency despite the incursion of the superstores and warehouses. The window was decorated in the cram-it-in school, a tangled hotch-potch of tools, display boards of picture frames and mouldings, lines of bottles and tubes of glues, door locks and handles and knobs. Notices that had once proudly declaimed 'Keys Cut' and 'Special Offer' in fluorescent splendour had now faded to a dull orange, suggestive of an ever-present air of dampness.

Capel pushed the door open. Inside, the shop was dim. High shelves lined the walls. Glass-top counters filled with obscure pen-knives and Russian doll families of padlocks surrounded a small space for the customers. The flooring looked like an early prototype for linoleum, worn through in places to a dirty wooden surface beneath. There was nobody behind the counter.

'I remember a place like this when I was a boy,' Ridge said in a hushed voice. 'I used to be fascinated by all the different tools and knives, but we only ever bought half a pound of nails, or some beeswax. I bet they sell beeswax.'

'Probably,' said Capel. 'Good morning.' Someone had come from the doorless alcove behind the counter, a middle-aged man with faded yellowish hair and a droopy moustache that could never have been fashionable. He wore a brown shop coat and under it Capel could see a darker brown cardigan, a checked shirt and, despite the early summer heat, the top of a vest sticking cheekily out of the gap in the shirt collar.

'Good morning,' said the shopkeeper, 'what can I do for you?' There was a strange chesty intonation to his voice, something more than the usual Somerset burr.

'Does, er, Ian Telfer work here?' said Capel.

'Hmm,' said the shopkeeper, in a ruminant fashion. Although the natural animal association that his moustache brought to mind was a walrus, there was something bovine about him. 'In a manner of speaking.'

'Is he out?' said Ridge.

'Out?' said the shopkeeper. 'No, not out.'

'Oh good,' said Capel, struggling to stay polite. 'So he does work here.'

'He certainly comes here to work,' said the shopkeeper. 'But his soul's not in it. Do you know what I'm saying?'

'I think so,' said Capel. 'Could we speak to him?'

'Hmm,' said the shopkeeper. 'I don't see why not.'

'That's very kind of you,' said Capel. 'Where is he?'

'In the workshop.' The walrus moustache twitched slightly. It was difficult to say if the obstructiveness was deliberate or the simple laid-back rural variety.

'Which is where?' asked Ridge.

'Oh, yes,' said the shopkeeper. 'It's, er, through the back.' He gestured over his shoulder, pointing through the dark recess. 'Down the stairs at the back.'

'Thanks,' said Capel. After some long seconds it became apparent that the shopkeeper had nothing further to say on the subject. He turned to a display of glues and started rotating the tubes so that the lettering all faced in the same direction. Capel raised his eyebrows at Ridge and lifted the flap in the counter, leading the way through into the private side of the shop.

The back room made everything they had seen so far look

sparkling and new. The special effects team of a horror movie could have learned a thing or two about cobwebs from that back room. Grey walls could occasionally be made out between greyer shelves, piled with cardboard boxes and old tins and an assortment of things which may well have been brown paper bags in their youth but were now well on their way through metamorphosis. They were clearly in the chrysalis stage. Capel wondered what sort of butterfly started life as a brown paper bag.

'It's like *Through the Looking Glass*,' he said quietly to Ridge. 'I mean that shopkeeper, and now it's making me think of strange insects. I'm not sure I fancy going downstairs.' He edged past an antiquated gas fire, luckily not in use in summer. Not that there was a lot of heat in the dim room. It was like being in a cave - the temperature of that grey grotto was independent of whatever was going on outside, a constant cool to chilly.

Ridge poked at an anonymous piece of grey furniture in the corner. 'I think that was a desk, you know. There are pigeonholes.'

'It could just as easily be a dovecote,' said Capel. 'Let's get on.'

The stairs were worrying. It was too dark to see what state they were in, but they were very steep and creaked ominously. Capel groped for a handrail, but all he could feel was the flaky plaster, coming away from the walls in large wafers. Only a thin sliver of light from under a door lit the small anteroom at the bottom. Capel found a handle on the rough, unsanded surface of the door and pulled.

A wash of light and sound spilled out. Just as he had opened the door, someone had started up some sort of machinery. They squinted against the yellow light, dim enough, but blinding after the gloom of the stairs. Capel recognised Ian Telfer, concentrating hard on feeding a large sheet of Formica through an ancient band saw. The blade screamed uneasily, sending a splinter of the material slamming into the wall by Capel's head.

'Mind yourself,' said Telfer, noticing them, but still

concentrating hard on the laminate. 'It's a tricky sod, when it's cut is this.' He slid the sheet forward until it parted and hit a big red button by his elbow. The motor died and the singing band slowed down, then stopped suddenly with metallic clunk.

'Shouldn't you wear goggles?' said Capel. Telfer's only protection was a pair of old gardening gloves. Like the shopkeeper he was wearing a brown shop coat, but he managed to look as if he had just thrown it on, while the shopkeeper's could well have grown on him.

'I tried it,' said Telfer, 'but I couldn't see a bloody thing in this light. Weren't you at the Schofield's?'

'That's right. I found Paul on the Tor. I'm just trying to do my bit to help.'

'So?' Telfer tensed. 'What are you doing here?'

'I wanted to talk to you,' said Capel.

'Who's he? Police?'

'Ed Ridge. He's a friend of mine. We've nothing to do with the police.' I ought to get a badge made, Capel thought. Nothing to do with the police.

'Talk, then,' said Telfer. He pulled himself up on the big workbench behind him. The ceiling of the cellar was quite low, bringing his face so near the unshielded light bulb that Capel couldn't make out his expression for the halo of light.

'I'm trying to find out what happened,' said Capel. 'Not for the police, but for myself. Or for Paul, if you like.'

'I can't see it'll do him much good,' Telfer said. 'Nosy, are you?'

'It's not that,' said Capel. I dearly hope it's not that, he added to himself. 'You saw Paul the night before he died, didn't you?'

'For a bit.' Telfer picked up a great curl of wood shaving from the bench and twisted it between his fingers. He didn't look at Capel. 'I was down the pub with my mates that night. It was Sunday, wasn't it?'

'That's it,' said Capel. 'I found him Monday morning. Which pub do you usually go to? I haven't found many decent ones round here yet.'

'I don't think it's your kind of place, mister. Not what you'd call decent.'

'You'd be surprised,' said Capel. 'I was in a prison before I came here.'

'Needlework teacher, were you? It's the Bottle, if you must know. The Slattern Bottle. At the east end of town.'

'I might drop in,' said Capel. 'Were any of Paul's other friends around that night?'

'I told you, I was with my mates. Dave and Kev. They were... Paul's mates too. He went out about ten, but we stayed on.'

Capel looked closely at the young man, but the light made it impossible to see any details of his face. He still stared down at the shaving that he twisted to and fro. There was something uncertain about him, something that gave to the touch, like the brown spot on an ageing orange.

'Are you sure?' said Capel quietly. 'Are you sure they were Paul's mates?'

'Yes!' Telfer jerked up, his eyes bright, defying Capel to disagree. 'He didn't have anybody else, all right? Paul wasn't the sort to have lots of friends.'

Not surprisingly if he went in for blackmail, Capel thought.

'We saw a friend of yours yesterday,' said Ridge. 'Or at least, someone who knows a friend of yours.'

'Who's that?' asked Telfer, looking suspiciously at Ridge.

'Harriet Watson,' said Ridge. 'I gather you're friendly with Harriet Watson.'

'Oh... Harriet.' Telfer's face lost its hardness, and a good few years. He could have been fifteen again.

'I've met Harriet a couple of times,' said Capel. 'She's nice, isn't she?'

'Nice?' said Telfer. 'She's not nice, she's incredible. I mean, she's so... You know, that hair, the way she looks at you with those eyes... What's she to you?'

'Nothing,' said Capel. 'Nothing at all. I've just met her over some business. I've got my own girl, okay? I was only saying she's nice.'

'I still can't believe it that she can even be bothered to speak to me. She must think I'm a real thick sod.'

'Harriet's not like that. Do you want me to mention you, if I see her again? Put in a good word, sort of?'

'No.' Telfer pushed himself off the bench and dusted down his jeans. 'No, I don't want helping. Are you done? I've got work to do.'

'We're off,' said Capel. 'Thanks for talking to us. We'll see you around.'

They squeezed out through the narrow doorway. 'I've got my own girl?' said Ridge. 'Very liberated and PC.'

'Pardon me, Mister New Man.'

Behind them the saw started up again. Ridge took the lead up the stairs, which were only wide enough for one. 'Your Harriet's really touched a nerve there.'

'She's not my Harriet,' said Capel from behind him, 'don't be ridiculous. It's strange, isn't it, how people's ideas of attractiveness change with fashion. I know what he sees in Harriet - she's a very likeable person and he's right about her eyes, but her hair's like a loo brush. I couldn't get excited about it myself.'

'She's probably kind to dumb animals.'

'Tactful as ever.'

The grey back room seemed a haven of light after the cellar. They manoeuvred out past the piled boxes and rags that littered the floor. In the sales area the shopkeeper had a customer. He handed over something in a crinkled brown paper bag and put some small change in the till. The whole transaction seemed to take place without the need for conversation. They watched from the alcove until the customer was gone.

'Just before we go,' said Ridge, popping out of the darkness with the suddenness of an automaton on an old clock, hoping to make the shopkeeper jump, 'I wonder if you could satisfy my curiosity. Do you sell beeswax?'

'We certainly do,' said the shopkeeper. He showed no surprise at Ridge's sudden arrival, but there was an air of excitement about him. His eyes were less watery, his back straightened. 'Not liquefied stuff in a tin. Good solid chunks of beeswax. Would you like some?'

'No thanks,' said Ridge. 'I was just enquiring.'

After they left the shop it was some while before Ridge spoke. Capel was familiar with the signs. There was a theory on the way. Ridge stopped suddenly as they were walking down the pavement, causing a woman with a pushchair to swerve and nearly hit a street lamp. She glared at him and muttered about drunks, but Ridge was in no state to notice.

'Well?' said Capel. 'What great revelation is about to be delivered on an uncertain world?'

'Nothing much,' said Ridge. 'But I know who did your murder.'

CHAPTER 11

'I thought this sort of melodrama went out with Maria Marten and the Murder in the Red Barn.' said Capel.

'If you don't want to know, I can keep my idea to myself.'

'Life wouldn't be worth living. And I want to get over to the county library, ideally before it closes, so I might as well get it over with. What's your idea, Ed?'

'Not here.' Ridge looked around with overacted suspicion. 'The walls have ears. Let's find somewhere we can get a coffee.'

The coffee was thick, bitter and surprisingly good. They had picked the first place they came to, an over-frilly teashop; decent coffee was an unexpected bonus. Ridge sipped his cup, spooned in a heaped pile of sugar and sat back to stir contemplatively. The steam had left a thin film of moisture on his wire-rimmed glasses. He ignored it.

'Consider the scenario...'

'Must I?' said Capel. 'Is this wise? You always said coffee had a bad effect on you.'

'You must. The key is Harriet Watson, your innocent little Harriet Watson.'

'You've not even met her.'

'So? Sherlock Holmes' brother thingy... you know? He used to solve crimes without even leaving his club. Everything leads back to Harriet. Henry Malkovski is seen at the scene. Do you like that? Seen at the scene.' Ridge pushed his chair onto its back legs, balanced precariously while he considered the impressive nature of his own eloquence. The teashop owner scowled at him from behind her counter.

Capel yawned.

'Yes, all right,' said Ridge. 'I blame television and YouTube - today's audiences have no time for dramatic pauses. Attention spans have been ruined. So Henry's at the scene - and who does he live with? Harriet. Telfer knows the victim very well and who does he fancy? Harriet. The victim was drowned at the well… and whose lodger is writing a book about it? Harriet.'

'Mycroft,' said Capel. 'Holmes' brother was called Mycroft.'

'Quite. We know that Schofield was blackmailing Malkovski. The chances are Harriet knew too. She wanted it stopped - they weren't exactly rolling in money. Then she finds out that this Telfer is drooling over her. Putty in her hands. So between them, they murder Schofield. I should think Telfer made sure that Schofield was pissed out of his skull that night. Easy work to get him into the well. Then the following morning, our friend Henry takes a stroll up the Tor, sees the body, realises what's happened - he knows Harriet well enough. Obviously he wants to protect her, so he does a runner.'

'Masterly,' said Capel. 'Utterly masterly. How anyone can be so selective with the evidence is quite unbelievable.'

'Standard police practice isn't it, guv?'

'The Home Office would not be amused. Your scenario is a bit thin, isn't it? Why should Harriet and Henry haul Schofield up to the top of the hill? Why not just leave him at the well? What about the letters on the wall? And the mysterious man with long hair? Not Henry, the other one? And how does this all tie in with Isobel Hunt?'

'Details schmeatails.' Ridge paused to take a long mouthful of his coffee. 'Why shouldn't they haul him to the top? Harriet's a bit of a weirdo isn't she? She probably thought it was the sort of thing a fully paid up druid should do. I mean, like it's mystically significant, man. The letters and the long-haired stranger are irrelevant. Coincidence. And as for Isobel Hunt, there is simply no connection. A different murder, different people, different reasons. It's a nasty, brutish world, young Stephen. There's a lot of unpleasantness about.'

'This is Glastonbury, Somerset, not Washington D.C. You're wrong, I'm afraid, Ed. Harriet isn't the right type. Your whole picture...'

'Scenario.'

'Your whole scenario doesn't ring true. It's great as a theory, but it doesn't work in practice and it doesn't fit the people involved.'

'You're just jealous.'

'Believe what you like, it stinks.' Capel drained his cup. 'Time I was off. Time, tide and libraries wait for no man.'

'So you keep saying. What's the great attraction of the library?'

'I want to find out more about Isobel Hunt. You can only get so much from websites, I want to get my hands on photos. I know you don't think there's a connection, but it's still possible. Anyway, you've got real work to do, haven't you?'

'Yes, but that's only what the taxpayer pays me for. Couldn't we just call and see Harriet, on the way sort of thing?'

'It's not on the way.'

'You said I didn't know her. It might help dissuade me from my terrible theories if I met her.'

'Should I care? Okay, we call in, just to check she's not got any problems. But no pressure.'

'Moi? The king of subtlety?'

'Exactly.'

~

They took separate cars to be able to leave Harriet's separately. Capel pulled up behind Ridge's big, dark blue Audi with a trace of a sigh tickling his mind. If he had stayed in his old job he would be driving something like that. Capel patted the steering wheel of his Fiat. At least it was easier to park. And used less petrol - more ecologically sound. Rationalisation is an easy art when you've had lots of practice.

'Oh yes,' said Ridge, posing self-consciously on the steps as Capel got out of his car. 'Yes, I can feel the psychic vibrations.

This is the place for peace, opposite the dead animal skin factory, man.'

'You look like something out of a low budget clothes catalogue,' said Capel. 'And by "out of" I mean something that was rejected. Now, please, best behaviour here. No digs about vibrations and stuff.'

'Scout's honour.'

Despite a smothered snigger when he saw the front door with its protective serpent, Ridge maintained his restraint. Capel hoped that Harriet wasn't in, but she answered almost as soon as he knocked.

'Hello?' Harriet sounded uncertain, seeing only two men for a moment, assuming the worst. 'Oh, Capel, hello.'

'Morning,' said Capel. 'We were just passing - this is a friend of mine, Ed Ridge - and we thought we'd call in and make sure everything was okay.'

'I think so. I was going out.' She hesitated. 'Is there something you wanted to ask me?'

'No, it's purely social,' said Capel.

'I'm interested in New Age thinking,' said Ridge suddenly. Oh shit, thought Capel, here we go.

'A lot of people who come to Glastonbury are,' said Harriet. 'We must have a proper talk some time.'

'Yes,' said Ridge. He had to back away a little to let her out of the doorway sufficiently to shut it. 'Do you think this murder business has any mystical significance?'

'What, black magic and ritual sacrifice and all that? It's not my sort of thing; I wouldn't know. Look, I really must go, I was late when I started. Will you excuse me?'

'See you,' said Capel. He glared at Ridge who subsided on the point of asking another question. Together they watched the small form, hair defiantly white against her dark shirt, walk away.

'There,' said Ridge. 'She was being evasive.'

'Ssh. Not so loud. She was in a hurry, that's all. She was perfectly polite. And look at her. Could she and Telfer have got a dead body all the way up the Tor?'

'Don't equate size with strength. My cousin Sarah can pick me off the ground, and she's only four foot ten.'

'Whatever; it was a waste of time as predicted. Do you mind if I get off now? No more little diversions?'

'I've nothing to offer at the moment. Where shall I meet you? How about this Slattern Bottle place?'

Capel thought for a moment. 'As long as you buy the drinks. Sixish? Six thirty? I don't honestly know when pubs open.'

'If they shut at all. Make it six thirty, I've got to get to Bristol and back.'

'Fair enough. But remember, you're buying.'

~

'There's something to be said for this life,' said Capel to himself.

'Sorry, what?' A librarian was collecting books from the nearby tables. Capel looked around to see who he was talking to. They were alone in the midst of a sea of empty tables.

'Did I say something?' said Capel. 'I'm sorry. I was just thinking that this isn't a bad life. There's something very restful about books and buildings like this. Libraries, even the modern ones, seem to have avoided the unpleasant urgency of the twenty-first century. I suppose it's because books are less pushy than the other media. Not so fast and flighty as newspapers or so condensed as radio and TV and web.'

'Very philosophical. But I'm afraid working in libraries isn't very exciting.' The librarian smiled at him. He seemed pleased to have someone to talk to.

Capel shrugged. 'I think I could cope. I did a stint on mobile libraries in my youth. I found the pace of life very appealing.'

'I don't suppose you saw all the boring bits. But don't let me keep you from your work. You've got quite a pile there.'

'Meaning "stop keeping me from what I should be doing". I'm sorry.'

'Don't be silly, it's a quiet afternoon, I don't do this job just for the books, it's the people too. What are you reading up on?' The librarian peered at Capel's collection.

'Lady Isobel Hunt. I couldn't find much. A couple of coffee table jobs, a rather detailed treatise on the development of Victorian style and a family history that stops when she was twelve. Do you think there's anything I've missed?'

'Isobel Hunt... she used to do those funny little TV programmes, didn't she? Oh, yes... are you writing a book on her, because of the murder?'

'I don't know yet. If I could find out a bit more about the last few years of her life, and what she was doing in these parts, it might help. It might be irrelevant, but it might help.' Capel pushed the open book in front of him away. 'You don't have local newspapers here, do you?'

'Only current ones. I assume you want last year's?'

'Exactly.'

'Hang on, I'll have a word with a friend of mine on the Observer. Not the real one, the local rag. Have you enough to keep you going for a few minutes?'

'Ample,' said Capel, pulling the bigger of the two picture books towards him. 'It's very kind of you.'

What was he doing exactly? Capel flicked through the pictures, looking for something, but not sure for what. Perhaps he wanted to defend Harriet; perhaps he simply wanted to be proved right. Or it could be a sense of neatness that insisted in a small, quiet, irritatingly impossible-to-ignore voice that coincidences like this were few and far between. He realised that he had stopped turning the pages. In front of him, spread across both leaves, was a stunning shot of Glastonbury Abbey – a black and white view of the ruins that had a powerful simplicity. The shadows were long; one of her early morning efforts he suspected. Although there was no one in the picture, nothing to show the time it was taken, it felt to be early in the day.

Capel put his finger in the page and turned to the front. It might not have been a recent photograph. But the imprint date was encouraging, this year. And there, opposite the publishing details, where the author might usually dedicate the book to 'Cuddles the Cat', or 'My husband for putting up with my spending a year in the garden shed throwing together my little treasure house' - there was a black bordered paragraph.

'Lady Isobel Hunt,' it said, 'was one of the country's foremost popularisers of architecture, bringing her sheer joy at the variety and beauty of buildings to a wide public. This book, incomplete at the time of her unfortunate death, has been finished as a tribute to one of the characters of our age.'

So here was a book that post-dated the tragedy. The photographs of Glastonbury were most likely those she was taking when she was killed. Capel turned back to the panoramic view. There was something unnerving about pictures taken on her fatal visit. He flipped back to the previous page, but it showed a supermarket in Oswestry; a different place, a different message. He turned on. Following the first, big photograph there were three pages on the Abbey. He skipped quickly over a set of views of the abbot's kitchen and the transepts. That left two shots of St Mary's chapel, the lady chapel, and two in the crypt, perhaps taken the very day she was killed.

The crypt. Capel lifted the book closer, peering at the tiny detail of the photograph, the dots of light and shade that could have been variations in the print, but could equally be small items of evidence. What evidence, he didn't know. Hardly a note saying 'I did it', signed by the murderer.

'They've got them.'

'What?' Capel jumped, dropping the book back onto the table. He had not been aware that the librarian had returned.

'Sorry, I startled you.'

I knew that, thought Capel. 'My fault, I was concentrating too hard. Did you say you'd got something?'

'My friend at the Observer, he says they've got back-copies from the murder. Do you want to see them?'

'I'd love to, if it's not too much trouble.'

'No trouble at all for me. The office is down the street on the left. You can't miss it. Ask for Martin, he's expecting you.'

Capel failed to find the office on the first attempt. There's something very tempting to fate about saying 'you can't miss it', something that makes opportunities to get lost arise where they have no right to exist. It was only when he had explored the entire length of the first street on the left, a suspiciously straight road called the Crescent, that he realised the librarian had meant that the office was down the street they were already in, on the left hand side.

The Observer had the usual display of photographs in the window: crowds of children at district carnivals and local celebrities opening anything that you could sensibly open with a ribbon and a pair of scissors. There was nothing that dated back as far as the murder, of course. Capel went inside and asked for Martin.

'The man researching the book?' Martin looked as if he had just been out jogging. He wore a track suit, the bright turquoise contrasting unpleasantly with a dark, blood-suffused face. He didn't look particularly happy.

'That's me,' said Capel, deciding that it was easier to go along with the misunderstanding. He didn't comment on the man's appearance. Practically anything he could say would cause offence.

'Yes,' said the man, Martin, slowly. His hang-dog look got deeper. 'Everyone can do it, writing, you see. Piece of cake. What's your real job; how do you earn your keep?'

'I'm a vicar.'

'Ah.' Another degree of coldness was added to the scale. 'That's it, you see. You don't get every Tom, Dick and Lucy reckoning they'd make a good vicar and performing services in their spare time, do you? But everyone's a bloody writer. Everyone could knock off a book, if they only had a bit more time. There's nothing special about us professionals: we're just the ones who can't hold down a real job as well as writing, so we're stuck with journalism.'

'It's not like that,' said Capel. He was getting involved whether he liked it or not. 'I don't have any serious plans for a book - certainly nothing weighty.'

'Oh no, not weighty like writing for a local paper,' said Martin. 'Do you get a local paper where you live?'

'I will do,' said Capel. 'I've only just moved in, you see. There hasn't been time.'

'My God, what you are missing. Did you see those pictures outside the building?'

'Yes, they were very nice.' I'm not cut out to be a detective, Capel thought. In the books people just trot out the relevant bits, not all this baggage. I don't really want to know about his problems, not today.

'And do you know why the paper carries those pictures? Why it so carefully reports the names of little Sally, carnival queen, and all her little friends?'

'Because there's not much hard news in a rural community?'

'Maybe there's not, but that's not the reason. It's because little Sally's mum and dad are going to go out and buy a copy - if we're lucky they'll buy three, can't miss the grandparents out after all - and that's the difference between profit and loss. The more names we mention, the more Sallys we photograph, the more papers we sell. That's the sort of Pulitzer prize winning material we churn out.'

'Look, forget it - okay. It's not that important, I was only following up an idea. Thanks for offering to help.'

'You might as well see the bloody things now you're here - I've had to cart them up from the basement. You could at least do me the courtesy of looking at them.'

'Whatever's best for you,' said Capel. He followed his verbal attacker into the office behind the counter. Two large bound volumes were open on a cluttered desk that was pushed up against a wall covered in articles from national newspapers.

'Yours?' said Capel, pointing to the cuttings.

'It's not quite all carnivals and amateur dramatics. I got fifteen column inches in the nationals when Isobel Hunt copped it.'

'You covered it, then?'

'Ah, yes, my great triumph. At least until someone publishes a book about it. That would rather outshine my efforts.'

'May I?'

'Be my guest.' Martin pulled a chair up for Capel.

'TV EXPERT MURDERED' yelled the headline in big enough type to overwhelm the paper's banner as the Taunton Observer for the 25th September.

'It makes her sound like an electronics engineer, doesn't it?' Martin commented close to Capel's ear. He was no longer aggressive, he seemed almost shy that someone was reading his work. 'It wasn't my idea, the sub always changes it.'

Capel nodded. 'Lady Isobel Hunt, popular presenter of architectural eccentricities and acclaimed photographer was found dead yesterday morning at Glastonbury Abbey. A member of the abbey staff found Lady Isobel's body, apparently clubbed to death as she photographed details of the crypt under St Mary's Chapel near the entrance to the buildings.'

'I would have said the west end, but the great unwashed isn't deemed capable of understanding such details any more.'

'Were you there on the day?' said Capel.

'Not taking many notes, are you? That's what us professionals do, we note things down, then we've a better chance of reporting the truth of what we see. Just a tip, you understand. No charge for advice.'

'This is ridiculous - there's been some confusion and it didn't seem worth untangling it. I'm not writing anything. I'm just trying to find out what happened. It's important to me because... because a friend's involved. That's all.'

'Forgive me, you touched on a sore point. What were you saying? Oh, yes, I was there. A blessed relief, to be honest. I was due to cover a council meeting.'

'I know it's a long time ago, but can you remember anything?'

'Of course I can. What sort of thing?'

'I don't know. Stupid isn't it? Anything which would count as clue if you were trying to solve it, I suppose.'

'Wow. I don't know, I mean you can read what I wrote then - feel free - but I can't imagine there'd be anything. The old girl got in early, none of the staff around. She'd got hold of her own key, you see. Liked the sunlight effects first thing, and it gave her a chance to get some shots in without the great British public intruding. She didn't have to cram half the occupants of Somerset into her photographs to sell them. The theory at the time was that some opportunist found the gates open - it would be in character for Lady I. to have left them unlocked - and went in for a bit of mugging, except he hit her just a little too hard.'

'Some things were stolen then?'

'Her handbag, bits and pieces of jewellery. Not a fortune; certainly not worth a life. But no fingerprints, no footprints distinguishable from the common press - there's a hell of a lot of people pass through Glastonbury Abbey in September. No one ever came forward as a witness, no one was nearby... as far as I'm aware the case is still open, but totally dormant.'

'What about her camera?'

'What about it?'

'Was it stolen?'

'She'd have had more than one. I can't be sure, but, as I remember it, the 35 millimetre DSLRs, the ones that'd be easy to sell, they did go, but they left her large format film beastie. Too readily identified, I guess.'

'Yes. Did she have an assistant or anything? Anyone who'd been around with her earlier on the shoot?'

'Nope. Bit of a loner, Lady I. She'd exchanged a few pleasantries with the old biddy who runs the souvenir shop...'

'I think I've met her.'

'Probably. I reckon she'll still be there. They have extras on for the weekends and the summer, but they only cover the peak hours. So it was Mrs Whatsit - it'll be in the paper there somewhere, like I said we're shit hot on names, and ages too, though God knows why - who found the body.'

'That's the one I met. Look, thanks very much. You've been

very helpful. If I could just finish reading through your articles I won't take up any more of your time.'

'You're welcome, mate. Enjoy.'

'Lady Isobel, star of three popular series on the buildings of Britain...'

CHAPTER 12

That Capel was a quarter of an hour late at the Slattern Bottle was not entirely his fault. On his return to Glastonbury he had spent some while at the Diocesan Centre, trying to smooth ruffled feathers. Apart from anything else, he felt an obligation to formally remove himself from the course; he somehow hadn't got round to it before. Then there was the matter of the accommodation. It hardly seemed justifiable for the diocese to put him up while he went about his own business. On that, however, he and the administrator couldn't see eye to eye. She seemed to feel that Glastonbury, if not the diocese, owed Capel something for the inconvenience of having been involved in their murder. And surely the police would prefer him to stay in the vicinity? Capel wasn't so sure, at least as far as the chief inspector was concerned. In fact at that moment, he wasn't even sure about a WPC.

Eventually he gave in gracefully on the hotel, but he still had to find the course tutors and try to smooth over their hurt. He had found that course tutors tended to be a delicate breed - it came from spending the whole day being so interested and committed, with a degree of frailty the inevitable consequence. By the time he had finished he was late getting back to the hotel and changing into something scruffier, and even later for his meeting with Ed. All of which was something of a shame, because had he, Capel, been first to arrive, there might have been less trouble.

The Slattern Bottle was a back street pub. Not the utterly remote back street pub that the brewery has totally forgotten about, more the sort of place where every few years the latest fresh young blood to join the brewery management tries something different to bring in a new clientele. Preferably one with a more sophisticated and expensive taste in drinks.

It had never worked, but the remnants of the efforts still clung to the surface of the building like the barnacles on a beached boat. The plaque on the outside explaining how Slattern Bottle had evolved from Slat and Beetle (a sort of hammer) - all that survived from the abortive attempt to make the place suitable for Glastonbury's tourists. A single Peruvian bank note was stuck to the ceiling - the remains of the last landlord but three's short-lived attempt to cover the ceiling in notes. Short-lived, because he lost two for every three he put up. The wrecked pool table that dated back to a brief period of enthusiasm when *The Hustler* was in the cinemas. All sad flotsam of wasted ambition.

In the end, changing a pub's character means changing the regulars, and the regulars of the Slattern Bottle were in no hurry to be changed. They knew what they liked, and they knew what they didn't like. They didn't like people with beards and sandals who went on about real ale. Beer was beer - the point of drinking wasn't to taste it, it was to get legless. And they didn't like folk music. The landlord who had got in a folk group to try to appeal to a potential hippy audience had been bitten by one of his customers. And they particularly didn't like men in suits.

Ed Ridge found this out soon enough. He had just bought two pints in a most inoffensive manner - none of the affable 'mine host' stuff, as Ridge could be entertainingly silly but he wasn't stupid - and had sat at a table in the corner, near the dartboard. He had expected to receive a certain amount of attention because it was the sort of pub where a stranger can't avoid attention, but that was all. Nothing more.

So, all in all, it was as much a surprise to Ridge as to Capel that he was backed into a corner, being threatened with the point of a dart, when Capel arrived.

'Oi!' Capel shouted across from the door. 'There's a copper

on the way down the street. You'd better leave him.'

It wasn't incredibly convincing, Capel couldn't remember what the current slang for the police was, but he was sure it wasn't copper. Even so, it was enough. The big man who was holding a dart to Ridge's throat - he looked familiar to Capel - backed off and turned towards the door. Ridge darted past and pulled Capel after him onto the pavement.

'Thanks. Where's your car?'

'At the hotel. I walked.'

'Oh, great.' Ridge grabbed Capel's arm again and started down the street at a trot. 'Come on then, mine's round the corner. I couldn't park any nearer.'

'What did you do, Ed?'

'Let's get to the car first.'

They ran on, down the car-lined pavement and into a smaller side street. Ridge's car was crammed into a tight space between a motorbike and a rusty van.

'Okay now?' said Capel.

'I'll be happy once I'm driving.' Ridge opened the door and was jerking the car back and forwards in the space before Capel had got his own door shut. Ridge glanced in the mirror. 'I don't think they are coming after us, but I'd rather be certain.'

'You and me both. What did you say to them?'

'Very little, they did most of the talking. Which way is it to the Tor? I could do with a bit of fresh air after that. We've got a while 'til sunset.'

'Left at the top, then round to the right, I think. Well?'

'Not exactly well, but recovering. That was a neat trick you pulled there.'

'You learn all sorts inside. Now come on, tell me what happened.'

'I bought a beer - two, actually. Yours is still in there if you want to go back for it. I'd intended to just sit quietly until you turned up, but the barmaid seemed quite friendly, so...'

'You chatted her up? I'm not surprised the natives revolted.'

'So I asked her if Blake and Gunn were in. Unfortunately

they were, and heard me asking.'

'Which they didn't like?'

'That's not the half of it. Guess who we threw out of the Abbey.'

'Why do I get a strange sense of foreboding?'

'With very good reason. I thought I'd try openness, win them over with my charm and all that, so I mentioned we'd bumped into a mate of theirs, Ian Telfer, the other day. They didn't like that at all. One of them knocked my glass on the floor - it was like the gunfight at the OK Corral, everyone stopped talking and looked at me, with the beer soaking into my best brown shoes. Then the bigger one - I think that's Gunn - pulled the dart on me and seemed intent on making me a pin-up. That's about where you came in.'

'Wonderful.' Capel put a lot of stress on the first syllable, soaking the word in irony. 'You certainly know how to soft talk a witness.'

They climbed the long path up the Tor in silence. The Tor itself had a lot to do with that. The steep slope discouraged conversation. By unspoken agreement, they walked round the tower rather than through it and stopped at the far side, enjoying the rich colours of the fields in the red-orange light of the setting sun. Capel's eye was caught by a scrap of plastic, part of a carrier bag, floating past on the light breeze.

Ridge picked up the direction of Capel's gaze. 'Not so windy as last time we were here. This is more like it.'

'Is that what you saw?' asked Capel. 'I mean, did that litter make you think of the wind?'

'Yes. Shouldn't it?'

'No reason at all why it shouldn't.' Capel began to pace up and down, marking a precise rectangle on the bare soil of the hilltop. His hand drifted up to his mouth, bringing the edge of his finger into nibbling range.

'And you?'

'Sorry?'

'It presumably made you think of something else. You were

looking at the carrier bag, I suppose?'

'Oh yes. I was looking at it.' Capel stopped abruptly. 'I've just realised how Paul Schofield was murdered.'

'We know that, he was drowned.'

'Yes. But I hadn't realised what a particularly unpleasant drowning it must have been. Come over here.'

He led the way into the shell of the tower. With the sun low on the horizon it was already getting difficult to see in there, but the outlines of the stones of the wall were still visible.

'Schofield was brought up here alive. He may even have come of his own volition. It was here that he was drowned.'

'Let's recap here, Capel. On top of the highest hill in the district, with no rain, no pond, no spring, not even a bloody puddle available, he drowned.'

'Exactly. You remember I found a rope, fixed to a peg in the wall.'

'Yes, and a mark round his neck.'

'Don't rush me. Suppose the rope had been round his ankles. Hanging him upside down. Then all it would take was a bag full of water. A carrier bag at a pinch.' He shuddered. 'I don't know why, but it seems particularly horrible, that he should be able to watch his killer bring the bag and stick it over his head, and not be able to do a thing about it. I saw a boy at the Abbey the other day with a bag full of water - carrying a fish, quite innocently. That's what made me think of it. The same thing, a bag of water - a life preserver or a murder weapon.'

'Very picturesque. Then I suppose they fixed it with a wire or something, round his neck to make sure he died.'

'Something like that. The mark on his neck was too thin for a rope, I thought that all along.'

'It doesn't change my theory, you know. In fact it makes it easier. Telfer and the girl didn't need to carry the body up the hill, it carried itself. Perhaps Harriet lured him up.'

'Ed!'

'You're biased, because you like her. I don't care what you say. Then Telfer strung him up and they did the dirty deed. It could have been Malkovski that cut him down, but that apart, I stand by my idea.'

'Hmm.' Capel wasn't convinced. As on their last visit he fingered the letters H and M. They seemed to glitter for a moment as a last ray from the sun struck them, then disappeared from sight.

'I know what you're going to say,' said Ridge. 'But there's no reason why the HM should have anything to do with it. It could be Helmut Mainz from Munich for all you know. Or... yes. Yes! Schofield gets a moment before they string him up. He already knows what they're going to do. He backs against the wall and desperately scratches. First H, H for Harriet, then M for murder. Harriet murdered me. It's all there but the action replay.'

'Really. What about Isobel Hunt?'

'What about her? I keep telling you, there's no connection. Or did you dig up conclusive proof in Taunton?'

'No.' Capel touched the wall a last time and walked to the nearer arch, the west-facing arch, which the setting sun rimmed with a fiery relief to the grey stone. 'I spoke to a man on the local paper who reported on the Abbey murder, and I can't come up with anything. Certainly no clear link with our man Schofield.'

'That's because there isn't one.' Ridge came over to stand beside him. 'You don't think her ladyship was another of your corpse's blackmail victims do you?'

'Hardly. I can't imagine they had a lot of contact. Don't worry, it'll come to me.'

'I should worry?' Ridge shrugged dramatically.

'Hardly at all. Perhaps we'd better start back. It'll be dark soon.'

'My mother would not approve of you keeping me out after dark. But someone's not bothered.'

'Sorry, what?' Capel had lost himself in the shapes of Glastonbury, dissolving into ill-defined shadows of the street lamp glow.

'Someone's not worried about being caught up here in the dark. There's somebody coming up the path.'

'Great. Probably exercising his Rottweilers.' Capel turned his back on the town and walked to the other arch, the one which would have lead into the nave of the church when it still stood in defiance of the lonely spirit of that hill. There was little to see now from that side. The fields had become a uniform, grey blanket in the dusk. A couple of lights twinkled on a farm; closer by the glow-worm trails of cars crossed the open spaces, but there was no feature to catch the eye, except the scarred, turfless skin of the Tor, a sickly dead-fish colour in what was left of the light.

'Are we going then?' Ridge was still at the other side of the tower.

Capel looked back, seeing Ridge as a black cut-out against the darkest blue imaginable of the sky. 'In a minute. I'm still thinking.'

'Okay, look, could you catch me up? I'll wait for you at the car.'

'If you like.' Capel didn't object to being left alone with his thoughts. The tower should have been an eerie place in the gloom. The wreck of a church, the site of a murder, lonely, isolated... and yet it hadn't got a depressing quality. It was restful, as if the many years of prayer - even years as far back as these - had imbued the place with a very natural peace.

He heard a scuff behind him, a foot catching one of the little stones embedded in the soil outside the tower. 'Get lonely did you?' He turned, smiling, but it wasn't Ridge. Even though it was now so dark that he could hardly see the outline of the arch on the far side, he knew that it wasn't Ridge. Capel took a step forward. And another. The stranger had reached the arch and was standing silently. He could make out a very faint shape.

'Hello?' For a moment, he wondered if he had done the wrong thing. He couldn't see, there wasn't enough detail to tell even if the person was facing him, but he was sure it was a woman. There was something about the stance and a suspicion of the outline of a skirt below the waistline. And that gave him pause, because it was hardly the place, hardly the circumstance, to make a sudden appearance out of the darkness. Capel tried to think of something suitably innocuous to say, but the woman saved him the effort.

'Capel?'

Capel teetered back against the wall of the tower in relief. 'Vicky. I can't really believe this is a coincidence.'

'We have our methods.' This close, very close, he could see the ghostly fairness of her hair, a glint of her eyes from the stray light of the stars. He was close enough to feel her breath on his cheek. Capel reached out and took her hand.

'It's good to see you. I thought I'd be off home tomorrow without a chance to say goodbye.'

'So did I. I mean, I thought you'd go too, that's why I've... taken a late lunch break. Can we sit down?'

'There's a sort of bench thing against the wall.'

'I've got a torch,' said Vicky, trying gently to detach her hand from his.

'Not yet. Wait until we're walking back down.' Capel lead her across the uneven flooring of the tower, feeling with his foot for the stone seat. 'There.'

'Thanks, I needed to get off my feet. The climb up the Tor was the last thing they needed after a day of doorstepping. If I have to ask one more person what they were doing on the night of Sunday the 14th, I'll give up and get a career change to selling replacement windows.'

'It's not going very well then, the murder enquiry?' Capel slipped his arm round her back, pulling them close together on the seat. Already the heat of the day had faded and there was a chill on the Tor.

'I don't know. We've got Malkovski.'

'That must have made Malcolm very happy. Has he charged him?'

'No. I'm not sure what he's up to. Malkovski won't say anything - rumour has it the chief's furious.'

'It wouldn't surprise me at all. Either of them, I mean. It's tricky.' Capel shivered, without actually feeling the cold. 'You don't mind being up here?'

'No. Why should I? That's what your friend Ed said as he went past.'

'Just that?'

'Well, that and he said it looked like he was going to have a long wait. He said something about finding himself a horse blanket.'

'We can't disappoint him then, can we?'

CHAPTER 13

Back in Thornton Down. It wasn't familiar enough to be home yet, it was like moving on to the next stage of a touring holiday. Especially Saturday morning when he had nothing specific to do, no eight o' clock service, no meetings, no visits to make... nothing better than to lie in bed until getting up was a necessity.

Capel drew back his curtains vigorously. Not that he had any intention of getting dressed yet; it was only half past ten. Another of the stunning blue skies that this summer seemed determined to deliver in defiance of British tradition greeted him. That and a parrot. Or possibly a parakeet. Capel stared in not-entirely-awake bemusement. He was no expert on birds, but to his recollection there was not a British species the size of a pigeon, bright, vivid green, and sporting a high, red beak.

He looked at the bird that perched in the cherry tree, the tree outside his window, uncomfortably close to the vicarage. The bird looked back at him. 'It's a parrot,' said Capel, aloud, as if determined to challenge the intruder. It looked back unruffled. The green birds he could think of, ducks apart, were finches and woodpeckers, and it certainly didn't answer any of their descriptions. It must have escaped, he decided. But who did you ring about escaped parrots? The police? The RSPCA? The RSPB?

He looked back at the bird, which cocked its head on one side. It didn't seem to care. For a moment he thought it was going to fly off, but it was only looking over its shoulder, anticipating the arrival of a second, identical bird, which landed on the branch beside it. A pair. They looked strangely exotic in the vicarage garden, backed by the yellow-grey Bath stone wall. Exotic and yet comfortable. Capel gave them a last look and hurried round his bed to the table to grab his phone. Some sort of action was obviously called for.

'Who are you going to call,' he muttered. 'Police? Surely not.' He looked back at the window, suddenly feeling the need for reassurance, that he hadn't imagined the whole thing. The phone slipped in his grasp; he grabbed for it, slamming it painfully into his leg. The pair of parrots wasn't there anymore. To be accurate, they could have been there, but it was impossible to be sure. The whole tree seemed to be bristling with the shocking green of their plumage, at least a dozen birds, roaming the branches like mobile limes.

Thirteen. He managed to count them in a moment of stillness. Thirteen parrots in a cherry tree. It was like a new verse of the Twelve Days of Christmas, drastically out of season. Capel shook his head. It wasn't right. He hadn't been drinking - not that he was in the habit of seeing parrots when he did indulge in the occasional drop. He looked down at his phone, still pressed against his leg. No way. There was no way he was going to ring the police and tell them there were thirteen bright green parrots in his cherry tree. It wasn't even a very big cherry tree.

A knock on the door disturbed his none-too-sound train of thought. Capel gave a last look at the intrusive green flock and stumbled down the stairs, pulling on a dressing gown. It was Alan Rhees. The chaplain looked Capel up and down, an unconcealed expression of distaste on his thin lips.

'Yes?' said Capel, not noticing Rhees's expression. He was too concerned with looking down the street for further evidence of parrots. There was none. The vicarage, situated squarely next to the church, faced straight down the narrow road that threaded through the centre of Thornton Down. There was not a tree in sight. A few cottages clustered tight on the pavement, and then, after the Forge, Thornton's sole public house, the solid congregation of structures that made up

Thornton Down School filled both sides of the road with a variegated patchwork of variations on the theme of Bath stone. No trees.

'I must speak to you,' said Rhees primly. 'Something very delicate has come up.' He paused to look pointedly at Capel's pyjamas. 'But I can see your week in Glastonbury has left you tired. Perhaps I should come back?'

'No,' said Capel, grabbing the chaplain by his sleeve. 'Come and look at this.' He ran back into the house and stopped half way up the stairs, stopping to look back like a bewildered dog. 'Are you coming?'

'I really don't think...' Rhees sighed sharply and followed Capel up the stairs and into his bedroom. 'Well?'

Capel looked at the tree, now bare of psittacine visitors, at Rhees, back at the window in the hope that something had changed and back to the chaplain. 'When I woke up this morning...' he pointed firmly at the cherry tree. 'When I woke up this morning there were thirteen parrots in that cherry tree. And now they're gone. Do you believe me?'

'Of course I do,' said Rhees, selecting from his working armoury the tones normally reserved for dealing with confused schoolboys. 'They're supposed to have escaped three or four years ago, from somewhere near Limpley Stoke I think. Been breeding ever since - they seem to cope quite well with our weather. Now could we get down to serious matters?'

'Yes, I suppose so,' said Capel, not sure if he was glad that he was believed or disappointed that Rhees could treat his remarkable discovery with such commonplace aplomb. 'What's the problem?'

'Not, er... not here,' said Rhees. 'It can wait half an hour, if you think you're going to be up and about by then. Perhaps I could meet you at the church?'

'By all means,' said Capel. 'I'll see you there.'

An uncomfortable sense of being out of place descended on Capel as he pulled on his most casual of weekend clothes and bolted down some muesli along with the remains of some dried apricots which didn't seem in too bad a state, despite being a month past their sell-by date. He had no doubt that Alan Rhees's emergency would be a penny discrepancy in the collection, or some equally dire misdemeanour. It was difficult to integrate these values with the reality of Glastonbury. His life had been churned up more by a week in that place than four years in Her Majesty's prisons.

The worst thing about it was the underlying certainty he felt but couldn't prove, that there was something very wrong with the arrest of Henry Malkovski. Capel had deserted Malkovski - and Harriet - when he should have been doing something to help. Only he couldn't think what was appropriate.

He finished an unsatisfactory cup of coffee, tainted by the flat, souring taste of powdered milk, and left for the church. He hadn't far to go. The squat vicarage stood in the shade of the unassuming church tower; he had only to go out of his front door, turn right through the gates and up the uneven path to the porch. In theory he needn't even leave the church land, as his garden backed onto the graveyard, but the back gate was rusted up and showed no sign of giving way to penetrating oil.

Inside the church, Capel stopped to look round. Rhees had not arrived yet. Capel surveyed the building with interest. He hadn't been there long enough yet to know every detail of the place. The interior was surprisingly light - tall, clear, lancet windows lit an unusually pale wooden interior, the first real indication of the Victorian nature of the bulk of the church. When Capel had visited, the wardens had been quite apologetic about its lack of ancient splendour, but he had brushed off their dismissal of its merits. He was fond of good Victorian architecture. Like Lady Isobel. Perhaps that was why he was so interested in what had happened to her, so determined to link her death with Schofield's.

Capel breathed deeply, taking in the subtle combinations of scents. The cool, slightly musty air that the hottest summer couldn't dispel; the furniture polish; the light sweetness of the altar flowers; from somewhere a tiny, bitter remnant of an earlier incumbent's love affair with incense. And a new smell, the touch of an acrid odour that was familiar, but he was unable to place.

Behind him, the door creaked. Capel turned to see Rhees, distorted by the poor quality glass of the vestibule. The chaplain bustled in and cast a hurried glance around the building.

'All in one piece, is it then?'

Capel was slow to respond, amused at the unconscious slip into a Welsh idiom that Rhees's irritation had pushed through his layers of urbane correctness. 'Shouldn't it be?'

Rhees's irritation grew. His lips seemed practically colourless in the very white light, like thin strips of tripe glued to his face. Position and pecking order were very important to Rhees. He would have felt entirely at home in a wild dog pack. When Capel had first arrived, Rhees had been concerned that the newcomer, by dint of his wider pastoral responsibilities, would assume the role of top dog. Capel's natural inclination to gentle teasing had not helped. Now, this morning, Rhees had felt that he had taken the upper hand, catching Capel in his pyjamas. He did not realise that the significance of the event had totally escaped his rival. So it seemed unfair that Capel was already re-asserting himself by doubting Rhees's judgement.

'Of course it should,' Rhees mumbled. 'I mean, it shouldn't, but it has been... No I don't, I mean it should have been but it hasn't until now, but now it is.'

'Of course,' said Capel, 'I see.'

'No you don't,' said Rhees, angrier than ever. 'This is serious, Capel, not one of your little jokes. Don't you take anything seriously?'

'Some things. Murders, for instance. Do you know anything about murders, Alan?'

'Stop the tomfoolery, can't you.' If Rhees had been a six-year-old he would have stamped his foot in frustration. 'While you've been enjoying your relaxing week in Glastonbury... well?'

Capel raised an eyebrow. There was obviously something about his expression that Rhees had interpreted as an interjection. He considered putting the chaplain right on what sort of a week he had had in Glastonbury, but, when he thought about it, he couldn't say himself. 'Nothing. I'll tell you later. Glastonbury had its moments.'

'No doubt.' The thin lips quivered. 'But while you've been having your moments, we have endured desecration.'

Surely he can't mean the royal we, thought Capel. The mind had to boggle.

'I can't blame *you* for it; it would hardly be fair...'

What's that got to do with it? thought Capel. Anyway, there was going to be a 'but'. The 'but' had signalled its arrival with all the subtlety of a procession of elephants.

'But it seems odd.'

Ah ha.

'Throughout the interregnum I struggled along on my own, managing to look after the parish as well as doing my full time, highly demanding job. Yet there wasn't a hint of trouble. Then, when you've only been in the parish for a few days and you leave things in my charge, it starts. I didn't know what to do - I considered calling you, leaving a message at the Centre, but I didn't think you would appreciate that.'

I certainly wouldn't have got it, thought Capel, and that would have made you even rattier. 'I'm here now. What's happened?'

'Haven't I told you?'

'Not in so many words, no.'

'It started on Tuesday. At least, that's when I discovered it. I came in to cast an eye over things. I like to do that every couple of days, one can't be too careful.'

It's worse with two, thought Capel irrelevantly and, sadly, irreverently.

'The altar had been desecrated. Despoiled. Candlesticks thrown over, candles smashed into fragments on the floor, crucifix overturned, frontal awry. I suspect Satanism.'

'Hang on,' said Capel, 'the evidence is rather scanty, isn't it? Are you sure you didn't leave the door open on a windy day or something?'

'Of course I didn't. What do you take me for?'

Don't tempt me, thought Capel. 'How about the kids? Could it be somebody from the school having a prank?'

'Thornton Down is not that sort of school. Anyway, there's more. By Thursday we'd lost two flower arrangements, the candles had been knocked over again and one of the server's robes had been partially shredded. Even if the boys and girls of the school could contemplate such an act, they couldn't get in. The church was locked; there was no sign of a forced entry, I checked myself. No, it was Satanism, one of the locals, the old families that might have a key from some previous generation churchwarden. I know that Satanism is on the rise in these country parishes. Don't look to the school, look to the farms.'

'I'll think about it, Alan. Okay? Consider the problem handed over. You've got enough to look after yourself without worrying about my troubles.'

'But it happened while...'

'I said don't worry. Leave it all to me. I'll keep an eye on the place.'

'If you need help - perhaps to hold a vigil in the church.'

'I'll let you know. Thanks for helping out, you've been great.'

Alan Rhees turned on his heel and left. Capel tucked the oddity away in a corner of his mind, not forgotten, but hardly to the fore. He would try to keep a watch on the church, but Glastonbury and the murders and Vicky all fought for his conscious attention. Not to mention writing a sermon for the morning. He had put that off long enough. Capel headed for his study, his thoughts in turmoil.

For a few minutes he sat in the old leather chair by the desk, breathing slowly, running through his favourite simple prayer in his mind. If he was honest with himself, he wasn't really praying, it was more like a calming mantra. Right, the sermon. Where had he got to? Capel had developed a system of noting themes in his diary for a few weeks ahead. It avoided repetition and saved effort when he came to write them. He pulled the small book from his inside pocket. A slip of paper, dragged out with the diary fluttered down to the floor. Capel bent to pick it up.

'We want to know how we can help you have a more pleasurable experience.' Capel's mouth twisted at the clumsy wording. Perhaps there was a subject for a sermon in there somewhere. But why had he got part of a hotel questionnaire in his pocket? He turned the slip over. There was a mobile phone number on the back. Of course, whatever-his-name-was, Andrea's friend. Capel had forgotten to ring back.

He dialled the number before he thought about what he had to say. It was a distinct danger when you always had a phone with you. In the old days just hunting down a phone had a slowing, calming influence that gave you a chance to get things in order.

'Hello?' It was a female voice with an Australian or New Zealand accent.

'Er, hi,' Capel said, playing for time. 'This sounds a bit stupid, I'm afraid. I'm looking for a man...'

'Waste of time, mate.'

Capel ploughed on. 'I thought it was his phone – I can't remember his name, but he's got a girlfriend in Glastonbury called Andrea.'

'That'll be Phil. He left his phone on the kitchen table. Hang on.'

There was a long wait. When he heard the phone at the other end picked up, Capel was expecting to hear that they couldn't find its owner, but there was a man on the line. 'Hello, Philip Hayes.' The voice was neutral, educated, without a trace of regional accent.

That was it, he was called Phil. 'Hello, my name's Capel. I met Andrea in the George and Pilgrim in Glastonbury. She said you wanted to talk to me.'

'You're the one who found Paul Schofield?' There was a sudden urgency in Hayes's voice.

'Yes.'

'I've got to talk to you. Why didn't you ring me back?'

'I have. And I rang a couple of days ago – I left a message.'

'I'm sorry. Can we meet? Can you get to Bath?'

'Quite easily. I'm not in Glastonbury any more, I'm only a couple of miles away in Thornton Down.'

'So you could get here this afternoon? Do you know the RPS?'

'I could make this afternoon. Where exactly...'

'Three thirty, in the coffee shop at the RPS. I'll see you there. Someone's life could depend on this.'

'Hang on, where's the RPS? What's the RPS?'

The line had gone dead. Phil Hayes had hung up

CHAPTER 14

It was a relief to discover that the RPS was the Royal Photographic Society. It sat squarely in the middle of a steeply sloping shopping street in the centre of Bath, half way up the hill. Capel walked in confidently. He wasn't sure if you had to be a member, but confidence got you past many barriers. He needn't have bothered. Inside was a shop selling posters and cards; beyond it, steps led down to a bustling coffee shop below the galleries.

Capel walked down, intrigued. He liked places that weren't what they seemed; this was a meeting spot for those in the know. Provided Hayes recognised him. He had changed into a clerical shirt and collar to help. Walking slowly between the tables, he felt like a model on the catwalk. Well to the back on the right a young man stood up and waved.

'Reverend Capel?'

Capel nodded and took a moment to look at Andrea's boyfriend. He was much the same height as Capel, of average build. Well cut hair; the sort of thing that used to be called a short back and sides. A student, yes, but not sort that would ever be seen in ragged jeans. Capel had little doubt that Philip Hayes had a dinner jacket in his wardrobe, an odd thought in this informal setting that brought a smile to Capel's lips. 'Capel will do. Philip Hayes?'

Hayes smiled slightly. His face seemed to have trouble with the action. He indicated a seat for Capel. 'I'm sorry to drag you out here, but it was very important.'

'As I said on the phone, I live nearby. Andrea said you were at teacher training college.'

'That's right - it's on the north side of the city. Quite a good spot. The thing is...'

'She's a nice girl, Andrea, isn't she?' Capel wasn't going to be rushed into things. He wanted to get a feel for the man.

'She's a bit of fun. You know how it is with local girls. You think the first half-decent girl you meet is wonderful until you move away, then you realise that your horizons were limited. It's all about growing up, I suppose.' Hayes tried to smile again with more success. 'You know what I mean.'

'I think I do,' said Capel. 'But you still see her? She seems to think things are still on between you.'

'I look her up when I get back to Glastonbury - why not? Like I said, she's a bit of fun. Unlike what I need to talk to you about. When Andrea mentioned...'

Hayes was interrupted again, this time by a waitress, asking Capel what he wanted. He settled for a latte and indicated for Hayes to go on with a gesture.

'Andrea told me that you found Paul Schofield's body.'

'You knew Schofield?'

'Slightly. I haven't seen him of late, but we were at the same school. There isn't much choice in Glastonbury. When Andrea mentioned you were involved I thought it best to speak to you. I didn't want to go to the police, I thought I might make matters worse, but I needed to talk to someone in the know.'

'I'm not sure I can help - I've no formal involvement - but I'm very happy to listen.'

'It's Ian Telfer, you see. He's an old friend of mine. Still lives in Glastonbury.'

'I've met Ian.'

'Really? That's good. I'm worried for him. I think he might be mixed up in this Schofield business.'

'You think Ian might have killed Paul Schofield? Why?'

'I'm not saying that,' said Hayes quickly. 'I don't know why anyone should kill Schofield. He wasn't exactly popular, but there was nothing wrong with him. Not a big enough person to dislike, if you know what I mean. Too insignificant; not enough to him.'

Unlike yourself, thought Capel. Young Mr Hayes appeared to rate himself on a different plane to his contemporaries. Capel nodded and thanked the waitress who appeared with his coffee.

'But Ian seems besotted with some woman at the moment. An older woman. I don't know who she is, but it seems to me that she had an interest in getting Schofield out of the way.'

'What gives you that impression? If you don't know the woman, how can you tell?' Capel held his cup to his lips, watching Hayes over the rim.

'It's little things Ian said; he's hypnotised by her. He specifically said he wanted to do something for her, something to prove he was more than just a kid.'

'It's possible that there's a connection,' said Capel, 'but it's all very tenuous. Have you heard anything to incriminate Ian?'

'Not exactly. I spoke to him on the phone the other day, when I heard Schofield had been knocked off. He was very wary, as if he had something to hide. You found the body - was there anything to make it look like Ian did it? Anything he left behind?'

'I wouldn't know,' said Capel. 'I'm not the police.'

'But you saw,' said Hayes. He took a sip from his cup and put it down hard in the saucer. 'You know what was there. Was there anything that could point to Ian?'

'Nothing,' said Capel slowly. 'A bit of orange string, one of those climbing pegs - pitons, aren't they? Nothing personal.'

'Right,' said Hayes. 'Perhaps I should go and talk to him. He's worried about something.'

'If you get a chance it would be a good idea. It's always good to have a friend to talk to. Perhaps you should see Andrea too; it sounds like you have some explaining to do.'

'Andrea's all right. She knows the way things are.' Hayes looked at his watch. 'I'm sorry, Mr Capel, I'm going to have to dash off. I've a tutorial this afternoon. It's been good to meet you, you've put my mind at rest.'

'I'm glad I could help,' said Capel. He shook hands with Hayes without getting up and sat back to enjoy his coffee. It looked like Hayes was a worrier. It was a shame that his concern for Telfer didn't stretch as far as Andrea.

The waitress came over, smiling infectiously. 'Will there be anything else, sir?'

'I don't think so,' said Capel.

'That's two coffees and a danish.' She handed him a slip of paper.

'Charming. He's left me the bill,' Capel muttered.

'I'm sorry, sir?'

'Nothing,' said Capel. 'Do you take cards?'

~

It was Tuesday evening before the phone rang. Three days during which Capel felt that the events in Glastonbury were moving into some mythical half-world. They were becoming unreal. Everything that had happened, even the people, had changed subtly in his mind. With the benefit of a week's distance he was seeing his discovery of the body from the outside, as if he were watching it on television. And the people - the Schofields, Harriet and Lillith, Henry, Telfer and his unpleasant friends, even Vicky, they were becoming fuzzy and soft focus.

He wondered if it was the association. Even with his experience of jail, murder was not a thing of the real world. Murderers, fine. They were ordinary blokes - and women, he supposed, though he had never worked in a women's prison - the man in the street. But *murders* were a thing of books and films and television. Of larger-than-life characters. So perhaps he was pushing his experiences in Glastonbury into the corner of his mind reserved for fiction.

To be precise, it started with the doorbell, not the telephone. It was ten past eight, one of those uncomfortable times when strangers tend to call at vicarages. Capel wondered if he was up to a lengthy doorstep discussion with Jehovah's Witnesses. When it was only Rhees, Capel was almost pleased. After all, he had to work with the man, so he ought to make an effort.

'Alan! Nice to see you. Come on in. Would you like a coffee? Or something stronger perhaps?'

'Neither.' Rhees had a wild look that sat uncomfortably on his pernickety donnish exterior. His hair was frankly out of control, his jacket buttoned on the wrong hole. 'I want action, Capel. This business in the church is not showing any sign of improvement. I just called in there on my way back from the refectory to pick up my copy of the Common Lectionary - I left it in the stall last week. Someone has defaced it. Look.' He held the book close to Capel's face. Deep scratches like knife cuts ran down the dark blue cover of the book. 'It's a special, leather bound version. It was a gift.'

'What a shame,' said Capel. He tried to put meaning in his voice, though he was sure that Rhees would regard him as a philistine when it came to books. Capel's study was lined with paperbacks, arguing that it was the content that mattered, and for any given budget he would rather have more books than a prettier binding. 'I can't see why anyone would do that.'

'I've given you a perfectly good reason,' said Rhees. 'But this isn't the worst of it. There was some sort of dead animal near the altar.'

'Really?' said Capel. 'That does sound serious.'

'Of course it's serious. You don't think I'd have been harping on like this if it wasn't serious.'

'We'd better go and have a proper look. There may be somebody still there.'

'*You* had better go and have a proper look. I've got evening study to supervise.'

'Surely it could wait ten minutes?'

'It's my job, Capel. Remember *I* have the sort of job where I can't be fluttering off whenever I like. I've drawn the subject to your attention; it's your responsibility to get something done about it. Good night.'

Rhees stomped off into the evening, leaving Capel on his doorstep. He glanced up at the church tower, visible over the corner of the vicarage. It looked big, isolated from the cosy collective safety of the village. Capel shivered. He was about to set off for the church when the phone rang.

'Saved by the bell,' Capel muttered unoriginally to himself. He pushed the door shut and walked down to the far end of the hall, where the telephone stood on the corner of a large packing case that he was yet to empty.

'St Swithun's Vicarage.' He was new enough that giving his name would only confuse half the people who regarded the vicar as a general purpose help and information line.

'Capel?' The voice was female, uncertain. It took a moment for everything to drop into place.

'Vicky! Hi, I've been trying to ring you since Friday.'

'It is you - I'm not sure I can get used to this "vicarage" stuff.'

'Neither am I,' said Capel. ' You should have rung my mobile. '

'I did. It went to voicemail. '

Capel grunted. 'Probably died.' He pushed the phone to the back of the packing case and squatted on the corner. As he turned, the cord pulled the phone over the edge, sending it crashing down onto the floor. Capel scooped it up and put it carefully back, then realised that he had been ignoring the receiver. 'Hello? Are you still there? I just dropped the phone.'

'I guessed. What's it like to be back in quiet village life?'

'Not so quiet, but I'll tell you about that later. Any news on the murder?'

'Fine. Don't ask how I am.'

'Sorry. Are you well?'

'Yes, I...'

'Great. Any news about the murder?'

'Thank you. There is, if you must know, but I'm not sure I'm going to tell you now.'

'I want to hear about you too, but I am involved in this

murder, remember. And you can't say I don't show an interest in your work.'

'No more thoughtfulness, I might cry. We're making progress. They pulled in Ian Telfer - you know, Schofield's friend - and he's spilled everything. Telfer and his merry mates went up the Tor with Schofield. Just having a bit of fun, he says. Had a bit too much to drink. So for a laugh, like boys will do when they're over the top, they decided to play a trick on Schofield. They strung him up and left him dangling from his ankles; said they were going to leave him there all night. When they came back to let him down an hour or so later he was dead. So they did a runner. They didn't want to be involved.'

'It sounds too elaborate for a practical joke. Do you think it's likely?'

'It's certainly possible. About three weeks after I started on a regular beat in Glastonbury I had to help out with a stag night joke. The groom's mates had chained him naked to the ticket machine in a car park. They'd painted his private parts bright red, and the rest of him was turning a delicate shade of blue, it being November. He could have had a serious case of exposure...' a snort of amusement from Capel stopped Vicky abruptly. She continued coldly, 'Oh, you know what I mean. He could have caught his death.'

'Was it a pay and display car park?' said Capel. 'Sorry. I should think your cheeks were red too.'

'You're not kidding. There's a limit to what college can prepare you for. But it shows what lengths some people - some male people - will go to to humiliate their friends.'

'Right. Does Malcolm have any great inspirations on this matter?'

'The Chief Inspector believes Telfer, I think. Not that the C.I. confides in me, other than to ask for another cup of coffee, but that's the word. He reckons that Malkovski chanced upon Schofield hanging there, saw a golden opportunity to get rid of his blackmailer, nipped back down to the well, broke in, got some water and took it up and drowned the poor bloke.'

'Has he admitted that?'

'Hardly. He won't say anything. But it fits. It might even explain why he broke into the well again the next day, to confuse any fingerprints. Not that it was worth it, because we couldn't get anything clear enough. Too many smudges.'

'It doesn't sound right,' said Capel. 'I suppose it keeps you busy though. That's why you've been out so much, is it?'

'Capel! You sound jealous.'

'Don't be ridiculous,' said Capel. He was very glad he was on the phone; an uncomfortable heat burned in his cheeks. 'You've hardly been home, I suppose.'

'I'm not at the moment, I just had a minute or two. It's not so bad, really. I do get home, but it tends to be odd hours, and all I want to do is sleep.'

'When it's over you'll have to take a couple of days off and come up here. It's an excellent place to sleep.'

'What would the parishioners say, Reverend Capel?'

'My intentions are purely honourable. Anyway if you came in uniform they wouldn't suspect anything.'

'They'd still talk. More so if you had police visiting - I was brought up in a small place, I know what it's like. Now be fair, you tell me something. What's been happening in Thornton Down?'

'Normally the answer would be "very little", but we have had our own little mystery. In fact Alan Rhees, you know, the chaplain at the school, I mentioned him, he thinks we've got satanists at work.'

'You don't, I suppose.'

'I've got an open mind. Things have been moved around and damaged, even though the church is kept locked overnight. And he claims to have found something dead, some sort of sacrifice.'

'What? It sounds nasty.'

'I don't know, I was just going over to take a look when you rang.'

'Sorry, I didn't mean to keep you.'

'Don't be silly, I was in no rush. Do you know anything

about Isobel Hunt?'

'Is she a satanist?'

'Lady Isobel Hunt, the photographer. The one who was killed in the Abbey last year.'

'Not a lot. I could ask around.'

'Please. I can't help wondering if there's some connection with Schofield.'

'I'll ask. Look, I'm going to have to go, the sergeant's calling. See you, Capel.'

'Yes,' said Capel, suddenly feeling a frantic urge to keep a link with Vicky, some fixed point in the future he could depend on. 'When can we see each other? I know you're very busy and everything, but...'

'I'll let you know as soon as things have settled down. There's no point arranging something now. I really do have to go. Speak to you soon.'

'Great. Bye.'

'Bye bye.'

Capel put the receiver back slowly. As soon as it hit the cradle the phone's ringer burst into life, making Capel jump, which knocked the phone once more to the floor. He scrabbled to pick it up. 'Sorry, did it again. Was there something you forgot?' He couldn't help a hopeful tone tingeing his voice.

'Not that I know of,' said Ed's rich voice. 'Have I called at a bad time? It sounded like you were going three rounds with the phone.'

'Oh, great. Humour in adversity. Where would I be without you?'

'There's no need to take that tone. I rang as a supportive, caring friend. I wondered if you'd heard anything from your floozy in uniform.'

'That's suppose to encourage me to confide in you? If you must know, they've got hold of Telfer, and he's admitted that he and his mates strung Schofield up for a laugh, but when they came back to cut him down someone else had got there first and drowned him. Do you know anything about inquests?'

'Not my department. It fits my idea of what happened, doesn't it?'

'Does it? No, the thing is, I'm fairly hot on the procedure with funerals, but I don't know when the inquest is likely to be. I presume they'll want me back.'

'Could be another week or two yet. Wheels of justice blah blah slowly blah. Of course it fits my theory - you can see that, can't you?'

'What theory's that?'

'Very good, very attentive. Your friend Harriet's off for a midnight ramble up the Tor. Getting some atmosphere for one of her mystical paintings or collecting magic mushrooms. Bumps into the ever-attentive Telfer, who tells her all. She twists him round her little finger and before you can say bubble and squeak the dirty deed is done.'

'It's all very circumstantial. Anyway, I can't stay here passing the time of day with you all evening. I've got a poltergeist to lay.'

'You just can't keep away from the women, can you?'

'It's an illness, your sort of mind. We have something odd going on in the church and I have to check it out. Happy?'

'Delirious. You couldn't wait until I can get over there, could you? I've always fancied a spot of ghost hunting.'

'You're going to have to sit this one out. I'll be in touch if I hear anything more.'

'And I will if I don't. Be good.'

'And you, Ed.'

Capel put the phone down and tried hard to laugh. Until he had spoken to Ed he had not taken the suggestion that there could really be anything in the church seriously. A creation of Rhees's overactive imagination, that was all. Now, as he lifted the church keys from the hook by the door, he was having trouble taking it so lightly.

CHAPTER 15

The last vestiges of dusk lent strange shapes to the still unfamiliar surroundings of the church. Something, probably a bat, fluttered overhead. Capel looked up, up the sky-clawing masonry of the tower. It made him feel dizzy, picking out the dark shape against the darker sky. There were no street lights - no streets - behind the church, nothing to lend an artificial but reassuring glow to the rural night.

Capel found the lock on the main door by touch. It had a big, overly decorated escutcheon that made it easy to guide the key into place. 'We ought to get some outside lighting,' Capel muttered to himself. 'One of those proximity lights.' He got the door open and stumbled over the step into the closed-off vestibule under the tower. The inner door wasn't locked. He was inside the church.

He stood for a moment, letting his eyes get used to the darker interior of the building. Somewhere, far away, but still inside the church, he thought he heard movement. His skin prickled with anticipation, a cold sensation generating painfully hard goose pimples in his upper arms. He listened intently, but now there was nothing at all. Only the inevitable noises of a large building, settling from the heat of the day.

Now he could make out the pews, islands of blackness in the faint grey sea of the nave. Capel reached for the light switch on the wall by the door. It wasn't there. It had never been there.

'Terrific,' Capel said aloud. Again, for a moment after his speech, he thought he heard something moving, something in the darkest of the shadows. He had a problem. He remembered now that the light switches, with elegant neatness, were built into a little panel inside the pulpit. It was probably just the thing if you wanted to do a sermon with an accompanying light show, but it lacked practicality when you simply wanted to see your way around. In the dark. With an unknown something desecrating the church. What he ought to do was go back for a torch - he should have brought one anyway, but he hadn't. And his phone was in the bedroom. What he ought not to do was try to find his way to the pulpit in the dark.

Of course, Capel told himself as he took a step forward, whoever - and it had to be a whoever, he didn't agree with ghosts, not in a boring Victorian country church - whoever was messing the place up was hardly likely to be there now. He still thought it was kids from the school. Hoped, perhaps. He took another step.

Something jabbed painfully into his chest in the darkness leaving a dull burning pain. Capel's mouth dropped in horror but no sound came out. He had been stabbed. Rhees's imaginings were more than fantasy, they had been a realistic warning. He was the subject of some horrific occult ritual. He waited for his consciousness to slip away, but nothing happened. There was no sound from his assailant. Trembling, he reached out in front of him, feeling the ungainly wrought iron arms of the floor-standing candelabra that was positioned at the side of the aisle.

'I'm a fool,' said Capel. He rubbed his chest, the pain already subsiding. Somewhere, it could have been in the vestry, he heard a crash as a metal vessel was dropped. 'Is there anybody there?' asked Capel loudly. His voice carried a firmness that he certainly didn't feel. There was no reply. He inched down the aisle until he could feel the plain wooden support of the pulpit. Carefully, feeling for each riser ahead of him, he half-crawled up the steps and stretched out his fingers for the switches.

A glare of light swathed down from the ceiling, all but blinding him. Capel held his hands in front of his face, peering through the cracks. There was nobody in the nave, only the offending candelabra. He pulled himself upright in the pulpit and looked all around from his vantage point. Nobody there. Nothing disturbed. It was funny really; despite himself, he had half believed Rhees's story. A distant clatter jerked his gaze to the vestry door. He wasn't in the clear yet.

'Who's there?' he shouted. In a fraction of second his voice was eaten by the deadening woodwork and there was silence. No attempt to reply. 'I'm coming into the vestry,' said Capel, whose experience of prison work had suggested that lack of information could lead to dreadful mistakes. 'I won't hurt you. I just want to talk to you. There's nothing to be frightened about.' So why am I scared? thought Capel. Why am I bloody terrified?

He had reached the vestry door. 'I'm opening the door now. All I want to do is talk.' Capel pushed the door open, keeping well back. No one jumped out at him. The vestry was still dark. It had its own switch inside the door. Capel slipped his hand in, expecting at any moment to be grabbed. The ancient fluorescents flickered reluctantly on. He couldn't see anybody. Crouching to bring his head unexpectedly low, Capel craned his neck round the door. There was nobody hiding. He straightened up and took a step into the room. The cause of the clatter was obvious. A brass bowl had been pushed off the safe and onto an adjacent table. Nothing else was out of place. He took another step forward. Something gave, squishily, under his foot. Capel looked down, looked at the sole of his foot and smiled. Then he laughed, openly and happily.

~

Capel often had disturbed nights, so it was no shock to see that the clock was showing 3.04 am when he peered at the lurid red digits. He rolled over and tried to go back to sleep, but the awareness of his effort kept him awake. There was something tickling the edge of his mind, like a tiny hair caught at the back of the throat. Hair. Yes, hair. It was nothing to do with his successful dismissal of Rhees's bogeyman, it was Glastonbury and hair.

He sat upright in bed. He wasn't going to be able to sleep until he had got this worked out, so he might as well let it play its course. Who had said something about hair in Glastonbury? Oh, yes. Why hadn't he seen it at the time? It was so obvious. He lay down again and closed his eyes. His mind, revving at double speed, started working through what had happened, imagining what might come next. He turned a couple of times, shifting the duvet half way across the bed.

When he talked the whole thing through with Ed a few days later, he had been unable to fill in how he got from his tangle in the bedclothes to being in the car, driving towards Glastonbury in the last shreds of the night. There had to be the mechanical processes of getting dressed, of going to the bathroom, throwing something into a bag... he must have had breakfast, because the dishes were there when he got back. But all this was in a dream state. It was only when he reached the A367 and the oncoming car lights were starting to look less bright in the hazy dawn that he was fully aware of his surroundings.

Capel arrived in Glastonbury at 7 am, much too early to do anything. It seemed presumptuous to park at the police station. He drove slowly round the almost deserted streets and found a car park next to a supermarket. The store was too small to be open all night and he sat in the car, listening to the radio, watching the supermarket employees come in one by one. At 8.30 the lights flickered on. They looked more blue-green than white, as if he was staring into a large-scale aquarium inhabited by a strange breed of tropical fish.

Watching the supermarket entertained him until 9 o'clock. That seemed a reasonable time to turn up at the police station. Rather than drive any further, Capel bought a car park ticket - it had seemed unnecessary while he was sitting in the car - and strolled up the street. As often happened, it struck him how dead to the world everyone looked. It was an illusion, he was sure, but each passer-by wore a mask of indifference to protect them from the rigours of the day. The police station was not far.

He recognised the man behind the desk immediately. It was Sergeant Moore, the sergeant who had gone with him and Vicky to see the body, back when Vicky was just an unfamiliar WPC. The recognition was not mutual. Moore looked at Capel with an automatic half-smile, but there was no sign of acquaintance in his eyes.

'Morning, sir,' said Moore, 'what can we do for you?'

'Good morning Sergeant... Sergeant Moore isn't it?'

'That's right, sir.' A look of suspicion was replaced by a self-deprecatory smile. 'Of course; the Schofield body, wasn't it sir?'

'That's the one. Capel's the name, if you remember.'

'Of course, sir. What can we do for you this time? Not found another one, I hope.' Sergeant Moore smiled broadly to emphasise that this was a joke.

'Not exactly, Sergeant. I wanted to ask a favour. When I was here before I saw Paul Schofield's parents and they told me that Ian Telfer was like another son to them. I feel some responsibility for them; I'd like to see Ian Telfer, if I could.'

'Ian Telfer, sir?'

'I understand you are holding him - something to do with the Schofield business.'

'How would you understand that, sir?' There as no smile any more. Sergeant Moore's face was blank, giving away nothing.

Capel thought hurriedly. He had a feeling that Vicky would not appreciate being given as a reference. 'As I said, I've kept in touch with the Schofields.' He felt a pang of guilt, but it was subsumed in the uncertainty as he played his next verbal card. Surely the Schofields would know about Telfer's arrest. 'They told me. It is my job to care for people.'

'It'll probably be all right, sir. Could you take a seat while I make a call.' Sergeant Moore watched Capel until he was sitting down, as if he expected him to make a run for it. 'Reverend Capel, wasn't it?'

'That's right,' said Capel.

He sat on the hard bench for a long time. Other people came

and went with their everyday problems, everyday experiences. Capel felt a freak, an outsider. He hadn't found a handbag, or got lost, or had his car towed away. He was trying to deceive the police.

'Mr Capel?'

'Hmm?' Capel looked round from watching a young couple leaving the station still arguing about who had failed to lock the car. 'Yes?'

'You can see Telfer now. We've had to hold him here, despite the lack of facilities. Overcrowding at county. Would you like to come this way?'

'Thanks.'

The sergeant lifted a flap in the desk and walked through. He led Capel without speaking down a dark, concrete-floored corridor. At the far end were two metal doors, thickly painted with scratched, light grey paint. Two cells. Each door had a viewing flap and a large keyhole - otherwise they were featureless. Something illegible was scrawled on a small whiteboard. The sergeant unlocked the left-hand door with a key from a ring he had carried very conspicuously in front of him. He pushed the door open.

'I'll be back in ten minutes. Give a bang on the door if you want to come out sooner.'

Capel doubted that he would. He couldn't see how anyone could hear a banging on the door in this gloomy hole. Telfer was sitting on a narrow bed, more a bench, his body pushed as far as it would go into the corner of the room. It was a depressing place, far more unpleasant than most of the prison cells Capel had seen.

'Hello, Ian,' Capel said. He perched on the other end of the bed, a reassuring distance from Telfer.

Telfer looked up for a moment, recognised Capel and looked away. 'Is it you did this?' His voice was a mumble, hardly audible.

'What do you mean?' said Capel.

'Put me in here. Someone must have done it.'

'It wasn't me, Ian. They didn't need anyone to finger you, you were an obvious suspect. How long have you been here?'

'Since Monday. They said they wanted to know what happened, how I'd be risking a murder charge if I didn't tell them. Then when I did what they wanted, they've gone and arrested me for assault.'

More like they need an excuse to hold onto you, Capel thought. 'I'm sorry,' he said. 'But I definitely had nothing to do with it. All I want to do is help.'

'Yeah. Doesn't everyone? But it's me that gets it in the neck. I bet they haven't pulled Dave and Kev in have they? Everyone thinks I'm soft, so it's me that gets it. It's always been like that, ever since school. Some other dickhead plays around and I get the blame.'

'I'm sure the police will sort this out quickly,' said Capel. He was also sure that they thought Telfer knew more than he was saying. 'Are you getting visitors?'

'Mr and Mrs Schofield have been. My mum won't come; she say it's my own fault I'm here and it's my own lookout. You get the fuzz to ask the Schofields; they know I didn't kill him.'

'So you think they're holding you for more than assault?'

'I'm not thick, mister. What do you think?'

'I don't know. Anyone else been to see you?'

'Only Wanker Hayes - beg your pardon, reverend - I mean, Phil Hayes. He was a mate of mine at school.'

'Oh, yes. I saw Phil at the weekend in Bath. He said he was worried about you.'

'Why?' said Telfer. His face was tense with suspicion, making his averted eyes look even closer together than usual. 'What've you been talking to him for? Why are you sniffing round?'

'I'm not sniffing round,' said Capel. 'Andrea... I don't know her surname. Andrea who's a maid at the George and Pilgrim asked me to have a word with Phil. He was concerned for you, that's all. But there was no one else came? Not even Harriet?'

Telfer looked straight at Capel for the first time since he had recognised him. There was disgust, or perhaps contempt, in his pale eyes. 'She wouldn't come here. It'd be... I couldn't see her here. It's not right for her.'

'Does she know you've been arrested?'

'I don't know - I don't want her to know. You mustn't tell her.'

'I thought I saw her on the way here.' Capel paused. He didn't want to put a direct question about Harriet to Telfer; it would make him suspicious and he needed Telfer's trust. 'It was her hair, of course. It makes her stand out in crowd with a cut like that.'

'It certainly does,' said Telfer. There was no contempt now. Only a dreamy contemplation of a more than perfect, more than realistic, memory.

Capel wondered what to say next. His subtle approach had failed. 'I was trying to describe it to someone the other day. I couldn't think of a good enough word for that colour.'

'I know what you mean,' said Telfer. He had the excitement, the forward lean of the enthusiast on his subject. He was talking about his idol, an idol for pure, heated worship. 'It's red, but not like ordinary red hair; it's certainly not ginger. It's sort of dark rusty gold.'

Capel sighed to himself. His guess was right. 'I've always thought that long, red hair was the most beautiful sight. How exactly did you say you met... Harriet?'

'I didn't say and I'm not going to. Why do you want to know?'

'Just curiosity, nothing sinister. I thought you might like to talk about her.'

Telfer flushed. 'I don't. Not to you, not here. All right?'

'Fine,' said Capel, 'it's not a big deal.'

~

Why? Capel asked himself, walking back to his car at a pace he would normally find painfully slow. Why would Lillith Cooper have passed herself off as Harriet to Telfer? What was there to gain? It made Ed's theory with Lillith substituted for Harriet much more attractive. He couldn't see Harriet taking part in such a killing, but Lillith was much more of a dark horse. He wanted to talk it over with somebody, to see if he was reading too much into this new knowledge.

He pulled out his phone and found Vicky's number. It seemed presumptuous to put it in Favourites yet. It started to ring. She probably wouldn't be able to answer - he'd thought it best not to ask at the station - but it was worth a try.

The ringing went on longer than Capel would normally hold. He was feeling the backlash of the lack of sleep, of the urgent demands he had placed on his body. He realised with a start that he had almost dropped off, standing upright in the street, listening to the dull, repetitive tone. It didn't go to voicemail, but there was no reply. He brought down the phone to disconnect the call. For a brief moment, before he touched the screen he thought the distant sound of the ringing had stopped.

Capel fumbled for the calls screen and re-dialled. This time there was no doubt. Within seconds the phone was answered.

'What?' Vicky made no effort to conceal her irritation. 'What do you want?'

'It's me, Capel.'

'I can see that. What the hell are you playing at, Capel? You get me out of bed, then you put down the phone when I answer. Wonderful. Then you wait until I'm half-way back to bed and ring again. I was asleep, you know.'

'Yes. I'm very sorry. I was only ringing on the off-chance. I didn't think you were in and I heard you answer too late.'

'Forget it,' said Vicky. She might have forgiven him, but she was in no hurry to sound too friendly.

'So how's it all going?' asked Capel, keeping his tone as light as he could.

'It was going quite well in the usual sort of sleeping way until you rang. I've been working all sorts of hours - I'm back on again at two. Look, I don't want to be rude, but I really need my sleep and I could do without a chat right now, okay?'

'Fine, I...'

'If nothing big happens, I've got a 24-hour break from midday tomorrow. Give me a ring then, okay?'

'I'll do that,' said Capel. It was obvious she didn't want to hear anything. There was no point in saying he was in Glastonbury. At worst she might feel obliged to stay up and see him, and that would only leave her in a bad mood. 'Sleep well.'

'See you, Capel.'

Hardly a brilliant call, he thought. Not exactly a brownie point for Capel there; quite the reverse, what would that be? A troll point, perhaps. He fumbled with his keys and dropped them as he tried to get back into his car. His state of alertness wasn't ideal for driving. The ticket in the windscreen had another hour to run. Plenty of time to get a coffee and to drag himself into a more conscious state.

CHAPTER 16

Like most towns popular with tourists, Glastonbury has a lot of little eating places. Capel had intended to find a coffee shop, but he was in the wrong area. Instead he breakfasted in a café, a classic greasy spoon. His first inclination was to walk past, but he was glad he stopped. They hadn't mentioned his dog collar, the tables were clean, and he'd been able to indulge his passion for a real English breakfast without any worries about being thought insensitive just because he wanted brown sauce on it.

Capel stirred milk into the last cup of coffee he had squeezed out of the crazed white jug that he had been given. The coffee was good too. He took a sip and looked out of the window. It was too close to the street to really see the passers-by. There were flashes of colour, dark clouds of suit material, varied heads bobbing past, but all too near, too quick for any detail.

What could he make of Lillith Cooper? He was going to have to talk to her again, and he didn't relish the idea. Capel wasn't the sort of man who normally found beautiful women intimidating, but with Lillith every conversation was a contest. The dark dregs at the bottom of the cup came into sight. Time to face up to it, to see her.

~

The dragon on the door seemed more aggressive than usual. Capel knocked hesitantly. He was certain that he wasn't so scared of Lillith just because he suspected her of murder, it was more that he was unhappy that he would say the wrong thing and give her an escape, a way to slip the blame onto someone else. She was blatantly capable of deception. Yet it didn't seem right to try to explain his ideas to the police. Not yet.

He was very relieved when Harriet answered the door. She looked a bit doubtful - his immediate thought was that she didn't like to be caught in her dressing gown, but then he realised that it was the first time she'd seen him in uniform. Sometimes the reality of a dog collar was more difficult to cope with than the concept.

'Capel.' Harriet must have found his worry obvious; a wide grin broke through her solemnity. 'I won't worry about the way you dress if you don't worry about me. Okay?'

'That sounds good to me.'

'Come in.' She stood back to let him pass. 'No coffee this time, I don't like to be too predictable. Do you like elderflower cordial?'

'Love it.' Capel let himself be lead into the little sitting room. Nothing seemed to have moved since the last time he was there.

'Don't get me wrong, I've not suddenly gone entirely flower power. It's my stepfather's idea of a good birthday present for someone like me. It tastes good though.'

'It was your birthday?' Capel took a glass, filled with the pale, yellowish drink. As he brought it to his face the subtle fragrance of elderflower brought fragmentary associations of summer childhood days and playing out in the newly cut hay, which was odd because he had never had elderflower as a child; the summer drink was always lemon barley water back home.

'It is my birthday. Today.'

'Really?' Capel's delight was genuine. He found it as easy to share in the joys of others as he found it difficult to leave alone a problem. 'That's wonderful. Happy Birthday.' He was filled with an urge to give her something, to show that she meant something to him as a person, but he had nothing appropriate on him. 'I'm embarrassed to admit it now, but I came to see Lillith.'

'I see.' Harriet pulled her dressing gown, which had drooped open to show a Snoopy nightshirt, tightly around her with unmistakable and probably intentional body language. 'You're having your usual luck - she's not here.'

'I'm not disappointed,' said Capel. 'I'd rather be talking to you.' One of his great strengths was that he could say something like that and mean it, and have someone believe he meant it. What could have sounded like a cheap chat-up line was genuinely sincere.

'A man of taste.' Harriet's eyes seemed wider than ever. They were remarkable eyes.

'I hope so. But I still need to see her, even if I'd rather not. Something has come up on this murder case. I've got to speak to Lillith to try to clear it up.'

'Ah.' Harriet put her glass down and stretched, comfortable and relaxed with Capel. 'She's on a sort of field trip. Over at Uffington. She's not due back until the end of the week.'

'What, the Uffington with the white horse?'

Harriet didn't bother to speak. She raised her eyebrows in affirmation.

'That's miles away. It's the other side of Swindon, isn't it?'

'Yes. Have you ever seen it? It's quite remarkable.'

'I've never been, but I've read about it.'

'I should think she's got a picture. Hang on.' Harriet pulled a cardboard box out from behind her chair. It was piled high with books, mostly glossy, large format productions. 'Here we go.' She flicked through and presented the book to Capel. It showed the Uffington white horse, tantalisingly foreshortened by seeing it from the ground.

'Oh, yes, I remember it,' said Capel. 'More like a dragon than a horse.'

'Exactly. You've spotted the second part of Lillith's usual in-depth research. She invents a dragon at Glastonbury and looks around for anything similar. Lo and behold, a mere fifty miles away, there's the Uffington horse. She's over there now trying to work up some connection. No doubt she'll succeed. If Lillith hadn't made it in her current field, she'd be a great fantasy writer.'

'Do you mind?' said Capel, pointing at the box.

'Help yourself.' Harriet recovered her drink and watched him, sipping the slightly astringent cordial.

'You've got a lot of Isobel Hunt,' said Capel. 'Pretty well the full set. Do you admire her work?'

'They're not mine, that box is Lillith's. I always thought old Isobel was fun, but Lillith had a very strange attitude to her. She bought every book she wrote the moment it was out, yet she used to call her every name you could think of. Lady Isobel thought Lillith was a fraud and didn't mind who she told. Lillith got quite an ear bashing from her once.'

'Lillith knew Isobel Hunt?'

'She met her a couple of times. I think it started at one of those literary luncheon affairs. You know the sort of thing - they get as many punters together as possible to enjoy the benefits of watching their favourite authors stuffing their faces. It's a bit like the chimpanzee's tea party at the zoo, except the chimps get paid a fat fee. Lillith and Lady Isobel shared a publisher who, in her wisdom, decided the pair of them would make a good double bill.'

'I should think they would.'

'Yes, but not quite in the way the publisher intended. They had a stand-up row, which it has to be said Lady Isobel won, because the lovely Lillith ended up storming out, her shawl flying in the wind. By third hand account it was superb. Isobel got a standing ovation for it too.'

'So she wouldn't rate amongst Lillith's favourite people.'

'Not by a long way.'

'Right.' Capel re-opened the book he had just shut at the fly-leaf. 'That's odd, then. Listen to this: "To Lillith Cooper, with all my best wishes." Signed by Isobel herself.'

'Let's have a look.'

Capel passed the book over and watched Harriet read the inscription.

'Oh, yes, it was when Lady Isobel was photographing the

Abbey - just before she was killed.'

'Can you read the date? I know what I think it says, but then I know what I expect it to be.'

Harriet looked closer. 'I think it's the 24th... the 24th of September last year, I reckon. That is just before she was killed, isn't it?'

'Oh, yes,' said Capel. 'How did Lillith happen to get the book signed? It hardly seems the sort of thing you do when the author's someone you can't stand.'

'I said Lillith had a strange attitude to her. She was staying with us then – Lillith I mean. It was before she'd started on her current book, while she was still getting ideas. She was drifting round the country, sponging where she saw fit. I mentioned that Lady Isobel was working at the Abbey and she hit the roof. First of all she seemed furious, then her mood turned quite suddenly, going on about how pleasant it would be to meet Lady Isobel again. Not at all like Lillith. She went off one morning early - it must have been the 24th - and caught Isobel at the Abbey before there were crowds around. She was remarkably pleased with herself when she got back. I suppose she'd patched it up somehow. She can be charming when it suits her. Then a day or two later Isobel was killed.'

'You don't get a paper?'

'Henry and I have never bothered.' She was suddenly sober at the mention of Malkovski. 'There's never any news we want to hear. Lillith found out about the killing a few days later.'

'Yes,' said Capel, 'I suppose word gets around.' He thought it was time to leave the subject of Lillith. 'Have you heard from Henry?'

'Nothing. I've no idea where he is, though he can look after himself. He does this sometimes, disappears for a few days. When he comes back he's filthy, been sleeping in ditches and living off what he can scrounge. He calls it "getting back to nature", but that's a joke - you know? He's not that pretentious.'

'He hasn't rung you?'

'No. He never does on these jaunts. Do you know something

I don't?'

'The police pulled him in on Friday.' Capel reached out to take her hand - Harriet's eyes were very wide. 'I'd have thought they'd have had to charge him or let him go by now. But I don't understand why he hasn't rung.'

'I'm going down there,' said Harriet, pulling away from Capel's hand. She stood up, her eyes searching the floor for something.

'Do you want me to come with you?' Capel stood as well.

'No. Don't label me weak and feeble, Capel. That's not me at all.'

'I wasn't. I want to help; is that so bad?'

'No. But I'm still going on my own. Finish your drink if you like - I'm going to get dressed.'

'I think I'd better be going myself.' Capel followed her through to the hall. 'I don't know where I'm going to be for the next few days - if there's anything you need me for, you can catch me on my mobile. Hang on.' He fought with his breast pocket to get a card out. 'That's got the number on it.'

'Thanks, Capel. Look after yourself.' Harriet reached for his shoulders and pulled his face down to her level to give him a quick kiss on the cheek.

'Thank you,' said Capel. 'And many happy returns.'

~

Uffington. Capel pulled his battered road atlas from the back seat of the car and looked for Uffingtons. Quite a choice: Lincs, Oxon, Salop, Northants, Suff. He supposed it had to be Oxfordshire, though he would have guessed Wiltshire. Of course it would have been easier with a sat nav, but there was no challenge with one of those. He flicked through to the page. There it was, just up the Ridgeway from Wayland's Smithy. Uffington - hill figure. He traced the route through an evocative list of towns. Shepton Mallet, Frome, Trowbridge, Devizes, Marlborough; it sounded like one of those romantic poems that reminisce on the age of steam.

'What am I doing?' Capel asked himself, pulling out into the gentle, mid-morning traffic. It was a long way to go to possibly see someone who might have something to do with a murder - two murders - with which he had no official connection. On the other hand, he was enjoying himself. He couldn't deny that. It was another sunny day, the roads weren't busy - driving was the positive pleasure it rarely manages to be outside of a car advertisement. He didn't even get stuck behind a tractor. Why shouldn't he go to Uffington?

The road billowed over one of the hills that littered his route. What would he say to Lillith? He wasn't sure - she wasn't predictable enough to be approached with a pre-set script. Yet the circumstantial evidence that she was involved, perhaps very personally involved, in the crimes in Glastonbury was difficult to deny. It seemed that she hated Isobel Hunt, yet she went off merrily to get Hunt's autograph - and got it the very day that Hunt died. She may have been the last person to see Hunt alive, yet no one seemed to know this.

Jump forward. Schofield had been a blackmailer. Why shouldn't he have something on Lillith, the murder of Isobel Hunt or something else? Lillith was very image conscious, an ideal target for blackmail. So she knows that she needs to do something about Schofield. Perhaps she mentions this to Telfer. She could only be stringing him along to use him in some way. Telfer wasn't even close to her type. Telfer tells her what's going to happen to Schofield, so Lillith takes the opportunity, goes up to the Tor and drowns him. With nearly every loose end tied up, she casts Malkovski as scapegoat. It's Lillith that scratches the initials on the wall, after the murder. Maybe she gets Telfer to cut the body down afterwards. Then she sends Henry to the scene to incriminate him. Capel nodded vigorously and switched the radio on. He may not have every detail, but it all fitted together like the insides of a watch.

He had driven between the handsome buildings of Marlborough school and into the very wide high street before he decided to stop for lunch. Why not, after all? Lillith wasn't going anywhere, and Capel found it difficult to suppress a holiday mood, despite the seriousness of his mission. He parked in the road dithering between the big hotel on the north side and a tearoom on the south. He chose the Polly Tearoom, just because he liked the name Polly. Come next Lent, he decided, he would have to go in for a third world diet. Food seemed to be playing much too big a part in his life right now. It was that strange, holiday spirit; cooked breakfasts, big meals were de rigeur for a good holiday.

The interior of the tearoom was so cool he shivered as he went through the door. Capel studied the menu - not bad, not bad at all. Everything was conspiring to make this a very rewarding day.

~

It was always a surprise to Capel, how fast his mood could change. Could he really have thought it was a good day? He surveyed the car park at Uffington, frowning. The meal had gone fine. The drive the rest of the way up to Uffington was pleasant enough. But what he found there proved only too well how little thought he had put into this expedition. The car park was big, scattered with trees, making it easy to miss someone. And, of course, he had no idea what Lillith's car - he assumed she had a car - was like.

Then there was the site itself. Gates lead through into open fields. A hill towered above, not unlike the Tor, but wider and more undulating. It was a huge place: he didn't know where to start. He did a circuit of the car park, peering in through the windscreens, looking for the sort of interior that might indicate Lillith. All he succeeded in doing was getting increasingly uncomfortable, especially when he realised that he was staring at a woman breast-feeding on the front passenger seat of a Volvo.

So much for the car park. He trudged up the hill, following the sign towards the horse. It was hot by now, too hot for this sort of exercise. He had changed out of his dog collar and grey shirt in a lay-by outside Frome, but even a cotton polo shirt seemed too much for a day like this. There were no obvious paths on the first part of the hill, but further up a rift was cut into the hillside, leading the visitor across the slope. Another sign gave him the choice of the castle and the horse. Capel chose the horse.

The path widened, a dusty, white track, quite dazzling in the sun. There were a good few people up ahead of him, though he hadn't passed any on the way. He stopped for a moment, looking for any sign of Lillith. To the far side of the small crowd that was gathered ahead, he saw the glint of long, red hair. When he got closer, he could see that the sightseers were collected around a notice, asking visitors not to go any nearer to avoid damaging the horse. He stood towards the back, openly looking at the hill figure while trying to keep an eye on the beacon of the woman's hair.

As a spectacle it was disappointing. It was difficult to see much of the horse, though Capel could make out enough to put it into context with the photographs in Isobel Hunt's book. It wasn't hard to argue that it was a dragon - the face came to a fierce point and the proportions were all wrong for a horse. The group in front of him, some sort of organised party all dressed in wildly fluorescent cycling shorts, moved away. Capel walked down the path a little way, still appearing to concentrate on the chalk figure, manoeuvring closer to Lillith. He realised that she was walking towards him, was likely to pass him.

Capel turned to face up the hill, hoping he could make it look as if he was contemplating climbing up to the castle. He looked his target straight in the face. 'Well, hello...' His throat dried as he realised he was looking at a surprised young girl. She certainly had long, red hair - but she wasn't Lillith. She was much younger with a pretty, open, freckled face that could never have been mistaken for the writer's dark beauty. 'This is going to sound really dumb,' Capel said, 'but I thought you were someone else.'

'Don't worry,' said the girl and continued down the hill. She couldn't have been more than about fourteen - Capel couldn't believe he had mistaken her for Lillith. He had been too busy trying to be sneaky and had never properly looked. So much for the horse - what about the castle?

Castle was a misnomer - the hill was crowned with an Iron Age hill fort, one of the ancient camps surrounded by a bank and ditch that have survived surprisingly well on a number of English hills. Capel trudged round the whole perimeter, even a way down the far side, but there was no sign of Lillith. He walked back to the car park, thoughtfully.

If she was still around, there seemed a couple of possibilities. There was an artificial mound, Dragon's Hill, nearby that was associated with the site - she might be there. Then there was the megalithic grave, Wayland's Smithy. So much he had gathered from an information sign by the gate to the car park. If in doubt, thought Capel, resort to eating. He had spotted an ice-cream van near the gate. His lunch was now some time behind him and the heat on that hill needed combating.

There was no one else at the van. The driver looked as if he was asleep, but he came round to the hatch, rocking the ageing van on its doubtful suspension, as Capel got closer. 'Hot enough for you?' The driver must have been a rock n roll fan in his youth. His hair was swept up in a full Elvis-like quiff. Only the colour let him down; the hair had greyed until it was a near match for the nylon working jacket he wore over a Hawaiian shirt.

'Plenty,' said Capel. 'Could I have a large 99?' He watched the ice-cream swirl out of the nozzle into the cone, mesmerised and drowsy in the heat. 'I don't suppose you've seen a very attractive woman - probably in her early thirties - with long, dark red hair?'

'Who's asking?' said the driver, pushing a Flake into the soft ice.

'A friend. We said we'd meet up here, but I was stupid enough not to ask exactly where.'

'That wouldn't be Lillith Cooper you were looking for, would it?'

'Yes!' said Capel, suddenly wide awake. 'Do you know her?'

'She's been keeping me in business the last couple of days. I can't understand how she keeps those looks, the amount of ice-cream she gets through.'

'Do you know where she is now?'

'I do. I reckon she's been pulling your leg, mate. She's gone down to Swindon; said she'd be there all day. "You're going to be lonely without me, aren't you, Bill?", she said to me. Might not be back until tomorrow. You've been had.'

'It looks that way.' Capel handed over his money and licked the soft ice-cream, enjoying the contrast of the cold on his tongue with his baking skin. 'I think I'll take a walk up to Wayland's Smithy now I'm here. Can you tell me which way to go?'

'No problem, mate. It's a nice walk this time of year.'

CHAPTER 17

A dull ache insisted on nestling into Capel's spine, levering its way between a pair of vertebrae as if it testing the nerves with a dentist's probe. He shifted uncomfortably. Not yet, he didn't want to wake up yet. Despite his best efforts the realisation that he was cold, thoroughly, unpleasantly cold, began to work its way through into his consciousness.

He stretched his arm out, only to receive a painful crack on the elbow. His half-active brain struggled to come to terms with these unusual circumstances. It took a remarkable effort to get his eyes to open, to bring the grey blur in front of him into focus as the door of his car. It was hardly surprising he was uncomfortable. Cerebration was running on all cylinders now. He remembered a pleasant walk up the Ridgeway. The dark, damp-earth smell and the sad scattering of rubbish in the remains of the long barrow that was known as Wayland's Smithy. The futile drive around Swindon, trying to spot that distinctive hair in the pedestrians. He'd nearly run into a bus playing at that game.

Capel pushed himself up and struggled to wind the seat back into an upright stance. He could see very little, the windows were terribly steamed up. His back complained some more. This was stupid; he had back problems as it was, a night in a car seat was an idiotic idea. Yesterday evening he'd stayed in Swindon for a meal, sitting alone in a chain Mexican restaurant, Chiquito's. Despite being aware how much he was straining his limited budget, he enjoyed eating on his own. There was an unusual lack of pressure about it - a rare opportunity for genuine relaxation. Not to mention the enjoyment of the part-overhead remarks of sympathy that anyone who dines alone seems to earn. After the meal he had come back to Uffington.

This time, he'd thought, there would be no danger of missing her car. His was the only one in the car park. He had taken a walk around, but had only met a dog, a small thing, not unlike a corgi but with longer ears. The dog had to be lost. He couldn't see where it could have come from, but it seemed perfectly contented, snuffling around the trees and bushes of the car park. It gave him a slow look, as if making sure he was no threat to its activities, then went back to sniffing with interest at a square-cut bush. There wasn't a lot Capel could do about it, so he left the animal to its own affairs.

His common sense had told him to go home. Everything sensible had told him to go home. Even the signs scattered around the car park told him that overnight stays were not permitted and thus, by implication, to go home. It had to be stubbornness that made him stay. For the first hour or two he had fooled himself that she might return to take some night-time psychometric reading, but no one arrived. He had listened to the radio for a while, until he began to worry that he was flattening his battery. In the end, sleep had been more demanding than common sense and he had made the best bed he could from his car seat and a dirty blanket that he kept in the back to protect his paintwork from the unlikely items that vicars were required to transport.

So here he was at six o'clock in the morning, feeling muzzy, the grainy, back-of-the-eye weariness that shallow sleep brought. He turned the ignition part-way on, enough to be able to start the windscreen wipers and set them sweeping across the glass. His view was still blank. There was nothing around to wipe the inside with. He took a tentative scrub with the corner of his blanket. The condensation smeared, picking up multi-coloured fibres from the cloth, but still he could see nothing. Capel shivered, dropping the soggy blanket onto the seat beside him. Gritting his teeth, he wound down the window.

Finally he understood why he was having trouble clearing his view. Even without the glass there was a white opacity to the air. The English weather, playing one of its regular jokes, had deposited a thick fog on the hilltop. For all he knew it might be a low cloud; the subtleties escaped him.

Capel eased himself out of the seat and stood beside the car. His back took the opportunity to remind him that it had no intention of staying quiet, but Capel was able to ignore it, fascinated by the isolation that the fog brought. It had to be the thickest he had ever seen, a solid wall of whiteness that cut off everything more that a few feet away. He closed the door; the thunk of metal on metal was eaten instantly by that white blanket, leaving him surrounded once more by a total silence.

If only to relieve his spine, Capel started to walk around the car park. The fog had the effect of bringing individual aspects of the place into sharp focus. Where he would normally look around and see the whole area without picking out anything specially, his limited sphere of vision meant that a particular plant, or a notice, or a bit of discarded rubbish was brought into an unnatural spotlight of attention. He was so wrapped up by the remarkable beauty of a single, isolated, wooden post that he almost walked into the car.

Not his car, he had walked straight away from it for a good few yards. This was an MG, a bright red MG that had loomed unexpectedly out of the nothingness. It had not been there when he went to sleep, that he was sure of, so it must have been driven up in this, in the deadly embrace of the fog, unless it had thickened since the early morning. He wiped the driver's window with his sleeve and peered in, seeing what he half expected. On the passenger seat was a notebook, an Ordnance Survey map, and the divining rod he had seen in Lillith Cooper's hand at Glastonbury Abbey. His prey had returned. She was somewhere on the site.

Capel smiled to himself, suppressing a small voice that assured him he wouldn't know what to say when he found her. If he found her, more like. The site covered a good few acres, which he would have to search in weather that would let them pass each other separated by ten feet without ever knowing. But the fog had its positive aspects. It limited the scope for wandering - sticking to the path was an essential - and Lillith was bound to have headed for the horse or the castle.

It was a slow trek up the side of the hill towards the chalk figure. There was no clear path for the first section, so he had to aim upwards and hope that he wasn't being fooled by some local variant in steepness. The fog kept his skin cold and clammy, which combined with the warming effect of the climb to make him feel feverish. Most of all, the total separation from the normal world imposed an uncomfortable vulnerability - he was at risk from some unknown, unseen attack.

When he reached the path, cut like a small gully in the chalk, it was a relief. He could readily have believed that he was climbing the wrong hill. For a little while now he could increase his pace, guided by the foot-worn surface. It was only when he came to the sign, the familiar 'go no further' sign that he stopped. If Lillith was at the horse, he was coming near; he needed to tread with caution. Caution was also needed just to get off the path and onto the horse itself. The land sloped steeply away and somehow it was much more treacherous going down than up.

Capel worked cautiously across to the white curve of the horse's head, never easy to see from close up, but rendered utterly meaningless by the isolating curtain of the fog. It looked as if it had been scoured recently. The chalk surface was clean and smooth. He stumbled his way past the simple, round eye and along the sinuous length of the back. It seemed to go on forever. The figure, a long 360 feet when visible, had stretched indefinitely. It was a relief to hit the end of the tail and turn back.

He explored each of the legs, the strange, malformed legs, and returned to the beak. There was no one there. Capel pulled his jacket tighter round him, caught by a sudden fit of shivering. He would have to try the castle. There had been a path of some sort, but he couldn't remember where. He searched either way from the horse's sign, but nothing emerged from the whiteout. Again he had to strike out up the wild hill, now steeper and less cultivated.

The castle was elusive. In places its surrounding mound was shallow - it was only being able to see the whole that gave it away. He wandered across the enclosure and only realised that he had already passed out of the far side of the castle when the hill started to fall away from him.

Typical. As Capel turned back he heard a sound. A slight scuffing, as if someone was scraping mud off their shoes. He ran as lightly as he could in that direction, pushing away the insistent thought that he could run off the edge of the world in the fog. In fact his downfall was much more mundane. He tripped over a jutting rock and hit the ground with his shoulder.

The impact drew a short cry from him, but he wasn't hurt. Capel sat up and listened. Nothing. If she was there, he had alerted her. Not only that, he was now totally lost. While he had been walking he had kept some sense of direction, but his reckless sprint had left him without any mental point of reference. He stood up, brushing the grass from his trousers, and started walking in even paces, counting each step as if the knowledge of distance travelled would provide him with a navigational log. He counted aloud, but only in a low whisper which was bound to be masked by the fog.

'Two hundred. Two hundred and one, two hundred and two...' Capel stopped suddenly. She was there, behind him. It had to be her, and there was certainly someone there. Apart from the pressure from whatever she was pushing into the back of his jacket, he could feel the warmth of her breath, tickling his neck.

'Don't move at all.' It was Lillith, her tone affected, almost melodramatic. 'I've got a knife against your back, which I'm quite prepared to use. Lie down on the ground, face down.'

'What...?'

'Down now!' She jabbed at his back. A sharp point

penetrated through his clothes and nicked his skin. 'Lie down and spread your arms and legs.'

Capel did as he was told. He had wondered what he would say to her. It looked like there was no need. It seemed she knew exactly what he suspected and was prepared to make sure that he didn't tell anyone else. The fact that he was being proved right hardly counted as a consolation. His visit to Uffington was a fatal error.

CHAPTER 18

'Any last requests?' Lillith seemed to be enjoying herself. Capel couldn't see the funny side of his position. In fact, he couldn't see much at all beyond the tuft of cold, muddy grass in front of his face. 'Let me make your position clear,' Lillith said, punctuating her remark with slight jabbing motions of the knife. 'I am not the feeble sort of woman you took me for when you decided to creep up on me. I am in charge of the situation. Do you understand?'

'Fully,' said Capel. It seemed that he had jumped the gun in thinking she was reacting to his suspicions. She didn't even know who he was. ' But I can't say the same for you, Miss Cooper. Is this the way you generally treat people who save your life?'

'What?'

Capel felt the pressure go from his back and relaxed. He turned his head, not risking a sudden movement yet. For a moment, a tiny moment, he saw doubt and concern in Lillith Cooper's face, before the habitual gloss and slickness returned. For that instant she had looked much younger.

'It's Capel.' A self-satisfied smile settled into place; once more he was seeing Lillith, the act. 'What can I say? An apology would be insulting, much too trivial. Do get up, Capel, you look a sorry sight down there.' She held out her hand to help him up.

Capel hesitated, contemplated rejecting her assistance and took the hand. Once more he noticed the length of her fingers. She somehow managed to stroke his wrist as she levered him up. When Capel was standing opposite her, the two of them as isolated as they could be in an anonymous hotel room she kept hold of the hand and pulled gently towards her.

'Do you always carry a knife?' said Capel. He disengaged his wrist and took a step backwards.

'Always when I'm alone. A woman has to look after herself these days.' She moved closer, so close that Capel could feel the material of her cloak brushing against his legs. He held his ground; she was in his personal space and he resented it, but he was sure that she knew it and refused to give her the satisfaction of acknowledging such a petty claim.

'It's risky, though. You wouldn't want to kill someone.' Capel was watching her eyes for a reaction.

Lillith reacted, but only with one of her slow smiles. 'You've got me all wrong, Capel. I should think Harriet has been feeding you stories. You've fallen for Harriet's little act, haven't you? Poor little girl, preyed upon by the heartless Lillith. Don't trust her Capel.'

Capel was going to argue, to disagree, but Lillith suddenly became brisk. She stepped back, emphasising the change of mood.

'I don't suppose you've come after me simply to pass the time of day. I love it up here, but perhaps we'd better go back down to the car. More appropriate for conversation. I've got some coffee.'

'That would be very welcome,' said Capel, relaxing for the first time since he had felt the prick of the knife blade.

'After you, Capel.'

Capel hesitated. She had done it again. The bloody woman had an uncanny ability to put him in a difficult position. As far as he was aware, he had done nothing to indicate his total loss of direction, yet she had picked it up. He decided that cheerful openness was the best way to defuse her advantage. 'I haven't the foggiest which way it is.' He couldn't resist laughing at his unintentional pun. The delay in Lillith's answering, patronising smile was a millimetre short of insulting. 'I've lost all sense of direction.'

Lillith turned sideways on to him, flicking her hair back over her shoulder. She stared, serious now, concentrating hard on the grey-white void. Capel was entranced, no, englamoured by her splendour. He'd been right, only the pre-Raphaelites could catch such cold beauty. She would have made a superb Lady of the Lake. Yet the glamour couldn't stick to his modern cynicism. Where a mediaeval peasant might have fallen at her feet in awe, Capel had the surety that she knew exactly how she looked, how it would affect him. He was still impressed despite himself, but in control.

'It's that way,' Lillith said, extending a hand languidly, pointing away to her right. The wrist was enclosed in a complex bangle, a woven Celtic design of some kind.

'You're sure?' said Capel, adopting the jolly idiot mode as a counter to her mystical charm.

'Sight is not limited to the eyes,' said Lillith obscurely.

'I'll take your word for it,' said Capel. He followed her meekly down the hill, focusing on the ground but keeping the woman's back in his peripheral sight. Whether she could truly see through the fog, or had kept careful track of her path, Lillith lead him unerringly back to the car park. Capel made as if to head for his car but Lillith touched his sleeve for a moment.

'This way. You did want a coffee.'

'I did.'

The interior of the MG was cold, but seemed to lack some of the dampness of the outside air. Lillith shivered. 'I'll get you that coffee in a minute.' She leant back over her seat, fishing for something on the floor behind. Her hair streamed out between them like a resplendent copper-gold curtain. Capel resisted a strong urge to touch it. There was something in the colour of that hair that went straight past the senses and hit deep in the emotions. 'Here.' Lillith flicked back her hair and smiled, offering him a blanket.

'You have it,' said Capel. 'Chivalry is not entirely dead.'

'I intended to share it,' Lillith said. She unfolded the dark purple-brown cloth and spread it across their knees. 'Better?'

Capel waited until she had found a small flask and was pouring dark coffee before replying. 'Thank you.' He took the offered cup and sipped the coffee. It was still hot. 'Would you do something for me? One little thing - it seems fair if you believe I saved your life.'

'Ask,' said Lillith. She pushed back her hair from her face.

'We're very alone. There's no audience, no one to perform for. Just this once, could I speak to the real you, not Lillith Cooper the popular author and undoubted character?'

'If you like.' She wasn't smiling now. She watched him very closely, as if his expression could give away something of his intent.

'Do you believe in all this? Mysticism and dragons and crystal power and dowsing. Is it all an act for the punters, or do you really believe it? There's no strings attached, I promise you. Nothing goes further than here - I have no intention of revealing all to the press. I'd simply like to know for myself.'

'Oh, so would I.' Lillith smiled at last, but it wasn't her usual, slow, calculating smile. It was a crooked twist of her mouth, nowhere near as elegant or as hypnotic, but much more natural and likeable. 'I did. A long time ago, I knew what I believed. I read the books - you know, ley lines and power patterns and everything of that sort - and I was impressed. It made sense, more sense than the sort of mechanistic rubbish they pumped out at school in the science class. It made sense that there was something beyond the physical.' She took a long sip at the coffee. 'Now I don't know. Are you familiar with the Tarot, Capel?'

'I've heard of it.'

'Say there are two fortune tellers who use the Tarot. The first has studied many years, knows every last detail of everything that has ever been written on the subject. The second read the blurb on the back of a cheap pack. The first makes predictions based on traditional interpretations, which have been passed down for generations. The second looks at the cards and says the first thing that comes into her head. Which is the genuine fortune teller?'

'That assumes there is such a thing. I believe in free will.'

'So you do, Capel, so you do. I belong to the second school. I've never bothered to study more than a couple of popular books. I look at things and I write the first thing that comes into my head - does that make me a charlatan or a true believer? I can't honestly say I believe or disbelieve what I write. I scribble it down and it sells. Who's to say it's not true? Is that an act? You tell me.'

'I don't presume to judge. I wondered if you knew.'

'You know as much as I do now.'

'Perhaps. There was one other thing.'

'Oh, yes.' The mask was returning. Capel silently cursed himself for wasting his moment of intimacy in satisfying his curiosity. 'There's always one other thing, isn't there Capel?' Lillith slid across the seat, getting as close to him as the gear stick allowed. She put her cup on the dash and slipped an arm around Capel's neck. 'Tell me about the other thing, Capel.'

'Ian Telfer - why did you tell him you were Harriet?'

'Is that all? He was a nuisance, he was pestering me; I thought it would be amusing to play a game with him. There's nothing more to it. What a disappointment, Capel, I expected something more... arousing from you.' She was rubbing the back of his neck. Capel was aware of her perfume. It was a different one from Glastonbury, but still intoxicatingly thick.

'I never said that was all. Let me tell you a story. A mystery story.'

'Excellent, Capel, I love mystery. Life is mystery; sex is a mystery.' She rested her head on his shoulder.

'A story,' said Capel, fighting the warmth of her proximity. He firmly told his hormones to switch off, this was a false alarm. He closed his eyes, but he could do nothing about her smell and the warmth of her touch. 'It goes like this. A writer of rather precious pseudo-historical books goes to meet a well-known photographer of historical buildings. This is an odd meeting, because there is no love lost between the two. Even more oddly, that very same day the photographer is murdered, yet the writer says nothing of her visit to the police.'

'Fascinating,' said Lillith. She rubbed her head gently against his shoulder.

'There's more,' said Capel. 'Somehow a young lout finds out what happened. He tries to blackmail the writer. But she is a very resourceful person. She befriends another local lad and gets him, with his friends, to string up her blackmailer on the Tor. While the heavies are away she drowns him.'

'A very dangerous sounding lady.' Lillith's other hand, the one that wasn't around his neck, came sliding across Capel's chest, searching for a gap in his shirt like a blind, new-born puppy searching for the teat.

'Oh, yes. But even that isn't enough for her.' Still with his eyes closed, Capel's hand closed over Lillith's and stopped its movement. 'She finishes off by trying to set up a close friend to take the blame. More than dangerous, wouldn't you say?'

'Certainly a risky person to be this close to, Capel. Especially when she has a knife. That's if you haven't got a death wish.'

Capel finally opened his eyes. 'I really thought you'd done it, right up until you told me how you wrote your books. Why did you go to see Isobel Hunt?'

'I admired her, Capel. She was nothing short of a heroine to me. I knew how she felt about my work and it hurt very much, but that didn't stop me admiring her. I'd already earned more from my first three books than anything she was likely to make out of writing, but I envied her the admiration she got from the intelligentsia. I'm not saying I'd rather have had that than the money - don't take me for such an obvious hypocrite - but I'd love to have both.'

'What can you remember about your meeting?'

'There wasn't much to remember. She'd pushed the gate closed, but she hadn't locked it. The crypt was the first place I looked - there aren't many spots you can be hidden in the Abbey - and there she was. Setting up a camera on a tripod. I had taken one of her books, I actually intended to tell her how much it had impressed me, but she didn't recognise me. That was the worst bit. I expected she would be all hackles and need a power of charming, but she just took me for a helper, one of the abbey staff. She was wittering on about some fool of a boy who'd been pestering her; she called him all sorts of names, poor sod. She could be cruel could Isobel. Not even recognising me, she thought I wanted an autograph.'

'If I still thought you'd killed her, that would be quite a strong motive. I don't suppose you enjoy it when someone doesn't recognise you. Especially someone like Isobel Hunt.'

'I was furious. She didn't show the slightest flicker of recognition when she asked my name. To put in the book, you know. I couldn't say another thing, I just stormed out of the place.'

'Did you see anyone else around?'

'I don't know, I wasn't looking. I was hurt.'

'I realise that, but Isobel Hunt must have been killed within minutes of you leaving her. You could well have seen her killer.'

'How terrible.' Lillith's grip tightened on Capel. 'But I didn't see anything. It sounds quite damning, Capel. Perhaps it's all a lie. Are you sure you aren't the teensiest bit nervous?' She pulled Capel's face round to hers and kissed him full on the lips. He detached her gently and pushed her back towards her own seat.

'Not any more.'

'It'd serve you right if I were to slip my knife between your ribs, just to prove that you aren't the great judge of character you think you are.'

'I'm reasonably confident of my own abilities,' said Capel, 'but I don't take undue risks.' He felt under his seat and pulled out Lillith's knife, rotating it between the finger and thumb of his left hand. 'I thought you'd be better off without it.'

Lillith snorted and turned half away from him, folding her arms across her chest. 'Humiliation complete, then, Capel? You'd better piss off and irritate someone else.'

'I will very soon. Just tell me about Peter Schofield's death. Why did he die?'

'Your guess is good as mine, Capel. I wasn't there. You can ask whiter than white Harriet, if you like. I was throwing up all over her carpet while she mopped up after me most of the night. Very domestic under her "look I've got short hair, I must be a modern woman" affectation is Harriet.'

'Ian Telfer said nothing about it to you?'

'Do you think I had deep, meaningful conversations with him? Telfer was just a joke to wind up Henry and Harriet.'

'Oh, yes, Henry. It was all a coincidence, was it? Henry's little excursion to the well and his early morning stroll.'

'If it wasn't, you should be talking to Henry, not me. I asked him to get me some well water, that's all. How and when he did it was up to him.'

'I suppose so.' Capel reached for the door handle, then turned back to face Lillith. 'Did Henry have any interest in Isobel Hunt?'

'He did,' said Lillith. Her face showed genuine surprise at the recollection. 'It doesn't seem at all like Henry, but he was very interested when I said I was going to see her. I think he wanted to come with me, but he didn't ask. That was the only time I've known him mention her.'

'Thanks very much, Miss Cooper, you've been a great help.' Capel opened the door and stepped out into the fog. It showed no signs of clearing.

'I wish I could say you delivered as much on promise,' said Lillith. 'Haven't you forgotten something?'

'Sorry? Oh, yes, thanks for the coffee, it was very welcome.'

'The knife, Capel, you've got my knife.'

'So I have.' Capel threw it into the nearest bush and slammed the door. Every instinct told him that Lillith had told him the truth, but it didn't do any harm to keep her separated from her weapon for a while longer. He heard her car door bang and low curses in a much less restrained voice than Lillith's self-image usually allowed, then the noise was absorbed by the whiteness and he was alone again.

Capel was pleased at the ease with which he got back to his

car. He had no illusions about the effectiveness of his sense of direction, but there was pleasure in succeeding nonetheless. He started the engine and coasted out of the car park, back down to the road. His headlights showed little more than a couple of feet of verge and the whiteness in front. Driving back to Glastonbury would be no fun.

~

An hour later he was still in the cotton-wool morass, still feeling his way at a crawl. He had given up on signposts after the tedium of stopping and climbing out to see them had become too much for him. Instead he was trying absolute navigation using an Ordinance Survey map. He counted roads on the left, the only landmark he could see clearly, and used this to log his position.

The constant concentration was a terrible strain. He had only met two other cars so far, two other people mad enough to venture out in that terrible cold embrace. Second road on the left and he turned off. A nice straight road for a couple of miles and he should hit a village. If they had a pub he was going to sit outside until opening time and get a pint inside him in front of fire. They had to have a fire in this weather even though it was June.

One. That was the first turning, a small road like an overgrown farm track. He switched on the radio for company.

' ...and a lorry has overturned on the westbound slip road of junction fifteen of the M4. The police are encouraging motorists to stay at home. Weather conditions should improve through the day, returning to the seasonal norm by late afternoon, but the band of fog will be very slow to lift. In half an hour on Radio Four, Woman's Hour, but first a rare interview with the murder writer Anthea Burton...'

'Spare me from murder mysteries,' said Capel to himself, turning off the radio. 'Damn.' He had passed the turning. He crawled back nervously, staring over his shoulder into the emptiness, looking for the ghostly headlights of another car about to speed out of the murk and hit him. Nothing came. He turned up the side road. This was more like it. The road was newly remade, with clear markings and cat's eyes. He speeded up a little, gaining confidence. Not too fast though. He glanced at his speedometer, taking his eyes from the road for an instant of time that under ordinary circumstances he would not have missed. As he looked back at the windscreen it shattered, showering pieces of glass into his face.

CHAPTER 19

That instant, as the glass flew out but before he was really aware of the yellow and black bar across his view, Capel's foot shot onto the brake. The car jerked to a stop. Capel looked up for the mirror to see if he had cut his face, then realised the stupidity of the thought. No windscreen, no mirror.

It was a barrier that he'd hit. The sort of thing they used on border crossings and at entrances to factories, a wasp-striped bar that had embedded itself in his car before snapping off its post. Capel shook himself, raining loose glass onto the floor.

'Are you all right, mate?'

There was someone outside. Capel started to wind down the window, then realised it was a bit superfluous with no windscreen. 'I think so; it was the shock, mostly. Where is this?'

'Evans Holdings. Didn't you see the barrier?'

'It wasn't easy. I thought I'd turned onto the Eastbury road.'

'You must have passed it. We're next on the left, that's how we direct people. Let's have a look at your head.' The security guard pushed his face close, avoiding the glass clinging to the edge of the windscreen. 'Cut your forehead, I reckon. Let's get you fixed up before we sort this out.'

'Thanks,' said Capel. He staggered as he stepped out of the car. 'Sorry, I'm a bit shaken.'

'That's all right,' said the guard, but he sniffed Capel's breath suspiciously.

~

It took a long time, not a very pleasant time for Capel, to sort out the damage. He managed to persuade them not to call the police, but there was still the insurance details to cover and he needed some sort of temporary windscreen. They gave him a sheet of plastic, apparently part of the stock in trade of Evans Holdings. By the time he reached Glastonbury it was late afternoon. There was no sign of the fog. As the day passed on it had thinned, but there was a point maybe ten miles outside the town where it had suddenly disappeared, a sharp edge to the mists. Capel stopped and looked back at it before he carried on. That fog had been more than a passive backdrop to his morning.

Glastonbury was performing normally, as if had not been touched by the freak weather. Capel drove through the town and stopped outside the low block of flats where he had dropped Vicky the last time he saw her. He took his time walking to the door. It was good to be out in warmth again without the clinging shawl of the fog around him. He wasn't too sure what reception he'd get either.

Vicky lived on the first floor, an uninspiring climb up steps fenced in by the metal pole and plastic handrail banisters that went with a cheap development. Her door was no different from any of the others, a uniform diarrhoea-brown hardboard face with an ugly slit of a letterbox and a bell push with the number written under it in uneven handwriting.

She had rubber gloves on when she answered the door. Capel looked at them pointedly, his eyebrows raised. 'I can come back if it's inconvenient,' he said. 'I don't want to disturb you if you've got company.'

'I won't even try to understand that,' said Vicky. 'You'd better come in. I never expected you to call. I mean, it's nice to see you, but I thought you'd just ring me.'

'But it is nice to see me?' Capel stayed on the doorstep.

'Of course it is. I could do with someone to talk to who isn't in the force. It all gets a bit much sometimes.'

'Consider me the ideal sounding board. Have I come too late to wipe? If you insist on keeping up this pretence that you're washing up.'

'You're just in time.'

Capel followed her, catching the tea towel that came flying out of the kitchen just before it hit him in the face. It was a small kitchen, very narrow, forcing them into an intricate dance to avoid each other as they moved about.

'I wouldn't be entirely honest if I didn't admit to an ulterior motive in being in Glastonbury,' said Capel. 'Not that I wasn't dying to see you, you understand, but I had an idea about the murder.'

'Give me a break, Capel. I've been living the thing solidly at work. Don't I get time off for good behaviour?'

'Let's see some good behaviour first. Do you mind if I continue with my story?' He took a slight nod as acceptance. 'I was worried by something Ian Telfer said, so I came to have a talk with him.'

'Well you can't, because he's banged up, which you would have known if you'd listened to me when I phoned you.'

'Don't move a muscle,' Capel said very loudly in her ear. 'Hold it just there.' He reached out with exaggerated caution and skimmed off a collection of soap bubbles which she had unconsciously deposited from her glove onto the end of her nose. 'Close thing.' He exhibited the bubbles, taking the opportunity to flick her fringe, sending the curtain of yellow-gold hair shimmering back into place.

'Idiot,' said Vicky without malice.

'Of course I listened. I hang on your every word. So I went to the police station and saw him there.'

'You've been already? They let you see him?'

'I'm not without influence, you know. Yes, they let me see him, and he told me what I wanted to hear, for what it's worth. Telfer had a crush on Harriet Watson, so he said, but he'd called her hair wonderful or something of the sort, which it certainly isn't. Not like yours.' He paused to stroke the back of Vicky's neck, sending a shiver down her spine. 'And, like I thought, it turns out that his Harriet was Lillith Cooper.'

'Lillith? Why?'

'It didn't seem unreasonable. I'd dreamed up a nice, convoluted plot with Lillith at the centre, murdering Paul Schofield and Isobel Hunt. Only, when I caught up with her she was innocent. No, not innocent, I can't imagine Lillith ever being innocent - but she didn't kill them.'

'Fluttered her eyelashes at you, did she? So you came all this way to see this Cooper woman with the wonderful hair, not me. It starts to make sense.'

'She certainly did some fluttering, and the rest. But, sadly, I'm convinced she isn't the killer. I don't suppose the Mighty Davies has come up with anything?'

'Complete blank. No one's saying anything more than we already know. Now could we change the subject, please?'

'Willingly. Would you like to hear about the dark mystery of the defiled church? Rampant Goings on in Rural Avon. Bath School in Black Magic Scandal. All that sort of thing. Good grief, I'm starting to sound like Ed.'

'No thank you, tell me some other time. I want cheerful conversation. How are you fixed for the rest of the day?'

'Is that the sort of offer my mother always told me to beware of, Constable Denning? Is my honour in danger?'

'You should be so lucky.' Vicky paused, appearing to reflect on what Capel had said earlier. 'What do you mean, "and the rest"? What sort of rest did Lillith Cooper do to you?'

'Very little, I was the epitome of carefulness. So what were you thinking of doing for the rest of the day?'

'You know I've got a twenty-four - I must have a bath...'

'I'm warming to this suggestion. Where do I come in?'

'You don't. Come into the bathroom at all, that is. For a vicar, you've got a very doubtful attitude.'

'I haven't asked you if I can wear your uniform yet, have I?'

'I should hope not.' Capel was delighted to see her blush. 'So I'm going to have a bath while you go down to the supermarket and get some food in. Then I'm going to cook you a meal and we can have a pleasant, brainless evening talking about nothing to do with murders, the police and crime. Fair enough?'

'No, not quite. I accept the conversation ban, though it reinforces all the worst things I've heard about the police and censorship. But I'm going to cook.'

'Don't be a prat, Capel, it's my house.'

'And you're the one who needs a break. Let me, I'd like to. Agree to let me cook and I'll go along with your censorship.'

'It's not... oh, never mind. You've got a deal.'

'Excellent. Anything you don't like? To eat, that is.'

'Aubergines and sago.'

'I can understand that. You're on. You get to your bath and I'll have a quick check round the kitchen then pop out for what I need. Fair enough?'

'I'm on my way,' said Vicky. 'There's a key on the table there - take it with you and let yourself back in.'

~

Capel walked to the supermarket in a light, fluffy sort of mood. Sometimes he had difficulty turning off a problem that was nagging at his mind, but today everything had sunk satisfactorily into the background and was not constantly teasing him and spoiling his concentration. There was probably something still going on in the mental crannies and backwaters, but nothing that penetrated through to his enjoyment of an ordinary, sunny day - and particularly his enjoyment of the people.

Supermarkets were one of his favourite spots for people watching, quite the equal of any Parisian pavement café. Even allowing for the delay caused by an unfamiliar layout that put dog food where the pasta should have been and transposed the fresh veg and the alcohol, Capel was a long time about his shopping. It was difficult to resist following the arguing couples, or staring in fascination at a running battle between a mother and her small twins, each determined to buy a totally different set of breakfast cereals. It beat Australian soap operas by a mile.

When he made it to the checkout he had a well-piled basket.

Vicky had very little in stock that contributed to his personal speciality version of spaghetti. She seemed to belong more to the tin, packet and microwave school of cuisine.

'Did you see the price on this?'

'What?' Capel smiled in bemused fashion at the boy on the till. He was holding a packet of fresh basil. Capel realised that he'd been on automatic pilot, thinking more about Vicky and her pantry than his purchases.

'There's no price.' The sales assistant gave him up as a bad job and rang a bell, holding the packet high above his head. 'Price please, fresh basil, small size,' he announced at the top of his voice to no one in particular.

Capel was taken with the thought that it was a good thing he wasn't buying condoms. The 'small size' which would be particularly galling.

' ... fifty three,' said the assistant.

'Sorry?'

'Twenty-five pounds fifty three,' said the assistant again with a sigh to show that he had better things to do than repeating things for muddled customers.

'Really?' Capel checked himself from remarking on how much everything cost. He wasn't ready for membership of the 'it was all cheaper and better in my day' club yet. 'I've only got twenties. Is that okay?'

It seemed it was, though the assistant examined the notes closely with a couple of suspicious glares at Capel. Perhaps he didn't look like the sort of person who could afford to use twenty pound notes.

Capel emerged from a close encounter with the automatic door humming one of his favourite hymn tunes, Down Ampney. The supermarket hadn't deflated his mood - rather the reverse. He walked back to the flat with a seraphic beam that encouraged several of the passers-by out of their workaday neutral frown into a surprised smile in return.

He couldn't put his finger on it, but she had done something to the flat while he was out. There was nothing he could point at and say 'that's changed', but there was an additional feeling of order and cleanliness. Even Vicky herself: it wasn't just the clean glow from the bath, she was less sloppy - no, not sloppy, less... just different.

'Supplies,' said Capel, holding up his two carrier bags.

'It was a meal you were supposed to be making, not doing the shopping for a fortnight. What do I owe you?'

'It's on me.'

'Come on, Capel, I probably get paid more than you do. Let me do it.'

'No. Especially not now you've said that. If you want to stay friends, this is my treat.'

'Okay. Dump it in the kitchen. It's too early to start on it yet. I've put the kettle on, would you like something?'

'Don't worry, I'll get it.'

'Like hell, you will.' Vicky came into the kitchen behind him and grabbed his hands. You can make the dinner, and buy the food, but leave me some of the entertaining. This is my flat, remember. Do you always take over like this? Coffee all right?'

'Yes. To coffee, that is. I suppose it's a habit from visiting inmates when I was at the open prison. And it'll be the same visiting parishioners, I imagine. It's quite often at a difficult time for them; they like you to take over and do things for them.'

'That's not me, okay?'

'Very clearly.' Capel patted her on the shoulder and went through to the living room. 'Is this more like it?' He shouted back to the kitchen. 'I'm on the settee, waiting to be served. I prefer dark chocolate biscuits.'

'You're getting Rich Tea, and liking it.' Vicky dumped a tray on the low coffee table, which wobbled precariously. 'Help yourself, the service stops here.'

'Thanks.' Capel took a sip of the coffee. 'Hot. Did you enjoy your training for the police? I trust that's far enough away from work to be acceptable.'

'You skip around a lot, don't you? Yes, I think so. After a while. You know what it's like to start with, you're a bit nervous, feeling your way.'

'A bit nervous nothing, I was terrified when I started training for the priesthood. It wasn't the theory, or the other students, it was the responsibility. To have to stand up at the front of a church and lead a service. I don't just mean the solo bits, even when everyone's saying something they expect the priest to give a lead. And the first time I had to go to someone's home and talk about a dead relation, talk them through it - it was very scary.'

'That's something we've got in common. Dealing with the bereaved.'

'You've had a lot of experience of that, I suppose?'

'There's no need to be sarcastic, I have done it.'

'Sorry, I can't help myself.' Capel gave her a quick hug. 'When I'm fond of someone this sarcasm seems to take over as safety net. I didn't mean anything. You can't have done too many, though. You can't be more than...' He stopped, flustered. 'I've no idea how old you are.'

'Old enough. You're thirty-four.'

'Thirty-three. Oh shit, no, it is thirty-four. How do you know?'

'We can't reveal our sources.'

'It was that bastard Ridge, wasn't it?'

'That's not the sort of language I expect from a clergyman, Stephen.'

'I said you were young. So how old are you? It's only fair.'

'Twenty-six; practically middle aged.'

'Ouch. Arithmetic is a terrible thing.'

'Balls.'

'That's not the sort of language I expect from a police constable, Victoria.'

'Well really, it's not as if age matters these days.'

'I've just added age to the list of banned topics. What was best at the police college?'

'I don't know. Sport, I suppose. I always loved sport.'

'I might have guessed. My sporting limits are a game of

backgammon and watching the Grand Prix on the telly. In my youth I was quite heavily into tiddlywinks. I think that's the most physical game I've ever excelled at. I played for the university.'

'Really? Tiddlywinks? That's, er, quite something.' Vicky was making a very bad job of trying to keep a straight face.

'I'm not joking. What did you play?'

'Netball, lacrosse and cricket. Cricket I enjoyed the most, but I was worst at.'

'You must have been quite a sight at the crease.'

'I was. You should see the photos.'

'Yes, please, I'd love too.' Capel put his mug down and sat forward on the edge of the cushion.

'No, I was joking.' Vicky put her hand to her mouth and leant forward, sending her hair cascading across her face. 'I hate having my photograph taken.'

'Go on. When you come to visit me I'll show you mine in return.'

'You'll be bored stiff.'

'I'll tell you if it gets boring - you can trust me to be unsubtle about it. Please. I love looking through pictures.'

'All right, but don't start complaining when you fall asleep. I should warn you, they're old-fashioned albums. I know everyone just uses their phone, but my mum always had albums and I liked it.'

Capel watched Vicky fishing around in a low cabinet, so low that she had to kneel on the carpet to reach into it. It was impossible to tell if she was genuinely reluctant to show off her pictures or if it was the conventional display of modesty. Probably a mixture of the two. She dragged out half a dozen dark blue bound albums.

'This is the lot,' she said, slumping down onto the couch next to him. 'Stop me when you've had enough.'

'We'll see,' said Capel, sliding across to be able to see the album better. Their legs touched, a light pressure that he found ridiculously enjoyable. 'I've been meaning to put my photographs in albums for ages. The old ones are still in the envelopes, stuffed in an old shoebox. Nothing so organised. And for the last few years they're just on my laptop.'

'I get it from my mum. Sign of a sign of a fussy nature.'

Capel watched in simple delight as she flicked through a stream of pictures, each page labelled in a careful, rounded handwriting. He watched Vicky grow from a round-faced schoolgirl, only just recognisable, into a somehow slightly pinker version of the present day while she was at college.

'Are you fed up yet?' Vicky left the fifth album closed, waiting for his response.

'I'm dying for more. This is wonderful.'

'You can't mean that.'

'I certainly can. Any more on the beach?'

'Dirty old man. I'll skip over last year's holiday when we get to it.' She opened the book. 'These are just after I started at Glastonbury. I told you I came from near Swanage, didn't I? I hadn't been to Glastonbury before, so I went round taking photos the way you do. You don't want to see all these.'

'I do.' Capel restrained her from flicking through. 'I'll turn. I stayed at the George, you know - of course you do. And here's the Abbey. It's difficult taking pictures somewhere like this. You never know if it's best to just have the buildings or to get people in the shots for a bit of interest. These days I always prefer...' He stopped abruptly, staring blankly at the page.

'Is there someone you know? Capel? Are you all right?'

'Oh, yes.' Capel looked up from the book, looked her straight in the eye. A mischievous smile bent his lips. 'Vicky, I'm going to have to break your rule. Do you know when the Abbey closes? I think I know how we can identify Isobel Hunt's murderer.'

CHAPTER 20

'Are you insured for anyone?' said Vicky.

'Sorry? Oh, the car. Yes, I think so.'

'I'll drive. I know Glastonbury better.'

'I never argue with a professional. Just remember that it's my car, not a high speed pursuit vehicle.'

'It'd be difficult to forget, wouldn't it,' said Vicky, looking doubtfully at Capel's car. 'Couldn't you afford a windscreen?'

'I had an accident on the way. I'll tell you about it later. Just keep the speed down and it'll be fine.'

'Is it possible to exceed the speed limit in a car like this?'

'Very witty.' Capel fastened his seat belt with ostentatious care. 'Reverse is there.' He pointed helpfully at the gear lever.

'You asked me to find out about Isobel Hunt, didn't you?' Vicky slid the car smoothly out of the parking space, judging the closeness of the bumper ahead with an accuracy that had Capel's toes curling. 'I didn't get round to it; we've had too much on. Is there a connection with the Schofield enquiry?'

'I think so. I think that Lady Isobel's murder and Paul Schofield's were linked. That's why I was so eager to see Lillith...'

'Eager to see her, were you?' Vicky changed up with insufficient clutch, dragging an anguished scream from the gearbox.

'Don't take it out on the car, it's suffered enough today. I wanted to see Lillith because she was with Isobel the morning she was killed. Like I said, I thought for a while she'd done it - Lillith, I mean. But it wasn't her.'

'So why are we rushing down to the Abbey?'

'Lady Isobel was taking photographs when she was killed. Postcards for the Abbey. Remember I was rabbiting on about photographs with people in them - I thought, what if Isobel had already started to take pictures when her killers arrived. She'd got the camera set up when Lillith saw her, which must have been some time before. They could be there, in the photographs, waiting to accuse themselves.'

'That's it, the great theory?' Vicky looked at him in amazement, so long that Capel had to point feebly at the road. 'You haven't got a good opinion of the police have you? They would have checked at the time. Shall we go home?'

'No, look, carry on. I'd thought of that. I'm sure they'll have interviewed everyone in the pictures, probably including the murderer. But they didn't have the Schofield business as a cross-check. Suppose someone in one of those photos cropped up in your current investigation, wouldn't that be interesting?'

'I suppose so. It doesn't prove anything, though.'

'We'll see.' They rounded the cross and pulled into Magdalene Street. 'Can you stop outside?'

'Not officially.' Vicky drew up on the forecourt of the abbey gateway. 'We're too late.' She pointed to the closed gates, the dark interior.

'There could still be someone there. Hang on a minute.' Capel jumped out of the car and ran up to the entrance. There was no sign of life. The Abbey had been shut for at least an hour.

'It'll keep 'til tomorrow, won't it?' said Vicky as he got back into the car.

'I suppose it will, but I wanted to know now.'

'You can't. Be patient, it'll keep.'

'And I'm going to have to book into a hotel room. I'm not going all the way home, especially not with this windscreen.'

'Why?' Vicky pulled back into the traffic.

'It might be good enough to get us to the Abbey, but I need something more permanent to get back to Thornton. Can you recommend anywhere?'

'Why do you need to book a hotel room?'

'Ah.'

It wasn't, perhaps, such a clever thing to do, Vicky thought to herself later that evening. It had been a spur of the moment thing, inviting Capel to stay, but she didn't know him that well, after all. She shifted against the pillow. It was only ten minutes since they had gone to bed, she in her room, him on the couch, very respectable. Capel had limited himself to a tactful peck on the cheek as a goodnight kiss as if he was aware of her concern. But the fact remained that she was about to go to sleep leaving a man she had known only a few days separated from her by five yards of carpet and an door she couldn't lock that was little more than cardboard.

It wasn't that she was incapable of defending herself - she'd had the martial arts training - but this wasn't the sort of thing she did. It was an unnecessary risk. Vicky never took unnecessary risks with people; the more she did her job, the more she realised how important that was. She held her breath, listening hard for sounds from the lounge. She heard the unmistakable squeak that her ageing couch made when it took a person's weight, then a regular creaking.

Vicky jumped upright in the bed, covering the noise from the lounge for a moment with the sounds of the pillows and duvet folding around her. She forced herself to hold still. There it was still, a regular, rhythmic creaking that the innuendo of a thousand TV comedies imbued with a perverted sexual connotation. Surely he couldn't be... not in her lounge. She slipped out of the bed, her mind skipping round the room, trying to remember anything in the dimness that could be used as a weapon.

There was nothing. Her hand was on the door handle, ready to rip the door open and confront him with a yell, but what then? The embarrassment of it. What could she possibly say? And what if he saw her in the doorway in her nightie, even though it was long and warm and anything but sexy. What if seeing her pushed him, already aroused, over the edge to assault her?

She eased the door open, holding the handle down so it didn't give out its usual groan as the spring relaxed. Through the narrow opening she could see him on the couch, but she didn't think he could see her. What she saw confused her. It relieved her and worried her more in the same instant. He wasn't doing anything disgusting, he was lying on the couch rocking from side to side, his knees raised high, his torso twisting with every turn.

There was something very disturbing about that rocking. She realised that she associated it with mental illness, that she linked this rhythmical distortion of the body with poor souls locked in mental torment. Or even the back and fro pacing of caged animals in old, barred, concrete floored zoo cages. She felt immediately sorry for him, wanting to comfort him, but also scared. She knew she shouldn't be scared, that mental illness was a reality of life, not something to fear, but she couldn't help it. All her life, from being a very young girl, two things had frightened her repeatedly. That she would lose her hair, lose those long, fair strands of her pride, and that she would go mad.

'Oh, I'm sorry,' said Capel from the couch. 'Did I disturb you?' He stopped rocking and sat up facing her, a sheepish expression on his face.

Vicky found herself looking at him properly for the first time, assessing him as a man. It's hard to say what it was that was attractive about him. Rather shorter than she normally liked. Not particularly well muscled, but at least not running to fat either. Hair nondescript. But there was something about his eyes, again showing a tendency to appear green, and particularly that wry smile... She realized she should have said something. 'I'm sorry, what?'

'Did I disturb you?'

'Not really...' said Vicky, fighting for a sensible explanation. 'I... I'd forgotten to brush my teeth.'

'It's embarrassing,' said Capel.

'No,' said Vicky too quickly. 'Not at all. Don't worry about it.'

'It's my pride, I suppose,' said Capel. 'It makes me feel old, having a bad back. I feel it should be the sort of thing that happens to old men, not to me.'

'A bad back?' said Vicky.

'The osteopath says it's all down to posture. That and lack of exercise. For nearly a year now it's kept me awake at night, but he's given me this course of exercises that are really helping. Especially that one; it loosens up the discs, I think. Gets mobility into the spine.'

'I'm glad it's helping,' said Vicky, taking a step backward into her bedroom. 'Carry on. Don't mind me.' She could feel her cheeks, hot with the burning flush of embarrassment.

'What about your teeth?' said Capel.

'Teeth?' said Vicky.

Capel mimed a toothbrush. 'Teeth.'

'Oh, yes,' said Vicky, feeling herself flush again. 'Teeth.'

~

'Who... what time is it?' Vicky's voice was heavily muffled.

'Eight o'clock,' said Capel, his mouth near to the closed bedroom door. 'I've got you a cup of tea, if you'd like one.'

'Come in,' said Vicky, slightly less muffled.

Capel transferred his own cup to the same hand as Vicky's and opened the door. The bedroom was very light. White walls; thin curtains, colour washed out in the bright sunlight; a cream duvet, tangled about her. It had been over her face, he decided, when he knocked. Her hair spread across the pillow in a near-invisible fan.

'Two sugars, wasn't it?' said Capel.

'Thanks.' Vicky pushed herself up and sat forward, slightly hunched. Her night-shirt was a big, floppy T-shirt; white again, with a chain of parachuting teddy bears down the front.

Capel sat on the edge of the bed. 'Very fetching. The teddy

bears.'

'I like them. Did you get to sleep okay? With your back and everything. You must have got up early to be dressed already.'

Capel looked down at himself. 'I slept wonderfully, but I thought the sight of me in my underwear would be too shocking for you first thing.'

'You should have borrowed my dressing gown.'

'I don't think so - that would have made things worse. I have to say that your couch was a significant improvement on last night's bed. After the car seat, it seemed positively luxurious.'

Vicky looked embarrassed. 'I'm sorry about that. We should have shared the bed, especially with your back - it's big enough. It's not that I don't trust you.'

'It was fine - I'm serious about it seeming luxurious. And you've got more trust in me than I would have.' Capel kissed her on the nose. 'Thanks for saying it.'

'I don't know why we didn't just... Capel?' Vicky looked up from her tea to see him peering at her phone.

'I wondered if you'd could ring someone for me. My phone's died.'

'Now?'

'If you don't mind. I want to call the Abbey; see when they open.'

'Oh, Capel!'

~

By the time they reached the abbey forecourt the gates were open, though there wasn't a roaring traffic at that time of the morning. Capel paid for them and took Vicky firmly by the arm, leading her past the shop and round the thorn tree to the ruins, lit by the clear morning sun.

'I thought you wanted to look in the shop,' said Vicky.

'I do,' said Capel. 'This was how it must have been, when Isobel Hunt was killed. So quiet. Peaceful.' He led her across the grass to the Lady Chapel. 'Imagine you're the killer.'

Vicky shivered. 'Must I? It seems a waste of a morning like

this. Remember, I'm back on duty in a couple of hours.'

'Live in the present, for goodness sake. You could be dead in a couple of hours.'

'Charming.'

'You know what I mean. You've got to enjoy what is, whatever it is, not always be looking to the future. Sorry, you've started me on a hobbyhorse. Here's our killer. Sneaked into the abbey grounds. May well have seen Lillith Cooper leaving. Crosses to the Lady Chapel, nice and quiet. What does he - she - want? An undisturbed look round? To mug the photographer; take all her expensive equipment?'

'Possibly. If he knew there was anything to steal.'

'Don't quibble. We approach the chapel quietly. There's Lady Isobel, perhaps on her own, perhaps talking to Lillith. We wait for the moment. Suppose we do intend to take her cameras. We wait until her back is turned and creep down on her. There's a rock. We pick it up. We don't intend to use it, just to threaten her. She's not as young as she used to be, after all. Or perhaps we intend to give her a gentle tap on the head to knock her out. It always works in the films and on TV. You hit them, they fall over and a while later they wake up, easy as that.'

'It's not like that in real life, though.' Vicky had caught Capel's mood. Her eyes were wide, excited. 'She wouldn't be intimidated, she wasn't that sort of woman. She probably laughs at us, tells us not to be silly. She turns back to her work, turns her back on *us*. So we hit her. Not hard; either way, we only wanted to knock her out. She falls down to the floor and we reach out for the camera.'

'But we notice she's very still.' Capel's voice was hushed. 'Even unconscious, there should be something. Breathing, some movement. We crouch down beside her. She's dead; we've killed her.'

'So we grab her bag and leave the less portable stuff.' Vicky mimed picking up a bag. 'We just run. At least as far as the gate. Then we walk away and mingle with the morning rush. One more person in a crowd. It's all over.'

Capel put his arm round Vicky's waist and squeezed her. 'It's very plausible, isn't it. Easy to see when you're here like this.'

Vicky shivered again. 'Very easy. Let's go to the shop.'

'Yes, let's.'

The woman behind the counter was familiar to Capel. It was the one who had found the body. Capel walked straight up to her. 'Good morning, I wonder if you could help us.'

'Yes? It looks like a lovely morning, wouldn't you say?'

'It certainly does. I don't know if you remember, I spoke to you a few days ago about Isobel Hunt's murder.'

'Of course.' Her eyes said she still didn't recognise him, but she was determined not to admit it.

'This is Constable Denning, from the police.' Capel felt Vicky take a breath to speak and put a cautioning hand on her arm. There were times when deception by omission was acceptable. 'Can you remember what happened to the film from Lady Isobel's large format camera? I believe she'd already set it up that morning.'

'The film? The police took the camera, of course.'

'They won't still have it now.'

'It'll have gone to Lady Isobel's family, I suppose.' The shop assistant was puzzled. 'I don't see how it matters, really, what with all this time gone past. The police were very thorough at the time.'

'Thank you,' said Vicky, accepting the compliment on behalf of the force. 'There's some new evidence come up. We can't keep records of everything, you understand. We thought that any film that was taken would have been returned to the Abbey. It was your commission, wasn't it?'

'Well, of course the Abbey arranged for the photographing,' said the woman. 'Do you mind if I sit down? My mother always used to say it helps the brain, concentrates the blood flow.' She came out from behind the counter and sat on a plain wooden chair at the side. 'But there was nothing to return - nothing for the police to find. Lady Isobel hadn't started taking photographs when she was attacked, she was still setting her equipment up. There wasn't even a film in the camera. I remember the policeman at the time, Inspector... oh, what was it? Inspector... no, it'll come to me in a moment... Inspector something...'

'It's not really important,' said Capel.

'It's so irritating when something sticks on the edge of your memory. Inspector ... no, it's gone. Anyway, the Inspector was most disappointed. He'd hoped they could tell something from the snaps.'

'Him and me both,' muttered Capel.

'It looks like we've wasted your time,' said Vicky.

'Not at all, dear.' The shopkeeper seemed put out at the suggestion. 'Anything but, I like a nice chat. These mornings can be very slow before the season really gets started. I was saying to Mrs Finch - she's the cleaner, lovely woman, though she does tend to go on - I'm tempted to bring in a good book and sit reading that, but I always find it off-putting to go into a shop and find the assistant reading. It's the same if they're eating; it makes you feel like an intruder - not at all comfortable. I wouldn't want that in our shop.'

'That's right,' said Vicky. She gave Capel an embarrassed look.

'Thanks for your help,' said Capel, 'we'd better be off.'

'Have a proper look round first,' said the woman. 'We've got some lovely things. Books, souvenirs - all sorts of unusual souvenirs, postcards... it's worth a look.'

'Thanks,' said Capel. He wandered across to the shelves and thumbed through a thick book on the development of the gothic arch. 'We'd better have a look for form's sake,' he murmured to Vicky. 'I suppose you've been here lots of times.'

'Only the once. I'm going to look at the cards.'

Capel pottered for a few minutes, keeping an eye on the woman who had returned behind her counter and was polishing a piece of crystal - cut glass, not the magical variety - with a bright yellow duster. He sidled across to Vicky. 'I think that's enough. I'll buy a few cards to keep her happy.' He picked a random selection of postcards of the Abbey and took them across to the till.

'Very nice,' said the woman, thumbing through his choice. 'Seven in all. Would you like a bag?'

'I'll take them as they are,' said Capel.

'It's funny, you choosing that one,' the woman said as she took his money. 'It was only taken the day before.'

'Yesterday?' said Capel. 'That's remarkable. I thought that postcards took weeks to produce.'

'Not yesterday,' said the woman. She gave Vicky a sympathetic look. 'He's funny, isn't he. Lady Isobel took it the day before she died.'

Capel felt something tightening painfully in his stomach. 'You've got postcards that Isobel Hunt took the day before she was killed?'

'It seems a trifle morbid, doesn't it?' The woman was stolidly cheerful, unaffected by the suggested unpleasantness. 'They weren't going to do it to start with, but then they said "why not", and you can't argue with that, can you? It's not as if it's disrespectful, after all. They were her last work, it'd be a shame not to use them.'

Capel turned the card over. There it was in small print in the bottom corner: *Photograph © Estate of Lady Isobel Hunt.* He turned back to the picture and looked closely. It showed the Abbot's Kitchen, a shapely building, alone against a vivid, cloud-flecked sky. The clouds framed the high chimney spire beautifully, no coincidence but the result of hours of patient waiting. There were no people in the photograph.

'How many are there all together?' asked Vicky. 'How many cards were there made?'

'Thousands, dear,' said the woman, 'we get them by the thousand. Oh, I see what you mean; it's a series of ten, they should all be there.'

Capel was already on his way across to the cards. Without speaking Vicky took the other end of the rack. They worked through the endless shots of the Abbey, scanning the back of the cards, moving on, occasionally keeping a picture out.

'The police went through it all at the time. They said we could use them. Surely we can't have done something wrong?' The woman seemed nervous.

'Nothing,' said Vicky. 'Why shouldn't you use them? Like I said, there's some new evidence, that's all.'

They took the cards back and spread them on the counter. 'I've got six,' said Capel.

'Me too.'

'There'll be duplicates,' said the shopkeeper. 'We can't keep them properly organised. People will take them out and put them back in different places. They've no sense of order.'

'Never mind,' said Capel. 'Let's see. Abbot's Kitchen - no one at all. Close up of Arthur's tomb...'

'Alleged, we have to say now,' said the woman. 'They take all the romance out of history these days. What's the point of getting to the truth if it's so boring that no one wants to hear it?'

'Arthur's alleged tomb,' said Capel. 'No people again.'

'I've got that one too,' said Vicky. 'Then one of the whole ruins. There's people in that, but not enough detail.' She held the card close to her eyes. 'I don't think you could recognise faces in this, even if you had it blown up. Has the Abbey still got the negatives?'

'I think they were transparencies, dear. They'll be in the archives somewhere, but I couldn't say where. You'd have to apply to the authorities next week; everyone's away at the moment. I don't have the right keys.'

'Terrific,' said Capel. 'Onward and upward. The Thorn, with a rather sweet little girl trying to touch it. I can't see that she's a suspect. Then one in the crypt; there's a woman there but I don't think I could recognise her, it's only a back view. It's certainly not Lillith or Harriet.'

'Let me see that, dear.' The woman took the card. 'Oh, that's me.' She unconsciously touched her hair with her fingertips. 'Lady Isobel caught me unawares.'

'Six down,' said Vicky. 'No, seven. I've got the crypt too.

Then a close up of some tiled paving. I don't remember that, is it in the kitchen?'

'No dear, near the crossing, up by the highest parts of the masonry. You ought to have a look, it's quite beautiful. There are a number of sections under little wooden flaps. You lift them up to see.'

'We'll remember that,' said Capel. 'Oh, I only had five. I had the Thorn twice. My last one's of the transepts. There are people again, mostly too far away except for this woman.' He showed the card to Vicky.

'Woman?'

'Here. In the trousers.'

'That's not a woman, it's a man with long hair.'

'How can you tell? I think it's a woman.'

'It's not, it's a man,' said Vicky firmly.

'I think it's terrible,' said the shopkeeper. 'These long-haired louts. There should be a law against it, it's quite unnatural.'

Capel took the card back from Vicky. He brought it close to his eyes in an effort to see more detail. 'Could it be Henry Malkovski without a beard?'

'Why Henry?' said Vicky. 'I thought you were sure of his innocence?'

'So did I,' said Capel.

Vicky pushed her head between Capel and the card. 'I've only seen Malkovski once. The hair's right but... you can't tell.'

'That's no use,' said Capel.

'It's down to me then,' said Vicky. 'Another Abbot's kitchen and that little chapel place. There's a family looking at it.'

Capel took a quick look. 'No. No one involved.'

'So there's two missing,' said Vicky. 'That's only eight different cards.'

'Typical,' said the shopkeeper. 'The temporary staff never tick things off properly. We have a nice little system, so we can tell when we need to restock the shelves, but they don't work it right. We get them from school - they've no idea how to work. I don't know what they teach them now, they seem to expect to come here and spend all day chattering and reading magazines. It's the parents' fault, of course.'

'Could we see the other two cards, please,' said Capel.

'It's not very convenient,' said the woman. 'I have to reach the boxes down off an ever-so-high shelf, and the one you want's always at the bottom. I could look them out for you at the end of the day, how about that?'

'We really do need to see them now,' said Vicky in her best official voice.

'If you insist,' said the woman. She led them into a back room, casting a quick look at the door. The entire time they had been there, no one else had come in.

Like the shop, the back room was modern and well laid out. 'They're up there,' said the woman, pointing at a high shelf. 'I'll have to find the steps.'

'Allow me,' said Capel. He dragged a step, one of those strange devices that roll on a central ball, across the floor and stood on it. 'Is it these?'

'Not them, the next ones,' said the woman. 'You want, er...' she consulted a list. 'Lady Chapel Upper and Abbey Barn.'

'You were right,' said Capel, 'they were at the bottom.' He dragged out the two packages and took them into the lighter shop area. A family with three small children came in, bringing a sudden burst of noise and movement.

'Come on,' said Vicky. She took one packet off Capel. 'Abbey Barn. I don't know that.'

'It's not on the grounds,' said the shop assistant, her eyes following the children warily round the shop. 'It's up the road, a fine building. No doubt someone will put a bypass through it soon.'

'It's beautifully shot,' said Vicky, 'but there are no people.' She got no response from Capel. 'I said it's beautifully shot, Capel.'

Capel had taken a card from the other packet. 'You were right,' he said. 'It wasn't a woman.' He pushed the card along the counter.

'It's the same person,' said Vicky.

'Yes,' said Capel. He stared at the picture, his head close to hers. Quite unconsciously he began to bite on his right forefinger. The card showed the Lady Chapel. There were half a dozen people on the bridge, mostly bustling across, bringing the imagery of the willow pattern to mind, but one, the long haired man, was standing dead in the centre, his gaze fixed on the camera or the photographer. His expression was clear, even from that distance. Very intense, absorbed.

'Do you know him,' said Vicky. 'I suppose it could be Malkovski without a beard, but I don't think...'

'Oh, yes,' said Capel. 'I know him.'

'One of those long haired bully-boys who were always around the place last summer,' said the shopkeeper, taking a moment from her surveillance of the children to look at the picture. 'One of those brutes who threatened us the other day, I shouldn't be surprised.'

'It's not Malkovski,' said Vicky. 'And it's certainly not Telfer or Blake or Gunn. I don't recognise him.'

'You wouldn't,' said Capel. 'He's called Phil Hayes. He's a student teacher up at Bath.'

'A teacher with hair like that?' said the shopkeeper, shaking her head. 'What are things coming to? Still, it shouldn't surprise me, they're all anarchists or bolsheviks these days.'

'You think it could be him?' said Vicky. 'Just because he's in the photograph, it doesn't prove anything.'

Capel's eyes glazed over. He stared blankly into mid-air. 'Wanker,' he said. 'Oh, my God.'

'I beg your pardon?' said the shopkeeper, mortally offended.

'That's all right,' said Capel vaguely. He grabbed hold of Vicky's hand. 'We've got to see Ian Telfer, now!"

CHAPTER 21

With Vicky there it wasn't difficult to get into the cell. Ian Telfer watched them come in with blank indifference. Capel was reminded of animals in a zoo, and felt a similar surge of repugnance at the need for captivity. It had never worried him in the prison for some reason.

'You again?' said Telfer. 'Who's your girlfriend? Bit of a cradle snatcher, eh, vicar?'

'This is Constable Denning,' said Capel. 'I want to ask you something about Phil Hayes, Ian.'

'What about him?' said Telfer. 'What's he got to do with you?'

'I know Phil,' said Capel. 'Remember, I told you I had coffee with him the other day. This stunt you pulled on Paul Schofield, did Phil know about it?'

'He might have.' Telfer looked unhappy.

'It's just that Phil seemed worried that you could have been the one. The one who killed Schofield. He was asking all sorts of questions; it wouldn't surprise me if he says it was all your idea.'

'That's good, coming from him.'

'So he did know about it?'

'Know about it? He thought it up. Very inventive, is Phil.'

'He was there?'

'Nah, course not. He was always like that at school; came up with of all the tricks, but he'd never do it himself. Got other people to be his mugs. He wasn't even in Glastonbury that weekend. Couldn't get away from his precious college.'

'Thanks,' said Capel. 'Thanks very much, Ian.'

'What for?' said Telfer.

Vicky waited until they were outside the cell to speak. 'It's not enough that he knew about it.'

'Let's see what Malcolm thinks.'

'The C.I.? You don't want to go to him do you?'

'We've got to, Vicky.'

Vicky's face was a mask. 'It's that way. And it's Constable Denning. Sir.'

~

'From what I've heard of Malcolm Davies, I should think you got a frosty reception.' Ed Ridge swallowed a third of his pint in a smooth, practised action. The Forge, Capel's local in Thornton Down had an excellent range of bitter, and Ridge considered himself a connoisseur.

'He wasn't well pleased,' said Capel, 'but he listened. He took his team straight down to Bath – they're looking for Hayes now. I don't think he'll prove a problem. He didn't expect to be challenged, you see. But it wasn't easy telling Andrea this morning.'

'Andrea?' said Ridge. 'I lose track of your women. Is that the police bird? Have you broken it off with her?'

'It's no use trying to wind me up. You've never called a woman a bird in your life. Andrea was the maid at the hotel. Hayes's girlfriend. I felt I had to go over and tell her, especially as she thought Hayes was so wonderful.'

'How'd she take it?'

'Badly. What do you expect? She still thought of him as Mister Wonderful, the man who was going to help her get away from her drudgery and her family and give her some independence and a life of her own. But he only ever saw her as a chance for a bit of fun. He had his career to think of.'

'That's what I don't understand. He seemed to move in a different world to the rest of them in Glastonbury. He had nothing to do with the hippies, he didn't hang around with Telfer and his mates. Why would Hayes want to kill Schofield?'

'We know Schofield was a blackmailer in his small way. He had to have something on Hayes. I don't know why it took so long to spot it. After Hayes pumped me in the RPS, making sure I didn't find anything incriminating, it should have been obvious.'

'That could have been simple curiosity. Or concern for Telfer.'

'I suppose so. Anyway, at the time I was determined to pin it all on Lillith. And the long hair threw me. The smart, well-trimmed look that Hayes had when he met me fitted him like a glove. I had no reason to think he'd had long hair until a few days ago, not until I saw the photograph Isobel Hunt took. If he had long hair last year, there's no reason why he couldn't have had it when Schofield was killed. When the eye-witness mentioned a figure with long hair, it was easy to think of Malkovski.'

'Ah, yes, Henry. What happened to Henry?'

'Not a lot. He was let off with a caution - he's gone back to Harriet, but I can't see it lasting. She deserves better.'

'So the HM on the wall, and Malkovski's walk and everything, was pure coincidence. But lucky for Hayes.'

'Yes, it was lucky. Of course Hayes made sure everyone knew he was stuck in Bath that weekend. Everyone except Andrea. She told me he had been visiting the first time we met, but it was a long time before I remembered.'

'Is that why you were so sure in the abbey shop? I can understand why you had your suspicions, but I'd have ferreted around a bit more before jumping for Davies.'

'No, it wasn't that,' said Capel. 'I...'

'Here you are.' Alan Rhees loomed up beside the table. 'I'm surprised you can relax under the circumstances.'

'Won't you join us Alan? This is Ed Ridge, an old friend of mine from the Home Office. Alan's the chaplain at the school here.'

'I haven't got time,' said Rhees. 'I wouldn't have thought you had, either.'

'Why?' said Capel. 'I've already written tomorrow's sermon. Have I missed something?'

'The church,' hissed Rhees with a dark look at Ed Ridge.

'It's fine,' said Capel, 'Ed knows about your church mystery.'

'It's your church, and your problem, which is why you should be doing something about it rather than sitting around enjoying yourself.' Rhees's expression made it clear what he thought about people enjoying themselves.

'There isn't a problem, Alan.'

'I don't suppose you've been keeping watch, have you?'

'There's no need. I've got a nice new cat at the vicarage.'

Rhees looked as if he could hit his fellow clergyman. 'Don't be ridiculous, Capel. There's no question of that sort of disarray being caused by mice. What do you expect your cat to do, ring the police if there's a disturbance? You seem to have no sense of proportion. As far as I can gather you've spent most of the last fortnight flitting off to Glastonbury for frivolous entertainment while God only knows what has been happening in your church.'

'Calm down, Alan. Are you sure I can't get you a drink?' Capel didn't wait for an answer - Rhees's face was answer enough. 'The cat was in the church. That's where I found it. It had been locked in for some days. It was responsible for the desecration. I got a bit of a clue when I trod in one of its calling cards in the vestry.'

'A cat?' said Rhees. He seemed incapable of further comment.

'A cat,' said Capel. 'I'm sorry if it upset you.'

'No, no, I wasn't upset. Simply concerned for you. New parish, new responsibilities, it takes it out of a man. Shouldn't have worried.' Rhees backed out of the narrow bar. 'Got to get on. Lots to do...'

'Is he real?' muttered Ridge.

'He's not as bad as he seems. He was genuinely worried

about the church. To tell you the truth, the night I found the cat I was none too happy myself. It's easy to mock when you're in a nice, bright pub, surrounded by other people.'

'Perhaps,' said Ridge. 'You were saying: about the revelation in the abbey shop.'

'Oh, yes, that. When I saw the picture of Hayes with long hair, I saw him immediately as the man the eyewitness reported on the Tor. I thought Telfer must have told him about the stunt - he had to be in touch, because Telfer said he had visited. Then I remembered what Telfer had called him. Wanker. Not a very nice name, but one that had probably stuck from school. Probably the name Schofield knew him by. So suddenly the initials HM scratched on the wall made sense. Remember, Schofield was hanging upside down.'

Ridge only took a moment to realise the significance, to raise a congratulatory eyebrow and to think of an objection. 'If he could scratch young Wanker's initials, surely he could rip the bag away from his face?'

'Not if his hands were tied behind his back. There were wire marks on his wrists.'

'Ah,' said Ridge, 'got you there. If his hands were tied behind his back, he couldn't have got hold of anything to write.'

'He didn't need to. Tied at the wrist, his hands had enough movement to scratch the initials. It was his ring, you see. It wasn't a soft metal like gold, it was hard enough to scratch the surface of the stone. It's only now that it's come back to me - when I was first up on the Tor with Vicky I saw that his ring had been damaged. And his knuckle; he must have scraped it on the stone as he tried to leave his mark.'

'Stone the crows, guv, it's a fair cop. Colour me impressed…'

Capel's phone began to ring. He held up a hand to stop Ridge, glanced at it and answered it straight away. 'Malcolm.'

Chief Inspector Davies sounded out of breath. 'We've got a problem. Hayes ran. He's got a part time job at the spa down in the centre of Bath, you know the one?'

'Yes.' Capel shook his head at Ridge who was pantomiming

that he wanted in on the conversation.

'The place is a warren. Took us a while to pin him down once he got inside. He's up on the roof – there's a swimming pool up there. Great views over Bath. Nice glass and metal barriers to stop you falling thirty feet to the pavement. Except Hayes is perched on the edge of it. And he says he's going to jump unless he can speak to you.'

'Me?'

'I don't understand it either, but it's what he says. Where are you? We'll send a car.'

'Don't worry, I'm not far – it'll be quicker for me to get down there.'

Capel cut the call before Davies could reply. 'Come on Ed, we're going. I need you to drive me down into Bath. Hayes is threatening to jump off a building.'

The drive down, Ridge for once almost silent, seemed like a dream to Capel. It was the same as he was hustled through the building, pulled along by two armed police officers as the spa guests looked on open-mouthed. Time hardly elapsed before he was there, staring across the startlingly blue water of the rooftop swimming pool that steamed into the cool evening air.

Around three sides of the edge of the roof was a tinted glass barrier, a little over waist height, topped with a shiny metal rail. Two of these sides looked out onto a lower floor of the building, but the third side gave stunning views over Bath, and across to the hills beyond. There was nothing to obscure the view – on this side the railing was at the very edge of the building with a sheer drop to the pavement, four tall storeys beneath. And seated precariously on the rail, facing in towards the pool, was Hayes. His face was white, his eyes wide as he watched Capel slowly approach. Capel was aware of Vicky among the police presence to his left, but could not spare her a look. His eyes were fixed on Hayes.

'Phil,' said Capel. 'You wanted to speak to me.'

Hayes muttered something in a low voice.

'I can't hear,' said Capel. 'I'll have to come closer.'

'Don't touch me!' yelled Hayes. His body twitched on the railing as if, for a moment he had lost his balance.

'I won't,' said Capel, speaking as calmly as he could manage. 'I'm going to get up alongside you. I'm not going to try anything, I'm going to be too busy hanging on. Okay?'

Malcolm Davies, standing the other side of Hayes started to speak, clearly horrified at Capel's suggestion, but Capel shook his head.

'Okay,' said Hayes.

Capel eased himself up on the rail, right next to Hayes. It was higher above the tiled walkway than he had thought and he felt horribly unstable, all too aware of the precipitous drop behind him. He could hear the distant sound of people shouting in the street – they were closing the road off below.

'What did you want to tell me, Phil?'

Hayes lifted a hand off the rail for the moment, wobbled and gripped desperately back on. Capel was transported for a moment back to the Lady Chapel, seeing Lillith teeter, nearly fall into the crypt. He shook his head. He had to concentrate. Hayes was speaking.

'When I spoke to you at the RPS I thought you were someone who'd understand. I need you to understand. I idolised Lady Isobel. Loved her, I suppose you could say. I've got this thing for archaeology. I was always collecting fossils as a kid and visiting ruined castles and churches when all my mates wanted to do was play footie. When I saw Isobel on the TV, she was so… she was wonderful. Then I found out she was going to be in Glastonbury and I had to go and see her.'

'At the Abbey.'

'Of course. I'd spend all day there, just watching her, everything she did. I spoke to her once or twice, but mostly I just watched her. I didn't think she noticed. She was too intent on her work. It was perfect.'

'What changed?'

'That red-haired bitch came. Spoke to her. They didn't know I was listening. I know every nook and cranny of that abbey, every hiding place. Isobel told the Cooper woman about me. And Isobel was laughing as she did it. Said I was pathetic, and how it had been funny to start with, but now I was just a pain in the arse. That's what she said. I was a fucking pain in the arse.'

'And when Lillith Cooper left, you confronted Isobel?'

'I didn't mean to do anything to her, just tell her what I thought. But she laughed in my face. Called me names. I picked up a stone. Just to threaten her. That's all I intended to do.'

'And you got away with it.'

'I was very careful. I thought there was nothing to connect me. But Schofield found out. He'd got a photograph somehow. And he started asking for money. It wasn't the money I was bothered about, though. It was my career. I had it all planned. I couldn't let him spoil it.'

'So you asked Ian Telfer to help.'

'Not to kill him. Telfer had no idea. He's weak, easy to manipulate. He never liked Schofield. I just encouraged him to get his mates to hang Schofield up in the tower for a laugh. They didn't know I followed them up the Tor with a bag of water. It was so easy to finish him and leave those jokers to find out something had gone horribly wrong. Schofield didn't even plead with me, you know. He seemed to realise he had it coming.'

'Okay,' said Capel. 'You've told me. That's the hard bit over. Let's just get down off this rail and go inside. It's getting cold.'

'There's only one way down,' said Hayes. He took both hands off the rail, holding them out towards Capel.

'No!' Capel reflexively put a hand out to Hayes. The sudden movement threw him off balance and he felt himself slipping backwards on the polished rail. Slipping towards the void behind him. Capel grabbed at the rail, but he couldn't get any purchase. He felt Hayes push him painfully hard and then he was falling and he heard a scream and he didn't know if it was him that was screaming and there was blackness.

CHAPTER 22

The universe was spinning around him. In front of his eyes, coloured bands of light broke the darkness, throbbing and pulsing. Slowly, very slowly, the colours faded to an out-of-focus mist.

'He's coming round.'

Capel was aware of a hissing in his ears and the face of Malcolm Davies swam into view, inches away from his own.

'Hello,' Capel said. It was inane, but he couldn't think straight enough to say anything else.

'Welcome back,' said Davies. 'You are very lucky to be here. Can you remember what happened?'

Capel shook his head, sending an urgent pain shooting through his forehead. 'I can remember sitting with Hayes, starting to fall… nothing else.'

'He saved you,' said Davies, 'they both did, Hayes and one of my officers. You were falling backwards, off the building. A goner for sure. Hayes pushed you the other way, back onto the roof. You hit your head on the side and went straight into the swimming pool. Luckily we had a lifesaver on the team to fish you out. I wouldn't have fancied jumping in after you in my best suit.'

Capel gently felt his head. There was some kind of bandage. 'And Hayes?'

Davies shook his head. 'Newton's law, isn't it? Pushed you forwards, went back himself. We couldn't do anything. Saves the taxpayer a fortune on the trial, I suppose.'

'I'm sorry,' said Capel. 'He didn't deserve that.'

'There's someone here that perhaps you'd like to thank,' said Davies. 'I don't know if you were introduced before.' He stepped aside. 'This is Constable Denning. She's the one who pulled you out of the water.'

Capel looked up straight into Vicky's eyes. 'Oh yes, we have been introduced. Thank you, Constable Denning. Thank you so much. I don't know how I can make it up to you.'

Vicky smiled slowly. 'I'm sure you'll find a way.'

ABOUT THE AUTHOR

Brian Clegg is a prize-winning popular science writer. His most recent books are *How Many Moons Does The Earth Have* and *Ten Billion Tomorrows*, with 20 other popular science titles including *Inflight Science, Before the Big Bang,* and *How to Build a Time Machine*. His *Dice World* and *A Brief History of Infinity* were both longlisted for the Royal Society Prize for Science Books.

Born in Rochdale, Lancashire, Brian read Natural Sciences (specializing in experimental physics) at Cambridge University. After graduating, he spent a year at Lancaster University where he gained a second MA in Operational Research, a discipline developed during the Second World War to apply mathematics and probability to warfare and since widely applied to business problem solving.

From Lancaster, he joined British Airways, where he formed a new department tasked with developing hi-tech solutions for the airline. His emphasis on innovation led to training with creativity guru Dr. Edward de Bono, and in 1994 he left BA to set up his own creativity consultancy, running courses on the development of ideas and the solution of business problems. His clients include the BBC, the Met Office, Sony, GlaxoSmithKline, the Treasury and many others.

Brian has also written regular columns, features and reviews for numerous magazines and newspapers, including The Wall Street Journal, Nature, BBC Focus, Physics World, The Observer, Good Housekeeping and Playboy. His books have been translated into many languages, including German, French, Spanish, Portuguese, Chinese, Japanese, Polish, Norwegian, and Indonesian.

Brian has given sell-out lectures at the Royal Institution, the British Library and the Science Museum in London and has spoken at venues from Oxford and Cambridge Universities to Cheltenham Festival of Science. He has also contributed to radio and TV programs, and is a popular speaker at schools. Brian is editor of the successful www.popularscience.co.uk book review site, blogs at www.brianclegg.blogspot.com, and is a Fellow of the Royal Society of Arts. Brian lives in Wiltshire with his wife and twin children. In his spare time, he has a passion for Tudor and Elizabethan church music.

OTHER TITLES BY BRIAN CLEGG

FICTION

Xenostorm: Rising

NON-FICTION

Science for Life
Final Frontier
The Quantum Age
Extra Sensory
Dice World
Gravity
Introducing Infinity
The Universe Inside You
How to Build a Time Machine
Inflight Science
Armageddon Science
Before the Big Bang
Ecologic
Upgrade Me
The Global Warming Survival Kit
The Man Who Stopped Time
The God Effect
A Brief History of Infinity
Roger Bacon: The First Scientist
Light Years

Cover image from Torre de Glastonbury – Interior by Josep Renalias

A LONELY HEIGHT

Printed in Great Britain
by Amazon.co.uk, Ltd.,
Marston Gate.